FINDING HOPE

FINDING HOPE

HALF MOON BAY BOOK 1

ERIN BROCKUS

Green Sage
Press

Ebook ISBN: 978-1-7358127-1-7

Paperback ISBN: 978-1-7358127-2-4

Large Print ISBN: 978-1-7358127-3-1

Hardcover ISBN: 978-1-7358127-4-8

CHAPTER 1

M arch 15...

As Hope Collins squinted at the enormous airplane roaring overhead, the icy sleet from an unexpected spring storm blasted her. She closed her eyes and grimaced, setting down her two suitcases to wipe her face before grinning as a flutter rippled through her midsection.

This is the last time—no more Chicago winters or spring surprises! Bending down, she wrestled her luggage through the automatic doors and into the departures section of O'Hare Airport.

It was nearly 9 p.m. and the hall's blinding interior assaulted her eyes after the darkness outside. Finding the reader boards for her airline, she joined the line of people snaking its way to the check-in desks. As Hope slowly made her way through, she smiled, trying to guess the stories of the people around her.

No one who knew her would ever guess what she was embarking on. Those she hadn't already told, of course.

An hour later, she was at the front of the line, and the agent called her up. "ID, please." His blue blazer was crisp, but he had the tired bearing of someone who had been dealing with grumpy airline passengers all day. His trim, dark-brown hair looked like he'd run a hand through it more than once. Hope handed him her driver's license. *Another plus of my new home—don't have to worry about all the international regulations.*

The agent brought up her ticket information on his terminal and brightened. "St. Croix! Oh, I'm so jealous! You definitely have the right idea. How long are you staying?"

"I'm moving there." The three words tumbled out of Hope's mouth as she bounced on her feet.

He set down her ID with wide brown eyes. "That sounds even better. Goodbye, Chicago winters! You know, if you're in the mood to celebrate, we have a discounted upgrade to first class for only $100. We have some unsold seats, so the price is pretty low for this route."

Hope hesitated before saying, "Why not? I'm sure I'll sleep better on the overnight flight. Upgrade me!"

This is your new start—splurge a little!

He processed her luggage and printed her boarding pass. "Your ticket includes access to our Club Lounge before your flight." He gave her directions and sent her on her way.

After a surprisingly painless pass through security, she continued to the Club Lounge. The check-in agent peered at her boarding pass as if he were a bouncer in a club looking to reject the undesirables. Finally determining Hope had a magic ticket, he gave her a big fake smile and welcomed her into the lounge. Refraining from rolling her eyes, Hope regarded the area as she walked toward the bar. She'd never flown first class before.

So, this is how the other half lives.

Armchairs were arranged in an area far larger than she'd expected. Table lamps cast a warm glow around the lounge, and several large flat-screen televisions broadcasted a national news channel with the sound off. After finding a comfortable stuffed

chair near the bar, Hope ordered a glass of
into the soft leather with a mouthful of ve
was worth the splurge.

Ninety minutes later, she sipped a glass c
celebrity after settling into her first-class seat
middle-aged businesswoman seated next to her

"Business or pleasure?" The woman, who had introduced
herself as Barbara, wore a navy-blue suit with a crisp white shirt
and a pencil skirt. Her navy pumps matched perfectly.

Hope thought for a moment. "A little of both, I guess. I'm
moving to St. Croix for a new business opportunity, but I'm
hoping it will be a pleasure." She paused. "It's really a complete
life change for me." The flutter of excitement was back.

Barbara's eyes sparkled. "Oh, that sounds dramatic—tell me
more."

"The short version is I've won a scuba diving resort there. I'm
flying down now to take it over and make it my own."

Barbara gaped at Hope before snapping her mouth shut. "I
think I'm going to need the long version. Good thing it's a long
flight and we get free drinks!"

Hope smiled and took a sip of champagne. Sitting here right
now, she couldn't believe how completely her life had changed in
only four weeks.

our Weeks Ago . . .

I AM NOT PREDICTABLE.

Hope opened the door of the shop, the warm coffee-scented air wafting out to her as she hurried away from the biting sleet of the winter's morning. As she frowned at the assorted pastries on offer, her mind returned to the conversation she'd had with her boyfriend, Kyle, the evening before.

"There's nothing wrong with being predictable," he'd said. "It's reassuring, like a favorite pair of slippers."

She glared at him as she crossed her arms. "I'm slippers to you? Seriously? I can be fun and spontaneous, but I'm also an adult and try to act like one. Are you saying I'm boring?"

"I didn't mean it as an insult. Forget I mentioned it." He sighed and went back to scrolling on his phone.

The problem was, she couldn't forget it. She unclenched her fists and took a deep breath of caffeinated air. They had been together for nearly two years, so maybe things *were* getting a little stale.

"Good morning, Hope! I saw you in line, so I made your coffee," said the barista, Ashley, in her crisp green apron.

Hope furrowed her brow as she swept back a lock of chestnut hair. "How did you know what I was going to order?"

Ashley's smile fell. "Oh! You always get a Grande Skinny Vanilla Latte. If you want something else today, it's ok. I'll make a new one."

Hope ran her card through the reader. "No, my usual is fine. I didn't realize I was so, uh, obvious."

Ashley's sunny smile returned. "We've got to have our routines, right?"

"Yeah, I guess so. Thanks." Hope grabbed the coffee, chewing on a fingernail as she walked toward the door.

Am I getting a wake-up call here? Kyle and Ashley?

The icy sleet once again pelted her as she left the shop and headed toward her car. Pulling her coat tighter, she had much more important things to think about. *You've earned this promotion. It's time to prove it to Terrance.*

Hope started her car, rubbing her hands together in front of the heating vents before driving the two miles to work. Pulling into the parking lot of Rosemont Inn & Suites, her trusty SUV only skidded a little. *I really hate snow.*

She inspected the tall building before her. Built fifteen years ago, the hotel still looked modern and upscale. The light-gray rectangular facade was broken up with rows and columns of windows. Royal-blue accent lighting was still on in the darkness.

Eduardo, the front-desk clerk, grinned from his computer as she passed by into her office. "Morning, Hope. It's another gorgeous day."

He soon appeared at her door, his black hair short and clean. Eduardo was thirty but looked fifteen—he complained he still got carded. "Hey, isn't your interview today?"

"Ugh. Chicago winters are the worst. And yes, my interview is this afternoon. Assistant general manager has a nice ring to it. If things go well, your sentence with me as front-desk manager will soon end."

Eduardo smirked. "Well, you've worked here forever. They'd be stupid not to promote you."

There was a poster on the wall of a runner breaking the tape as she won a race. The caption read, *Good Things Come to Those Who Don't Give Up*. "Sometimes it feels like forever, but it's been ten years. And thanks for the compliment."

∾

LATER THAT MORNING, Hope sat in her office looking over occupancy lists when raised voices drifted in from the front desk. She smiled at Eduardo's soothing tone as he tried to calm a customer.

"What do you mean you aren't giving me an upgrade? Don't you know I'm a Gold member?"

"Yes, I see that, and we thank you for your loyalty. Unfortunately, we don't have any suites to upgrade you to. Our check-in time isn't until 3 p.m. If you'd prefer to wait for a better room, I can see what opens up between now and then and call you immediately." Eduardo used the extra-sweet tone he always took with awful customers.

The man bellowed, "This is completely unacceptable!"

Ok, that's enough.

Hope rose and approached the front desk, finding a very large and very red middle-aged man looming in front of the counter. He wore a rumpled suit, and his graying hair stuck up on one side.

She peeked at Eduardo's computer screen to scan the details before putting on her best professional smile and introducing herself. "Hello, Mr. Goodson. Eduardo is absolutely right about no suites being available, but I have a great corner room that just opened up. Would that work? I know it's an inconvenience, but our options are limited when checking in this early in the day."

Goodson deflated. He'd been puffed up, spoiling for a fight. "Ok. I guess that could work. I've been flying all night, and it was a terrible flight."

Hope's face hurt from smiling so hard. "I understand completely. Red-eyes are the worst." The fire in the hearth gave a loud pop, making Goodson jump. "I'll let Eduardo finish getting you checked in. Our restaurant is open if you'd like to get breakfast."

He shook his head, still grumpy. "At this point, I only want to get some sleep."

"Our rooms are soundproof, so that should help. Please let me know if there is anything else you need. I'm here to help." Hope handed him her card. "I'll leave you in Eduardo's expert hands."

"Thank you," Goodson said, flushing now.

Hope smiled and walked back to her office. *Entitled Elite Number One handled for today.* He wouldn't be the last, but she could handle people like him in her sleep.

At 12:58, Hope walked through the door of the executive conference room with her back straight and shoulders squared. Terrance, the general manager, sat at the conference table with the food and beverage manager and the current assistant general manager on either side of him.

"Good afternoon, Hope." Terrance smiled. "Please have a seat." As usual, he looked like he could have stepped out of *Inc. Magazine*. Not a wrinkle in his suit, and his salt-and-pepper hair perfectly groomed.

After exchanging pleasantries, Lydia, the F&B manager, narrowed her eyes and asked, "What is your experience here, Hope?"

She straightened and met Lydia's eyes. *As if you don't know. We have lunch once a month.* "I've worked here ten years. Four years as a front-desk assistant and the past six years as front-desk manager. I know the ins and outs of a wide variety of hotel operations."

Terrance steepled his hands in front of him. "You've done excellent work here, Hope. How do you feel your current position has prepared you for assistant general manager?"

"I'm good with people. When I took this position, the front-desk associate turnover was sky high. Nobody wanted to work the front desk." She shifted her gaze to Mark, the outgoing assistant manager who was taking over their hotel at the Denver airport. He was also the person she had replaced as front-desk manager. "I haven't needed to hire an employee in over a year. I don't think any other department manager here can say that."

Hope turned back to Terrance. "The assistant manager needs to know every detail of the hotel and make sure the small things are done right. The front desk is the first point of contact for guests. We deal with everything, and I've just about seen it all. My department also has the highest guest-survey ratings in the hotel."

Lydia looked impressed, and Terrance had a warm glow in his eyes.

"I've been here for a long time, and I'm one of the most experienced employees you've got. Terrance, we've had multiple discussions about increasing my responsibilities here. In short, I think you'd have a very hard time finding anyone *more* qualified for this position."

SITTING BACK IN HER CHAIR, Hope looked at the wall clock, surprised it was nearly 3:30. Still on a high after her interview, she smiled as her phone vibrated with a text from Kyle.

Kyle: Dinner tonight? I made a reservation at Olive Tree for 5:30. Ok?
Hope: Perfect! See you then.

OLIVE TREE WAS one of her favorite restaurants, and she was definitely in the mood for a celebration. *Hopefully, he wants to make up for being an ass last night, though he might have a point. This new job could be exactly what I need to shake up my routine a little.*

Eduardo ducked his head into her office. "So tell me! How did the interview go?"

"Great." Hope smiled widely. "They still have more candidates to interview, so they won't announce the position quite yet. But they didn't throw me any major curveballs, and I've certainly paid my dues here."

"Well, you get my vote. Ok, I'm out of here." He turned to look at her, one hand gripping the door frame. "You're not working late again, are you?"

"Nope. Dinner date at 5:30."

He disappeared out the door as she rose to help with the afternoon check-in rush, happy and excited now that the tension of the interview was over.

She may have started her day in a funk, but she was confident it would end on a high note.

CHAPTER 3

*H*ope pulled down the driver's side visor and opened the vanity mirror. Reapplying her lipstick, she ran a hand through the slight natural wave of her shoulder-length hair. She touched up her eyeliner as her hazel eyes stared back at her. Unfortunately, she couldn't do anything about her winter-pale skin.

Tonight was a celebration, and she wanted to look good. Kyle might not be the man of her dreams, but he was a solid, dependable guy, though a little distant sometimes. She'd certainly done worse in the boyfriend department. *Stop. Do not go there. It's been years—are you ever going to get over it?*

She closed her eyes and took a deep breath.

Some of their best dates had been at Olive Tree. Even the weather was cooperating. The sun had set, but the wind was holding off its onslaught for the moment. The restaurant had a charming, bohemian vibe, with colorful tapestries draped along the ceiling. Candles in metal lanterns sat on tables covered with brightly colored tablecloths in tie-dyed patterns.

Hope walked through the bead curtain at the front door, inhaling the aromas of garlic and fresh pasta. Kyle sat at a secluded table. With a smile spreading across her face, she made her way over. He spotted her and ran a hand over his accountant-perfect brown hair.

Kyle gestured to a glass. "I ordered you a glass of Malbec."

"My favorite. Thanks." She studied him. His face was somewhat bland most of the time, but tonight it was pinched. "How are you doing?"

"Fine." His voice was strained.

Ok, I guess I'll start the conversation.

"My interview went well, I think. Terrance seemed enthusiastic about me in the position. He had told me *not* to interview when this job last opened up four years ago because I didn't have enough experience. But I do now." Her smile faded. Kyle wasn't listening to her. Hope tried again. "So, this is a great night for a celebration dinner. I'm trying not to get too excited, but I honestly feel like I have—"

He looked her straight in the eye as he interrupted. "Hope, stop. I'm sorry, I forgot your interview was today. I didn't ask you here to celebrate." He rubbed the back of his neck as he dropped his gaze to the table. "God, there's no easy way to say this. I don't want to continue this relationship anymore."

At first, she didn't think she'd heard him correctly. Then, as his words sunk in, her heart started pounding. "Wait. What did you say?"

He sagged and put his head in his hands, his manicured nails on full display. "I don't think this is going anywhere." He looked back up at her. "And now, I'm just done, ok? I want more excitement in my life. I want a woman who's *there*. I told you last night, this relationship has become too predictable. I'm ready for something else."

"More excitement?" Flames ignited her cheeks. "You're a corporate accountant, for God's sake! I tried to plan a weekend away last month, but you weren't interested because you had to work overtime." Hope's voice rose. "You brought me to my favorite restaurant to *break up with me?* Out of nowhere? What, am I not good enough for you?"

"Keep your voice down." Kyle glared at her before lowering his eyes. "And I didn't say that. We're both in our mid-thirties now. This isn't working for me anymore. I'm sorry I did this on your big day—that wasn't my intention." At least he had the decency to look abashed.

"Of course it wasn't your intention. It never is. And last night, you said being predictable was fine. At least I can make up my mind." She scraped back her chair with a loud screech. "Fine. If you want to end this, consider it ended."

Standing up, she drank the rest of her wine in one shot and stormed out of the restaurant.

~

HOPE MADE it halfway back to her apartment before the tears came in force. Her hands shook as she gripped the steering wheel. *I can't believe what just happened. How could I not see this coming?*

She pulled into her covered parking space and sat in her car, still gripping the wheel as she leaned her forehead against her arms. Taking a shaky breath, she wiped her eyes and looked up at her apartment building. It was a beige, rectangular box, and tonight she saw it through new eyes.

Is that what I am? Bland and dull? Have I shut myself off so much I don't even see it?

She nudged open the car door that could have weighed a hundred pounds, needles of ice pelting her as she walked to the front door. Entering the code to open the door, Hope sighed at the blast of heat coming out of the building. She rode the creaky elevator to her one-bedroom apartment on the ninth floor.

Walking into the living room, she took out her cell phone. There was one person she could always call and vent to—her little sister, Sara. Four years younger than Hope, Sara was a free spirit who didn't take life too seriously. She lived in Charleston, South Carolina because she hated the midwestern winters. Dialing the number, Hope took a deep breath.

Sara could also be as sharp as a knife.

She picked up on the second ring. "Hey, big sister, how's it going?"

"Oh Sara, I don't even know where to start."

"Uh-oh. Do I feel another tale of woe coming on?"

"Kyle broke up with me."

A long-suffering sigh emanated from the phone. "Oh no. Really?"

"Don't fall over with sympathy for me."

"Look, I'm sorry you and Kyle broke up, but how long did you expect this to go on? And I've tried sympathy before." Another pause. "I know you're hurting, and that kills me. But you won't commit to anyone. Hell, you refuse to even get close to anyone. Can you blame him for wanting to move on?"

"Yes, dammit!"

"Oh, come on! You know I love you, but—"

"I had no idea it was coming. We've been together for almost two years. I'm not sure I wanted to marry the guy, but the relationship seemed to be humming along." Now the tears had started again. Sara was the only person she didn't mind crying in front of. "At least I thought so."

"Two years, Hope! Have you even gone on a long vacation together? Look, I've never been president of the Kyle fan club, but you're pretty much married to your job. Maybe he wanted to find an actual wife someday."

"Whose side are you on, anyway?" Hope stomped over to the gas fireplace and flipped the switch. It whooshed to life. She swiped the tears off her face with a furious palm.

"I'm not even going to dignify that with a response. You are your own worst enemy. You need to get out of this rut." Another deep sigh came from the phone as Hope returned to the couch.

"You're a beautiful, smart, successful woman. Any man would be lucky to have you. You deserve someone *much* better than Kyle. But if you want to shake up your life a little, then *do* something about it! You've always been so focused and driven."

Sara paused, and Hope could practically see her lips pursing together. "And how many times do you and I need to keep having this same conversation about men?"

Hope closed her eyes, drained. "I'm trying, Sara. I just . . . can't."

"There's someone out there for you. But you have to take a chance to find him. What's your idea of your perfect man?"

"Not Kyle." In fact, if Hope were being honest, she'd always thought Kyle was something of a boy pretending to be a man. Maybe that was why she considered him safe.

"There's a revelation. I'm serious. Do you even know what you want in a guy?"

"Yes! He'd be a man who's strong enough that I always feel safe with him but had no fear of him myself. He'd be smart and funny, and good looks would be a bonus. A man who believed in honor and being faithful, and who loved me above all else, of course."

"Good God, Hope. No wonder you're single. Where do you propose to find this paragon?"

"I don't. I'm done with men for a while. I need some time alone." She grabbed a tissue and wiped her face before changing the subject. "I do have some good news, though. I interviewed for a new job today. Maybe this will be the new direction I need." Making her way to the kitchen, she opened a bag of chips.

"Ok, this sounds promising. Was your interview for a totally new job?"

"It was for a promotion to assistant general manager at the Rosemont Inn." Hope collapsed onto the couch again and closed her eyes. "Oh no, that sounds kind of boring, doesn't it?"

"Well, maybe the universe is telling you it's time for a change.

You've been in Chicago forever. Let's brainstorm a major life shift for you. Any ideas?"

"No! I'm pretty confident about this promotion." She bit a chip in half. "This job could be exactly what I need, even if it's not the most stimulating thing in the world."

"You're no fun. And stop talking with your mouth full." Sara paused. "You know . . . I might have an idea."

Oh no, this conversation had been going so normally for Sara. "What idea might that be?"

"Remember Marissa, the friend I work with?"

"Yes. Should I be scared where this is going, Sara?"

"Of course not. You know I only have your best intentions at heart. Always. Anyhoo, she just got back from a vacation in St. Croix in the Virgin Islands. And there's a dive resort there being offered up in a raffle. The current owner is retiring or something. She told me all about it and gave me the brochure."

"So what?"

"Think about it. You buy a raffle ticket for $100, then the owner picks a random ticket. And voila—you own your own resort. In the Caribbean! Well, after they make sure you're not an axe murderer, of course. You could enter that! I mean, really— white sand, warm sea, cabana boys. Scuba diving in the clear blue sea . . . You have the hotel experience to make it work, you know."

Hope froze, a chip midway to her mouth. "Have you lost your mind? What if I won? I can't pick up and leave my life behind. Besides, I can't even scuba dive. An entire life shift might be fine for you, but it would never work for me."

"You need to give yourself more credit. Seriously, you are one of the most capable people I've ever known." She stopped for a big breath, and her voice got firm again. "Stop settling. You have been doing this for years! How many more will it be before you finally start living?" She paused as Hope put her feet up on the coffee table. "Hope, things have a way of working out. I'll say it one last time—you are definitely better off without Kyle. You deserve a man a lot better than him."

"Thanks, sis. You can be a bitch sometimes, but you can also be right on occasion." Sara laughed. "If I get this promotion, maybe it will be the change I need. Love you."

After the call, Hope went into the kitchen to make a cup of chamomile tea before drawing a hot bath. As she slowly sank into the bubbles, she snorted.

Winning a resort in the Caribbean. How ridiculous . . .

CHAPTER 4

*S*unlight filtered through the clear blue water, casting rippling beams onto the vibrant coral reef. But dive leader Alex Monroe was immune to the beauty at the moment. He blew an irritated stream of bubbles out of his regulator.

Where is that guy?

He craned his neck. The man's wife was right where she should be, following behind Alex, but her husband wasn't. He looked up. Sure enough, the guy swam right along, but thirty feet above the rest of the group. Alex signaled to Bob (or was it Bill?), asking if he was ok. The guy signaled back ok, so Alex gave him the submerge deeper sign and turned around to lead on.

He checked his wrist dive computer. They were at sixty feet. Even at that depth, the reef glowed with soft and hard corals in shades of green, pink, and purple. Alex led the group out of the coral channel as a large school of blue tang swept by, swooping down to eat algae on the reef.

His destination was a large outcropping in the middle of the sand that housed two leaf scorpion fish. The white one was out and easy to spot as it sat motionless on a coral branch, looking iridescent with its long serrated dorsal fin, its body waving back and forth in the gentle surge. He showed it to the rest of the group and hunted for the bright purple one. There! It hid deep in a crevice. Alex pointed it out, then swam off a short distance to wait while the divers enjoyed it and took photographs.

No one had indicated to him yet that they had half a tank of air left, which was a good sign as they had been down for over thirty minutes. Still, this group wasn't very experienced and might not be tracking their air closely. Alex tapped his open palm in the standard signal for an air check and pointed to BillyBob, who fumbled with his dive console and looked at his computer. His eyes grew large behind his mask before he hesitantly held up three fingers.

Three hundred pounds left? Are you kidding?

Alex rushed to him and tilted the dive computer toward himself to verify. Yes, only three hundred psi of the original three thousand left in his tank. The man was nearly out of air. Alex stared at the guy and his wife and jabbed his thumb upward, signaling they needed to end the dive and surface together *now*.

The wife looked confused and gave the safety-stop signal with a shrug. It was standard procedure to end each dive with a three-minute safety stop. Alex shook his head and repeated the thumbs-up gesture. The two headed toward the surface at a safe ascent rate, so Alex led the other four divers on.

He turned and brought them down a canyon, a sandy channel with twenty-foot-high sheer coral walls on both sides. Alex glanced up to make sure the two divers were still ascending safely. Movement caught his eye. A whitemouth moray eel poked its head out of a hole in the coral wall, rhythmically opening and closing its mouth as it breathed. Alex motioned the rest of the group over, checking once again as the two divers surfaced. Soon after, the boat engines started as Tommy steered the boat over to pick them up.

With his problem divers safely on the boat, Alex could relax a little. He wasn't about to cheat the other four divers out of the rest of the sixty-minute dive. The group was rewarded near the end of it when a squadron of four eagle rays glided by. With flat, triangular-shaped bodies, they were gray with white spots covering their backs. Six-feet-long tails trailed behind each one. Alex relaxed as they slowly swam by.

This is why I love diving. You never know what might pass by.

Soon the group was back on the surface, and Tommy motored over to pick them up. Alex took his usual position adjacent to the stern ladder so he could help the divers remove their fins and hand them up to Tommy. Finally, he scrambled up himself and shrugged off his tank. The remaining four divers now sat on the side benches near the stern of the boat, their tanks with attached buoyancy compensation devices lined up behind them as they exclaimed about the eagle rays.

Alex glanced at the couple who had nearly run out of air. The woman had a frown on her face. "Brent, calm down. He told us before the dive he would send up divers alone who needed to go up early."

Brent—that's right!

He stared right at Alex, fists clenched. "You should've surfaced with us. I could've run out of air, and you're supposed to be responsible for us."

Alex raised his eyebrows. "Oh? *I'm* responsible that you didn't check your air until I asked you halfway through the dive?" He shook his head. "Sorry, Brent, this one's on you. You're a certified diver. You should have *never* gotten down to three hundred psi without knowing it."

He straightened, parking his hands on his hips. "And your wife was your extra air source if you ran out, not me. You're the only diver in the group who was low—the others had plenty of air left to finish the dive." Brent had taken a step back at his aggressive posture, so Alex relaxed his arms. "If it makes you feel better, I kept a close eye on you until you surfaced to make sure you were both ok."

Brent's wife sighed, squeezing the water out of her black hair. "Brent, sit down. You know he's right."

He flopped down on the bench, mumbling to himself as Alex took a deep breath and counted to ten.

Tommy turned around from the wheel, spreading his arms wide with a grin on his dark face and his brown eyes crinkled. "Hey now—no bad vibes on my boat!" He pointed to Brent. "You learned somethin' new today, and everyone else got to see eagle rays. Sounds like a good mornin' to me. Now let's have some fun on the way back!"

He turned up the reggae on the boat radio, doing a quick head count to make sure everyone was aboard before he started dancing as he drove the boat. Tommy was not a small, lithe man, and it broke the tension, even getting a smile out of Brent.

Alex relaxed and turned toward the stern of the boat, watching as the St. Croix sun glinted off the water. He smiled as half a dozen flying fish skimmed along the surface next to them for several moments before diving back into the sea. He joined Tommy, pulling on his royal-blue staff T-shirt as he said quietly, "Thanks for defusing that."

"No problem." Tommy grinned. "There's always one on each boat."

"All's well that ends well, I guess." The boat made the turn into Half Moon Bay and the resort with its bungalows spaced behind the white sand beach came into sight.

Just another day in paradise.

~

AFTER THE BOAT returned to the pier, the guest divers quickly disembarked, leaving the chore of removing the tanks and scuba equipment to Alex and Tommy. Tommy walked down the pier to the dive shop and retrieved a cart for the tanks. His red Half Moon Bay Resort rash guard tightly hugged his body, complements of his wife's cooking. Alex transferred the tanks from the boat onto the cart, then glanced at Tommy.

"Go ahead and take off. I know your daughter has school conferences today."

"You sure? There's still lots to do."

"Yeah, I'm sure. See you tomorrow." Alex rolled the cart to the air compressor room. He'd need to refill all the tanks with fresh air for tomorrow's dives, but that could wait until after lunch. *It's not like I have anything better to do, anyway.* Next, he removed all the scuba equipment and wetsuits, rinsing everything in fresh water and hanging it in the gear storage room to dry.

Alex walked past the dive shop to the side of the pier, where a flight of stairs led up to his apartment. He headed straight for the shower. After rinsing off the salt water, he changed into a clean pair of board shorts and grabbed a new staff shirt, returning to the bathroom mirror to finger comb his short sandy hair. He frowned at his chest and shoulders.

For sure not combat ready anymore.

He leaned his hand against the vanity and glared at himself. "Stop it. You're damn lucky to be here right now and you know it. And you're plenty healthy enough to do your job. So drop the self-pity act."

With a sigh, he returned to the combination living room/kitchen and looked around his apartment. It was bare and sterile, but he didn't care. The only important item sat in the corner—a set of adjustable weights.

Keep at it. You're getting it back.

Leaving his apartment, he walked to the end of the pier and sprayed down the fiberglass deck of the boat, thoughtful now that the action of the day was over.

This might not be the life I had planned, but it could be worse. As long as I keep busy, I can't think too much.

CHAPTER 5

*B*eep, *beep, beep* . . .

Hope cracked open a resentful eye and stared at her phone, hoping she was dreaming and didn't have to get up yet. No such luck—it was 6 a.m. Groaning, she silenced the alarm and sat up on the edge of the bed.

February twenty-fourth. Today marked her thirty-sixth year around the sun. It was also the day management would announce the winner of the promotion. Hope stood with a smile. *Couldn't ask for a better omen . . .*

She padded into the kitchen and brewed herself a cup of coffee before opening up her laptop to check her email. Kyle hadn't contacted her since their breakup two weeks previously, but he might still wish her a happy birthday. Her inbox proved her wrong. Hope sighed and closed her laptop.

After finishing her coffee, she headed into the bathroom, peeling off her sleep shirt as she walked. Glancing in the mirror, she stopped for a moment, the three-inch tattoo on her right shoulder making her pause. The chrysalis was a muted green, with a looping black line that led to a brilliant butterfly, resplendent in the same green as well as bright yellow with black accents. She stroked it then met her gaze in the mirror. "You'll get there, Hope. Believe."

After changing into workout gear, she headed to the apartment gym and climbed onto a treadmill to start her usual thirty-minute run, which was a breeze for her. She'd run a half marathon last summer and was looking at a repeat this year.

No self-doubt today. You ARE going to get this promotion. You've given a lot to this hotel, and now it's about to pay off. Today was literally her day.

Hope increased the speed on the treadmill.

THE MORNING PASSED in a haze of anxious anticipation. Hope endured not one but two endless teleconferences from corporate while she refreshed her email every few minutes. She pictured herself as a cog in a vast machine—the effects of working for a corporate behemoth.

Instead of a friendly face-to-face meeting with Terrance about the job, she had to wait for the email blast that would be sent to all applicants. She ordered a sandwich and soda from the hotel restaurant to eat at her desk and smiled at Eduardo.

"Nothing yet?"

"Nope. My stomach is so knotted up I probably won't be able to eat."

"Well, it can't be long now. Hang in there, Hope. If I were doing the hiring, you'd be a sure thing."

"Too bad you're not deciding. Thanks for the vote of confidence."

"Any time."

There was a snowstorm forecasted, so the hotel was sure to book up with expected delays and cancellations at O'Hare. At about 3 p.m., she was looking over the staffing report to make sure there were enough people scheduled when her email pinged. She looked up—it was from Terrance Bartlett.

Subject: Decision approved for position N43678A

Even though she had been waiting for it all day, her heart dropped into her stomach. With shaking hands, she reached for her mouse before hesitating.

Come on, Hope. It's only what you've wanted for the past four years.

She double-clicked the subject line to open the email.

WE WISH to extend our sincere thanks to all who applied for the assistant general manager position. We were humbled by the number and quality of applicants. This was an extremely difficult selection to make, but we are pleased to announce Greg Parsons has accepted the position. Greg has a solid background as food and beverage manager for Paragon Airport Hotel, and we are looking . . .

HOPE CLOSED the email and laid her head on her folded arms. She had met Greg a time or two at local meetings. Tall and confident, bordering on cocky, he was probably ten years younger than she was and much less experienced. Worst of all, Greg was from an outside hotel chain and knew nothing about this hotel.

Raising her head, she opened the email again and read it. Nothing had changed except her heart pounded. She dug her fingers into the desk.

What was Terrance thinking? What do I have to do to get ahead with this company?

Tears threatened, which only made her angrier.

Absolutely not. No one sees my tears.

Hope bit her bottom lip, stopping the tears in their tracks. Then she leaned back in her chair, a hot furnace kindling in her gut at the sight of her motivational poster, which now looked pathetic. The threat of tears was gone, but her anger was increasing like a steam engine building speed.

Those bastards. I'm sure they think I'll meekly accept this and go on being dull, predictable Hope. How could they have selected Greg over me?

Only one way to find out . . .

Hope marched toward the executive wing. Seeing Terrance's door open, she walked straight into his office before she could second-guess herself.

"Do you have a few minutes? I'd like to discuss the promotion with you." She worked to keep the edge out of her voice.

"I'm sure you're not thrilled right now. I'm sorry." He leaned back in his chair, wearing a charcoal-gray suit and blue tie today. Still right out of *Inc. Magazine.*

A flush rose up her neck and face. "Could you please tell me how you believed that a *man* ten years younger than me, with much less experience and from an outside company, was more qualified for this position?"

Terrance sighed and shifted in his chair. "This was one of the hardest decisions we've ever had to make. It was really close between you two. We simply felt Greg's long-term prospects were a better fit for this hotel." He leaned forward, one finger pressing into his blotter. "This does *not* mean we don't appreciate you or the excellent work you do. You're a key part of this operation, and your experience here isn't lost on any of us."

Hope fought to hide her anger. "Oh yes, experience. This position last opened up four years ago. It was you, Terrance, who told me I didn't have enough experience to apply. And so I waited and got that experience, yet here we are. You still gave the position to someone much less qualified."

Terrance narrowed his eyes. "No, he is not less qualified than you. We simply thought he was a better fit for this position."

Oh, bullshit.

He leaned back in his chair. "Look, you still have a very promising future here."

"Oh, do I? It doesn't seem so from where I'm sitting. In fact, it seems like the handwriting on the wall is pretty clear right now. The only future I have here is as front-desk manager, and I'm ready for more." She was breathing hard now and inhaled deeply as she came to a decision. "If I can't get that experience here, I'll look for opportunities elsewhere. It's not like there aren't any other hotels near one of the biggest airports in the country. There's plenty of competition around here. And you've proven that outside candidates are extremely valuable."

Nope, not letting a man push me around. Never again.

"So, I am officially giving my notice of resignation. I'll write it up and give you a formal letter on Monday." She started to walk out, a wave of pride sweeping through her gut.

"Hope!" Terrance's voice radiated alarm, much to her satisfaction. "Don't do this. Today is Friday—take the rest of the afternoon off. You'll feel better by Monday."

She stopped and looked back at him. "I doubt that, Terrance."

HOPE PULLED her stocking cap down, ducking her head from the wind as she rushed back to her car with a bottle of wine. Her triumph of pride after leaving Terrance's office had turned into a morass of anxiety. Her apartment was only a few miles from the Rosemont Inn, which meant it was also only a few miles from countless other hotels surrounding O'Hare Airport. That made her feel a little better about her prospects for a new job.

Entering her apartment, she opened the wine and poured a healthy glass, taking a sip as she turned on the fireplace. She slumped onto her couch before opening her laptop and bringing up a job search site. *Let's see . . . lots of openings at hotels in the area. Plenty of entry-level jobs, but I want something more challenging than what I do now.*

She tipped her head back and rubbed her temples.

Is this really what I want to keep doing? I have a business degree, for God's sake. That should apply to lots of positions.

She shut the laptop and took another drink of wine. She was dizzy, and it wasn't from the alcohol. It was hard to believe how much her life had been turned upside down in a few weeks.

Hope was equally elated at and terrified by her present situation. Elated at herself for standing up to Terrance and terrified at having no safety net now. Safety had always been her top priority. She watched the sliding-glass door as the wind blew sleet against it, the needles leaving dots of water on the glass.

This isn't the first time you've had to start over, and it's certainly not the first time you've faced a difficult situation.

Hope snorted and lifted her glass in an imaginary toast. "Dad, you might have been a Class-A asshole, but you taught me how to survive without you. I'll survive this too."

CHAPTER 6

*A*s Hope took a sip of wine after her toast, her phone rang. Sara's name flashed on the screen. Hope thought about not answering, but Sara could be like a terrier chasing a rabbit when she was determined. She swiped to answer the call.

"Happy Birthday, big sis!"

Hope laughed and threw an arm over her eyes. "Thanks. Would you believe I completely forgot it's my birthday?"

"Yes, unfortunately. That's why you're so lucky to have me in your life. I always look after you. So, how is life after Kyle? You doing ok?"

"Yeah. I just feel numb. I wasn't head over heels in love but getting dumped stings, you know?"

"I'm sorry, sweetie. You'll meet your perfect match when the time is right. You'll see."

"Oh God, Sara." Hope laughed. "You sound like a call-in radio host. Real life isn't a movie. People are messy and complicated. I certainly am." She got up to pour more wine.

"There's nothing wrong with messy and complicated. That's what keeps life interesting. And you deserve the happily-ever-after, Hope."

"I already told you a man is the last thing I need. And real life isn't a fairy tale. Can we change the subject, please?"

"Certainly, since it's your big day. So, any big plans for tonight?"

Laughter erupted. It came out shrill, so Hope cleared her throat to cover. "Well, today is my thirty-sixth birthday, and I'm currently drowning my misery in a bottle of red wine. I quit my job this afternoon."

"Are you serious right now?"

Hope sighed and closed her eyes again. "Not only did I *not* get the promotion, they gave it to a guy ten years younger, much less experienced, and from an outside company. It's total bullshit. I'm much more qualified than he is."

"Honey, you are definitely having an awful month! Did you really quit?"

"I told my boss I'd have my written resignation for him Monday. I quit in the heat of the moment, but I haven't changed my mind since. I can't believe I gave that company ten years of blood, sweat, and tears, and this is how they reward me. I'm an idiot."

"I take it you don't have another job lined up?"

Hope gave another slightly-unhinged laugh. "Nope. For the first time in a very long while, I'm flying blind. Everyone keeps saying I'm too predictable, so I guess I'm trying to shake things up a little."

"I'm so sorry this happened to you. Do you remember my telling you a couple of weeks ago that maybe the universe was trying to tell you it was time for a change?"

"Yeah. This wasn't the change I had in mind, though." After ending the call, Hope stumbled straight to bed, exhausted and depressed.

~

SATURDAY MORNING GREETED her with a steady snowfall accumulation building on her balcony. Hope sat on her couch in her fuzzy pajamas and slippers, drinking coffee as she searched for employment. What had started as fluttering butterflies escalated the longer she spent with her laptop. Now Mothra flew around in her gut.

There weren't as many positions available as she'd thought. She'd been glued to her laptop for several hours now, searching every position near O'Hare, then widening the search area further. She found several management positions at hotels, but they would be lateral moves, and she wanted to move up.

I've had enough of sideways.

HOPE WAS THINKING of midlife career changes by Sunday, possibly finance or project management. She had moved her brooding job search to the armchair, hoping it would be better luck than the couch.

The problem was, she liked her job. She enjoyed working with a wide variety of people and interacting with the guests, the occasional idiot notwithstanding. Sitting up straight, Hope resumed the search.

She had some savings and wasn't going to be out on the street anytime soon, but this was definitely an unsettling position for her. The only thing she was sure of was the piece of paper sitting on her coffee table.

She smiled at her letter of resignation.

∼

MONDAY MORNING BROUGHT new iron to Hope's spine as she walked through the hotel lobby with her official two weeks' notice in hand. She smiled at Eduardo but didn't stop to talk, heading straight to her office instead. *I need to hand this to Terrance before I say anything to anyone else.* By mid-morning, she figured enough time had passed for him to deal with any emergencies left over from the weekend.

Hope knocked on his open door. "Got a minute?"

He frowned at the sheet of paper in her hand. "Of course. Please sit down." He straightened his tie. Red silk today. "Look, I thought about you a lot this weekend. Let's come up with a plan to get you working toward a position you feel you've earned."

"I'm sorry if I intruded on your Sunday sports, but the problem is that the position I *feel* I earned has already been awarded to someone else." She paused, pleased when he shifted in his chair. "But you're right about one thing—my career needs to move in a new direction. So as promised, here is my two weeks' notice."

"Come on, Hope. You don't want this. I don't want this. We can work it out." He stared at the piece of paper like it might have the plague.

A ripple rolled through her stomach. Surprisingly, it was relief. She smiled. "Terrance, my decision is final. It's time for me to move on."

She rose and left his office.

Eduardo was stricken when she told him. "You can't leave me! I'll probably end up with some horrible boss who knows nothing. Then I'll have to do his job *and* mine, and I'll have a heart attack and die. Do you want all that on your conscience?"

"Oh, stop being such a drama queen." Hope laughed before giving him an appraising glance. "Maybe you'll get my job. You want me to put in a word for you?"

He reared back in horror, his brown eyes flashing. "God, no! The last thing I want is all that responsibility. I only want to punch my time clock and go home at the end of the day. I'm going to miss you, though." His eyes misted, and he gave her a hug.

Hope went back to her office. She placed her hands over her

keyboard, but they were shaking so badly she couldn't type. Hope closed her eyes.

You've survived worse than this. You'll make this work. You always do.

≈

SHE MADE herself dinner when she got home from work and was adding the croutons to her salad when her phone rang. It was Sara's ringtone.

"Well?" Based on her tone, Sara was practically jumping up and down. "Did you give your notice?"

"Yes, I did. In two weeks, I'll be a free woman."

"Ha! I can't believe you actually did it. I thought for sure you'd back out. Did you find another job over the weekend?"

Hope ignored the lurch in her stomach. "No. I don't know what the hell I want to do. I'm terrified."

Sara paused and sucked in a large breath. "Maybe I can help you with that. I have a birthday surprise for you."

"In case you forgot, my birthday was last week, back when the world was still somewhat normal."

Sara giggled. "Well, you did say you needed a change in your life."

Then she took another deep breath, and Hope's stomach dropped.

What is she up to now?

"Ok, here's the thing," Sara said. "When we were talking about that raffle for the dive resort in St. Croix, you seemed so sad that night." It came out niiiigghttt. This was never a good sign. "And that was on top of your breakup with Kyle. So, I thought I would be a great little sister and buy you a couple of tickets for it. As a birthday present, Hope! Well . . . I bought three. Happy Birthday!"

"Uh, thanks, Sara."

"Oh, you're very welcome. Have I told you lately how smart and beautiful you are? Um, well, here's the thing . . . uh . . ."

"Sara, what did you do?"

Hope was familiar with the tone of her voice, and it always meant trouble.

"Congratulations, Hope! You won the raffle for the resort. Isn't that amazing? Aren't you super happy about it?"

"WHAT?"

"I used my email address but entered in your name. I just got the email from the resort a couple of hours ago announcing Hope Collins as the winner. Isn't that great? Isn't it the best? Please?"

Hope snapped her open mouth shut as she paced between the living room and the kitchen. "Sara! I told you I wasn't interested, and you entered me anyway?"

"Yes! Don't you see? It's fate! I told you things have a way of working out. This is the change you've been looking for."

"You have completely lost your—"

"I looked it up online. It's called Half Moon Bay Resort, and it's in St. Croix, in the Virgin Islands. It's really cute, not too big, and on a gorgeous white sand beach. It's an amazing opportunity —you're very lucky. You should be extremely grateful to me, Hope."

Hope poured herself more wine as she tried to stay calm. "Great. You accept it and move down there! I like my life in Chicago."

"I'm perfectly happy here in Charleston, and I love my job at the salon. Also, I'm not the one who just broke up with her boyfriend, suddenly found herself unemployed, and wanted a change in her life. Hope, the timing could not be more perfect for this if you had planned it. You know you love me."

Hope took a large gulp, then set the glass down and scrunched her hair. "My God, Sara. I know you mean well, but why can't you ever leave well enough alone? I can't drop everything to become a beach bum." She was close to pulling out a tuft of hair, so she opened her hand and pressed it against the cool quartz countertop.

"You'd hardly be a beach bum. You've already got lots of experience with hotels. It wouldn't be *that* different. I'm going to email you all the documentation as soon as we get off the phone. Please check it out. Hope, I'm not kidding when I say this is an incredible opportunity."

"No, dammit!"

Sara's voice turned firm. "Hope, knock it off. I'm serious now. This is *exactly* what you need. This isn't just a great chance for you —it's the chance you need to finally start living your life. You've always made sure I'm ok. Now I'm trying to do the same for you."

That got to her. Tears built in Hope's eyes. "Oh, all right. Send me the information. I'll look it over, but I'm not making any promises."

CHAPTER 7

*H*ope had been staring at Sara's email for several minutes. She couldn't get past the obnoxious headline or the knowledge that its contents could change her life.

Oh, Sara. What have you gotten me into?

She clicked on the headline and opened the email:

RE: URGENT! OPEN ASAP! Half Moon Bay Resort raffle entry

Dear Hope Collins,

We are thrilled to announce you are the winner of our raffle for full ownership of Half Moon Bay Resort in beautiful St. Croix, USVI! Here are the steps we need to process your winning entry:

1. Please email stevej@hmbresort.com within 48 hours to confirm your prize.
2. In the same email, please also confirm it is acceptable for us to use your name and likeness in promoting your win.
3. Legal transfer of the property is contingent upon approval from current property owner, Steven R. Jackson, and his

legal counsel. Raffle winner is also encouraged to obtain
legal counsel to expedite the property transfer.

Please respond ASAP. If we don't hear from you within 48 hours,
we will have to draw another winner! Click on the following link to
learn more about our resort, a favorite with divers and beach lovers
since 1998. We take great pride . . .

HOPE'S HEART pounded in her ears, and her stomach did gymnastics. She read the email four times. Finally, she clicked on the link that brought up the resort's website, and her eyebrows flew up at the cover image. It was an aerial shot of a beautiful crescent of white sand with the turquoise-blue ocean lapping the shore.

Half Moon Bay Resort was situated on its namesake bay. It was a boutique resort with eight individual bungalows spread along the stunning beach, four on either side of the restaurant and central complex of buildings. Palm trees lined the back of the beach. She could practically hear the tropical breeze in her ears. She clicked on another page, which showed a long infinity swimming pool with an attached pool bar overlooking the ocean.

Scuba diving seemed to be the primary activity and had its own tab, discussing a daily dive trip with instruction available and equipment for rent if necessary. Hope thought back to snorkeling on a trip to Jamaica several years back. *I bet the snorkeling in St. Croix is great.*

Another picture showed a long wooden pier, complete with an attached dive shop and classroom halfway down. The dive boat was moored at the end of the pier, next to a thatched palapa.

The overall effect of the resort was peaceful, not to mention breathtaking.

Hope sat back on the couch, breath heaving and shoulders tense. She rolled her neck.

This is all mine for the asking.

Opening a new tab, she googled Steven Jackson, clicking a link to a local newspaper article about a large charitable donation to the humane society in St. Croix. There was a large picture of a craggy-faced man who looked to be in his sixties and a woman of similar age, both holding kittens and smiling at the camera. The following link went to a major vacation review website. Half Moon Bay Resort had a 4.5-star rating, mostly due to strong repeat business with divers.

Hope closed her laptop, tapping her fingers on the lid as she stared out her sliding door at the snow falling in the glow of a streetlight below. She smiled, no longer completely disregarding the idea anymore. After taking another drink of wine, she yawned. "You still have to work tomorrow, you know. You should go to bed now." She plugged in her laptop and headed for her bedroom.

HOPE WAS BACK UP at 3 a.m. checking out the resort website again. She looked at the cover image of the beach and serene ocean for the hundredth time.

I'm surprised they don't have staff listed on their website. I'd change that if I were in charge . . .

She clicked on the email. It sat there, daring her to reply and beat the clock—**within forty-eight hours or we'll have to choose another winner!** Hope finally hit the reply button, writing that she was ecstatic to win and was accepting the entry. She noted her updated email address but left out the part about her sister entering her unknowingly.

With her heart pounding in her ears and her finger hovering over the send icon, she groaned. Hope opened another tab and stared yet again at the home page image, memorizing the beach, waves, palm trees, and beautiful pool as her fingers trembled above the keys.

Make a decision!

She hit send, her breath bursting from her lungs. Clapping her hands over her mouth, she laughed.

THE NEXT DAY, Hope sat in her office and listened to Eduardo chat with a guest as she nursed her fourth cup of coffee. Her phone vibrated, and she froze when *Unknown Number* appeared on the display. She'd been expecting a call, but not this soon.

"Hi, Hope. My name is Steve Jackson, and I'm the owner of Half Moon Bay Resort. I wanted to call and congratulate you. I got your phone number off the raffle entry. Is this a good time to talk?"

"Of course." Hope got up and shut her door. "I'm still in shock. It's very nice to speak to you. I have to admit to being a little overwhelmed by the whole idea."

"I'm sure I would be too, if I were in your shoes. I wanted to go over a few formalities before we can officially declare you the winner. I assume you're all right with us running a background check on you?"

She laughed, pushing her cup away. "I'd be concerned if you didn't. Don't worry. You shouldn't find anything alarming."

"Good. I'm glad." He laughed. "So, do you have any experience in the hospitality industry?" Hope explained her background. "Ok. Things will be different down here, of course. But having some prior hotel experience will be a big help. Have you ever been to St. Croix or the Virgin Islands?"

"No. I went to Jamaica with some friends a few years ago, but that's the only time I've been out of the country. Is St. Croix part of the United States?"

"It's a US territory, along with St. Thomas and St. John, the other two US Virgin Islands. That makes it easy for Americans to travel down here, or move for that matter. My wife and I relocated here and started the resort back in the 1990s. We didn't find the transition too tough. There are more resources available now, and of course the resort is well established."

"What made you decide to part with the resort? Are you retiring?"

He hesitated for a moment. "This resort has been a real labor of love for myself and my wife, Susan. We raised our kids here, but they both moved back to the mainland. Susan passed away from cancer last year, and this place hasn't been the same for me, so I've decided to retire and move to be closer to my kids."

Hope raised a hand to her mouth, her stomach lurching. "Oh, I'm so sorry for your loss. I can understand why things would look different for you now." She paused. "Why the raffle, though, instead of just selling the resort outright?"

"I liked the idea of the resort going to someone who could never have afforded to purchase it otherwise. Beachfront acreage isn't cheap here, you know." His warm laugh made Hope smile. "And we sold a *lot* of raffle tickets, so I'm coming out of this with a pretty tidy nest egg. It seems to be a win-win situation for both of us. Plus, it's been done elsewhere and worked out well for everyone involved. I thought it was a great idea."

"I'm certainly not going to argue! But I do have to admit to being a bit nervous. Do you have a plan for the transition?"

"Sure. I'll hang around for a while. I'm committed to staying here for six months or so. We can get you set up in one of the guest bungalows. They're pretty comfortable."

Hope blinked, hardly able to believe it. "That sounds amazing. Really."

"The sooner you can move down here, the more time we have for me to show you the resort operations. By the way, do you scuba dive?"

"No, I don't. I know it's primarily a dive resort, so I imagine I'll need to learn at some point." Hope wasn't about to admit to him that the idea of being fifty feet under the ocean surface scared the hell out of her, and she had no intention of learning to dive. He'd be gone before it became an issue.

"There'll be plenty of time for that. We have a great dive staff here. Our instructor Alex is as good as it gets."

"It all sounds great, Steve. I can't wait."

"As I said, we have some formalities to clear before we can officially proceed, but do you know when you can move down here? I'd like to get an idea."

"You know, it's funny. The timing of this is pretty incredible." Hope rested her head in her hand. "I gave notice at my job last week because I realized it wasn't going anywhere. And my apartment is now on a month-to-month lease, so there's not that much holding me back. I could probably wrap things up within a few weeks."

"Maybe it's fate then. Forgive me for the personal question, but no husband or kids?"

"No, I'm single."

"I understand. Assuming you pass the background check, the next step will be the damn lawyers. Sorry about that, but we have to." He paused to laugh again. "It was nice talking to you, Hope. We'll keep in touch."

"Thank you, Steve. It's a big relief that you're going to stay on and make sure this transition is as smooth as possible."

After the call ended, Hope stared at her office walls but imagined palm trees and clear turquoise water.

CHAPTER 8

*a*lex lifted the final two tanks out of the water bath and carried them to the other side of the room, lining them up with the other full tanks. He turned off the air compressor and removed his protective ear cans, relishing the quiet. The late afternoon sun, combined with the heat from the compressor and the tanks as they filled with air, made the small room stifling. He escaped out the door and stood on the pier, letting the breeze wash over him before heading for the bar. It had been a long day, and he wanted a drink.

Alex walked toward the pool bar, surprised to see Steve seated at a table. The water whispered over the edge of the infinity pool as he passed by, and several guests relaxed under umbrellas. Alex smiled and nodded at two sisters walking down the beach. They'd been on the dive boat the last couple of days. Steve motioned for him to sit as he smirked.

"What?"

"I was getting concerned those two women might give themselves whiplash when you walked by."

Alex shot him a dirty look as Clark, the bartender, brought

over two Leatherback beers. "You keep me busy enough without more complications."

Clark smiled, showing his silver incisor, which sparkled against his dark face. "You want anythin' else?"

Steve and Alex shook their heads, and Clark returned to the bar with its thatch roof. Alex looked around, surprised there weren't more guests scattered around the sandy bar area. It was late afternoon and a beautiful day, with puffy white clouds drifting across the sky.

Steve took a long pull of his beer. "How were the dives today? Seems like we've got a good group of guests right now."

Alex nodded. "They're pretty good. Minimal babysitting and Oscar came out for a visit." Oscar was an extremely large resident green moray eel. Alex hooked a thumb over his shoulder with a grin. "Thought I was going to have to rescue those two. They weren't too happy about a six-foot moray doing circles around them." Then Alex sobered. "Tommy told me when we got back to the dock the bilge pump is acting up again."

Steve waved him off. "You guys can fix it. We're too busy to do a deep inspection of the boat."

Alex tried to keep from tensing. "Easy for you to say. You're not the one out on the boat every day. But I imagine we can get the pump working again, and then I guess it becomes the new owner's problem."

Steve smiled at a family playing in the ocean. "Man, I'm going to miss this place. I'm ready to move on, but I have to admit, it's harder than I thought it would be."

"You sure you're doing the right thing here?"

Steve looked at the bar, then at the tables scattered about in the sand. "Yeah, I'm sure. Doesn't mean it's easy, though." He ran a hand through his graying hair. "I talked to the winner of the raffle, Hope Collins, a few days ago. First impression was good. She seemed nice. And she has experience in the hotel business."

Alex snorted. "Well, I'm glad she's *nice*, since we're the ones who will have to deal with her."

Steve winced. "I wouldn't leave you guys with someone impossible. We ran the background check on her and it came back squeaky clean. She seems pretty normal to me."

Alex stared at him. "Sounds fabulous."

Steve laughed. "Oh, give me a break. I'm doing the best I can here." Then he sobered. "My lawyer Al is working on all the paperwork to get everything transferred. He's planning on sending it to her attorney in Chicago for signatures."

Alex shrugged, not caring about the details of how his life was about to change drastically.

Steve sighed. "Can I give you some parting advice?"

"What, are you going to bolt tonight?"

"Relax, it's a figure of speech. I'm still planning on staying six months. Or less if she's a fast learner." He leaned forward. "Look, I know what you've been through. Don't let it define your life."

Alex stiffened as he darted a glance around to make sure they weren't overheard. "Trust me, you don't know. You can't."

"Alex, you've been here *five years*, and I've never even seen you with a woman."

He straightened and crossed his arms, glaring. "What? You want me to start screwing all the female guests now?"

"Don't pull that intimidation crap on me. It won't work."

"Ok, *Dad*. But I can't believe we're having this conversation right now. This isn't exactly any of your business."

"All right, I surrender." Steve leaned forward again. "Almost."

Alex groaned and closed his eyes. "Oh my God."

"Look, you prickly bastard. You're one of the best people I've ever met in my life. I know better than anyone what it's like to be alone. That's my life now, and I accept it. But you don't have to. You deserve better, Alex."

He met Steve's eyes, his jaw locked. "Thanks. I'll take it under advisement. Can we change the subject now?"

"Fine." Steve looked like he was biting the inside of his cheek as he tried not to smile. "You know, the new owner says she's single."

Alex gave Steve a tight smile. "That sounds like an incredibly bad idea on so many levels that I don't even want to start."

Steve finished his beer as Clark brought another round. "Ok, ok, you win." They clinked beers.

"Is she at least a diver?"

Steve grinned wider. "Nope, never dove."

"Oh, great."

"I'm sure you can certify her if she wants to learn." Alex shrugged, and Steve narrowed his eyes. "You're not getting itchy feet, are you?"

"What? No, this place suits me. Been here for five years now. I don't have any thoughts of moving on."

Steve sighed, his shoulders relaxing. "Good. That's an enormous weight off my shoulders. I feel better about leaving, knowing that you're around to keep an eye on things."

Alex scowled. "You said you thought she'd work out fine."

"I do, but she doesn't have your experience here on the island, and she sure doesn't have your background. Alex, you can't hide out forever."

ALEX STOMPED down the pier toward his apartment, fuming. He ripped off his shirt and shoes and dove into the water, cargo shorts and all, with no goggles. It was night anyway—not like he could see anything. He sliced through the water, his powerful stroke the result of years of practice.

Who the hell does Steve think he is, raffling off the resort to a complete stranger?

He had worked very hard over the last five years to build the resort dive operation from a side business featuring a revolving door of dive professionals to a well-respected and safety-focused mainstay that brought back guests year after year.

And this is the thanks I get—some woman who doesn't know the first thing about diving.

CHAPTER 9

 *resent Day . . .*

HOPE TOOK A DRINK OF CHAMPAGNE. Her throat was dry after the long explanation about winning the resort and wrapping up her life in Chicago. The airplane air didn't help either.

Barbara gaped at her. "What an opportunity. You're not nervous?"

"I alternate between euphoria and terror at equal intervals." Hope took another sip, the bubbles tickling her nose. "I still can't believe how easy it was to settle my current life." *Kind of depressing, actually.* "A woman in my apartment building was thrilled to buy my car. I sold some of the stuff in my apartment, donated the rest, and now here I am."

"You know, I'm a corporate attorney. Real estate is definitely not my area of expertise, but you got this checked out, didn't you?"

Hope laughed, easing back in her seat. "Yes. Background check passed. Attorneys pored over the documents, and we signed a week ago. I am the official owner of Half Moon Bay Resort." Her heart pounded just saying the words.

"The name sounds romantic. Is it one of those resorts with non-stop activities and aerobics in the pools?"

"No, I don't think so." Hope smiled as the flight attendant refilled her glass. "It looks like it's mainly a scuba diving resort."

"Oh, that's awesome!" Barbara turned more toward her. "I got certified around fifteen years ago but haven't been diving since I had kids. You must be an avid diver then?"

Hope shook her head. "I've gone snorkeling and enjoyed that. Diving seems scarier, though—what if you run out of air? No, I'll have plenty to keep myself occupied without adding drowning to the list."

"Well, it sounds wonderful and a terrific opportunity for you. Few people have the courage to cut their ties and jump into a new life. I wish you all the best."

⁓

AS THE PLANE DESCENDED, Hope kept her face glued to the window. The ocean was a mixture of impossible shades of blue. She didn't know colors like that existed in water—dark indigo indicating deep water, to royal blue, cobalt, and finally turquoise before shading to the lightest aqua near the sparkling white sand beaches.

She glimpsed a town as they passed the north shore. Then they passed over jagged emerald peaks and headed back out to sea to begin their final approach. The plane descended lower and lower until they finally bumped down safely in St. Croix.

As they gathered their belongings, Barbara said, "Good luck on your new adventure." Hope wished her well and stood to depart from the airplane.

Soon, they were walking down the staircase from the plane to the tarmac, their plane one of several lined up in front of the small airport. The warm, humid air caressed Hope, and she took a deep breath.

She closed her eyes, becoming dizzy as the impact of her decision hit her.

This is my home now. This is my life. I will *make a success of this.*

Hope opened her eyes, lifting her chin and marching into the terminal. *Besides, it's not like I'm totally alone. Steve will be there to help me learn the ropes, thank God.* She made her way to the baggage carousel, and her two suitcases appeared within minutes, tagged as first class so they would come off the plane first.

As she made her way to the taxi line, a Black man in wrinkled trousers stepped away from his elderly sedan and bowed in front of her. "Malcolm Adams, at your service, miss. Where you headin' today?" He seized the suitcases from her, a smile creasing his weathered face.

"Half Moon Bay Resort, please."

Malcolm manhandled her suitcases into his trunk. "What you got in here, rocks?" He laughed, taking a handkerchief from his back pocket to wipe his face and curly gray hair.

"Just my whole life." He opened the back door for her before climbing into the driver's seat.

"Well, that sounds pretty serious, now. All this for a dive vacation?"

Hope settled into the back seat as Malcolm started the car. Despite looking dubious, it started right up. "No, I'm not on vacation. I'm moving here."

"Is that a fact? Welcome to sunny St. Croix!" He pulled onto the highway and headed west.

Hope couldn't resist his infectious attitude and smiled back. "Thanks. It's great to be here."

"Half Moon Bay is a very nice resort. Good people. You gettin' a job there?"

"You could say that. I'm the new owner of the resort."

"No! You're the one who won that lottery?" Malcolm slapped the steering wheel, and Hope laughed.

"Yes, that's me."

"Really? What's your name, miss?"

"Hope Collins. I'm excited to have Steve show me the ropes before he moves to the mainland to retire."

"Hope, you'll be just fine. You ever been here before?"

"No. But I'm loving my first impression." They were motoring around a bend in the road next to the ocean. The sun sparkled on the water. "It's so beautiful."

"It is. And St. Croix is a welcoming place. Half Moon Bay is on the western end of the island. Very green and lush. The east side is totally different. Desert-like, with cacti all over the place. We're coming up on Frederiksted now. That's the nearest town to where you'll be. The other major town and capital of the island, Christiansted, is on the north coast."

"I saw it as the plane landed." Hope peered out the window as they drove through Frederiksted. They were driving down a main street with the ocean on one side and multicolored buildings on the other. "It's so pretty! The town looks straight out of a postcard."

"That's the Danish architecture. St. Croix is famous for it. We also have forts you can tour, plantations, and lots of pirate legends."

They left Frederiksted behind and traveled north, the road winding through the lush jungle. Shimmers of ocean appeared periodically.

"Half Moon Bay is right ahead."

Hope's pulse pounded in her ears as they crested a hill and a wide crescent of sandy white beach came into view—the bay was aptly named. A pier jutted out into the aquamarine water in the middle of the bay. They turned left at a sign for Half Moon Bay Resort and started down a narrow paved track. Towering jungle vegetation created a tunnel over the road.

Would she need permanent mosquito repellant and a machete? She had just formed the thought when the jungle stopped, and they pulled into a clearing with a cluster of buildings scattered about and a glimpse of the ocean behind. Malcolm stopped the car at a roundabout in front of a charming one-story cottage-style building. Light yellow with white trim, it boasted a wraparound porch and black shutters.

He popped the trunk and unloaded her suitcases. "You'll be just fine here, Miss Hope. Don't you worry."

"Thank you so much." She handed him a twenty as a tip. "I'm off to a great start already. I'll take it from here."

"Thank you so much. You have a wonderful day now."

Malcolm rumbled away, leaving Hope alone. Some distant noises came from inside the building, but the area was almost silent otherwise, with only the occasional birdsong. She closed her eyes for a moment, taking a deep breath and turning around.

Picking up a suitcase with each hand, she climbed a few steps and entered, noting the lobby sign over the door. The propped-open doors were made of beautiful tropical hardwood. Hope glanced around the lobby. There was a seating area with couches and armchairs preceding the front desk.

Two dark-skinned women behind the desk were having an intense conversation. On the other side of the lobby was additional seating, along with a large table set with cookies, infused water, and fresh fruit. Hope walked over and helped herself to a glass of water, parched from her long journey.

As she drank, one woman from behind the counter walked over. She looked to be in her late fifties and had a fuzzy halo of black hair. Her name tag read Patti Thomas, Manager. "Good mornin'. How may I help you?"

Here we go.

Hope smiled and put all her confidence in it. "Hi Patti, I'm Hope Collins, the new owner of the resort." She held her arms out from her sides. "Here I am! And I can't wait to meet Steve. Can you let him know I'm here?"

Patti winced, her ample frame turning away slightly. "Oh dear." Then she faced Hope. "It's very nice to meet you, and everyone is excited you're here. But we've had a terrible shock this mornin', so we're all of out of sorts."

She sighed and took Hope's hands. "Steve left suddenly last night. He didn't say a word to anyone. None of us knew." Patti squeezed her hands as Hope's breath came faster and faster. "When he didn't come out of his house this mornin', I got concerned and went to check on him. He was gone, and he didn't leave any information on how to reach him. Even his cell phone number is disconnected." Patti wrenched her eyes shut before opening them again. "I can't believe he'd just up and leave!"

Hope's pulse pounded in her ears as her head spun. "He left? How am I supposed to take over the resort?"

CHAPTER 10

*H*ope raised both hands to grip her hair, her breath heaving as Patti's warm brown eyes opened wide. She put her arm around Hope's shoulders, steering her to a couch. "Now you sit down, child. I can't have the new owner passin' out on me, now can I?"

"Steve promised he was staying six months to help me transition," Hope said, her voice rising. "I don't know anything about this place. How could he just leave? What am I going to do?"

Patti squeezed her hand, her eyes filling with warmth as she scooted closer. "When I went into his house this morning, there was a letter for me. He said he was terribly sorry to be leavin' in the middle of the night, but he couldn't bear to stay on and felt he had to leave straight away. There was also an envelope with your name on it, so it looks like he wrote a letter to you too. But we'll let that sleepin' dog lie for now."

Hope pressed both palms to her eyes and leaned forward. "I left everything behind for this. I can't turn around and go home again. This is supposed to be my new start in life. How on earth am I supposed to figure out how to run this place?"

Patti smiled, transforming her face as her white teeth lit up the room. "Why, child, you don't have to worry about that! I've been the manager of this resort for a long time now, and anythin' I don't know isn't worth knowin'. Half Moon Bay has been here a long time. I run a tight ship, and we're all hard workers here." She touched Hope's cheek for a moment. "Steve might have thrown us a curveball, but I'm not goin' anywhere. You and I will make this all work out, you'll see."

Hope gave her a brave smile. "Thanks, Patti. I'm glad you're here." She looked around the lobby, taking in the colorful paintings of local plants and scenes of sunsets and green mountains. "This place looks beautiful. I know I'm very lucky, but I'm still in shock."

"It is beautiful, and no mistake. Let me give you a quick tour of the resort and introduce you to some of the people. I knew you were comin' in today, so I have the Hibiscus bungalow set aside for you, thinkin' Steve would still be in the owner's residence. No matter. Let me start by introducin' you to Martine, who works the front desk . . ."

ALEX UNSCREWED the yoke of the regulator and hung it over the tank valve. They were on their way back after the second morning dive. He worked quickly, trying to get as much done as possible before they returned to the resort. It had been a great morning, culminating in seeing three Caribbean reef sharks on the second dive.

The group consisted of four couples who liked to take dive vacations together. They were excellent divers, which made his job much more enjoyable. A corner of his mouth turned up as he watched the flat blue sea, not a cloud in the sky.

Tommy had the radio up as usual, and several guests were singing off-key to Bob Marley. Alex smiled wider and shook his head. Everyone was in a good mood. Mark, one of the husbands, stood next to him. "So, Alex, I couldn't tell. Are you a divemaster, or an instructor?"

"Both, I guess. You have to become a divemaster before becoming an instructor. I got my instructor cert about eight years ago."

"You've been at this a while then. You have to take a special course for instructor, right?"

Alex nodded. "Most dive shops can teach up through divemaster, but you have to take a specialized course for instructor." He coiled up the regulator and hung it over the tank valve.

"Oh yeah? Where'd you take yours?" Mark's wife Lucy had handed him a towel, and he rubbed his dark hair.

"Don't let him pester you. He can talk scuba all day." Lucy laughed and returned to her seat.

Alex grinned. "Can't we all? Nothing wrong with that." He turned back to Mark. "I did my instructor course in the Red Sea. The diving there is *great*."

"Man, I'd love to do this for a living. What's the instructor course like? Is it hard?"

Alex added his wetsuit to the pile on the floor. "It's a lot harder than basic open water certification for sure. But it should be—you're responsible for people's lives. Here at Half Moon Bay, I mostly lead dives. I do some certifications, but most people are here to dive, which is the fun part of the job anyway."

Mark closed his eyes and took a deep breath of the marine air. "I could definitely get used to this."

Alex moved to the next tank. "Well, it's not so enjoyable when it's pouring rain and the seas are six feet. But I agree, on days like today, it's the best job in the world."

Mark went back to sit next to his wife, and Alex redressed in his staff T-shirt before continuing to remove the regulators and BCDs from the tanks so he and Tommy could get the tanks off the boat quickly once ashore. As they tied up to the pier, Patti and another woman walked toward them. He held out a hand to help the divers off the boat.

"You look like a group of happy divers. That's what I like to see!" Patti wore her trademark smile.

"Fantastic morning!" Lucy said with a broad grin. "Give Alex whatever he wants to stay here. He is a wonder at finding things underwater."

"He is, that's for sure. We're proud to have him and Tommy both. Enjoy your lunch."

The group continued down the pier toward their bungalows as Patti and the woman headed toward the boat. Tommy stayed aboard and started handing Alex the dive gear so they could rinse it in fresh water.

"Good afternoon, gentlemen," Patti said, stopping in front of Alex. "Sounds like a successful mornin' of diving."

"It was," Alex said, turning toward them and lifting his sunglasses onto his head. "Can't go wrong on a day like this. We even saw a couple of sharks." The very pretty woman standing next to Patti looked to be in her mid-thirties and of average height, with brown hair being blown around by the wind. She seemed preoccupied and didn't really meet his eyes, like he wasn't worth noticing.

"I'd like to introduce you both to someone," Patti said. "This is Hope Collins, the new owner of the resort. Tommy, standin' in the boat there, is our captain. And this is Alex, our dive guide and instructor."

"Welcome!" Tommy scrambled off the boat and onto the dock to shake her hand. "It's so good to have you here! You're gonna love it."

She gave Tommy a tight smile. "Thanks. It's been quite a morning, but everyone has been so friendly."

"Hi, I'm Alex." As he shook her hand, tension radiated from her. Either she was just uptight, or something else was wrong. She didn't seem overly friendly. "I figured Steve would be showing you around himself. This resort is his baby."

Patti and Hope shared a dark look.

What is going on here?

Patti breathed a sigh. "That brings me to the other big announcement. Steve is gone. He left last night."

Tommy dropped the BCD he'd been holding. "Huh?"

"What do you mean he's gone? He left the island?" Alex asked, stepping closer to Patti. "He never said anything to me about leaving now."

Patti met his gaze. "He didn't talk to *anyone*. When he didn't come into the office this mornin', I got worried and went to his house to check on him. I found a letter sayin' he was leavin' right away."

"I can't believe this! Did you try to call him?"

Hope took a step back and narrowed her eyes.

"Of course I did! I'm not an idiot, you know." Patti's eyes flashed. "His number has been disconnected."

Alex held up his hands. "Sorry, only thinking out loud. He told me he was finding it harder to turn over the resort than he'd thought it would be." He turned to Hope. Now her attitude made more sense. Her lips were set in a thin line. "Are you ok? I'm sure this isn't how you thought your arrival would go."

"No, this is definitely *not* how I had pictured it." She lifted her chin. "But I'll be fine."

The steel in her spine made Alex take another look. She met his gaze head-on, as if daring him to tell her she'd fail. He still wasn't sure he liked her, but he thawed a little. Alex appreciated people who weren't afraid of a challenge.

"I've been giving Hope a tour of the resort and introducing her to people. We'll let you two get back to work." They turned and walked back down the pier.

"What are we gonna do now? I can't believe Steve bolted on us!" Tommy stood with his hands on his hips, indignant.

"Me either. I didn't think he'd make it the full six months he talked about, but I never thought he'd cut and run." Alex grimaced.

I didn't think he'd do this to me.

"Maybe it was too much for him to take," he continued. "He did say he wasn't looking forward to saying goodbye. Pretty crappy thing to do to the new owner, though."

Alex had a sinking feeling his quiet, predictable life had just been turned upside down.

CHAPTER 11

*H*ope was still dazed as she and Patti walked back toward the resort. They stepped off the wooden pier and onto the soft white sand. Directly in front of them was the infinity pool, and music came from the attached pool bar to her left. Behind the pool sat the open-air restaurant.

"We just opened for lunch," Patti said. "Let's head over there and get you somethin' to eat." She led them over to a secluded corner table. "This is where Steve and his wife ate their meals. It's in the corner to create some privacy, but he liked to be out with the guests in case they had any questions or concerns. The rest of us eat in the kitchen. Of course, you can pick any table you'd like."

Hope made an effort to pull herself together. "This one is fine. And I agree—sitting in the restaurant with the guests is a good idea."

As Hope sat, Patti beckoned to a young woman standing near the edge of the restaurant. "Charlotte, come on over please, and bring a menu." She turned back to Hope. "Charlotte is one of our servers. Order whatever you'd like to eat and drink. We've brought your bags to the Hibiscus bungalow, which is on the other side of the restaurant. Why don't you have a bite to eat, then spend the rest of the afternoon relaxin'? You can try out the pool too."

"That sounds like a great idea." Hope sat down. "Thank you for your help, Patti. You've been a lifesaver."

Patti squeezed her shoulder. "You're welcome, child. I'm sorry we didn't get off to a smoother start. I've got some things to take care of, so I'll leave you to your lunch."

Charlotte handed Hope the menu and gave her a shy smile. "Pleased to meet you. Can I get you a drink? It sounds like you've had a shock of a mornin'."

"That sounds perfect, but I don't even know what I want right now." Hope immediately warmed to Charlotte, who was a slim young Black woman with her hair pulled back in a slick bun.

"Oh, don't worry about that! I'll have Clark, our bartender, mix you up somethin' special."

As Charlotte hurried toward the pool bar to place her drink order, Hope surveyed the restaurant. Several cooling fans spun overhead, and a row of tables stood directly at the edge of the beach, with several more next to the pool area. The décor was casual tropical, with potted red and yellow bougainvillea scattered throughout.

This is such a beautiful place, and I've never felt so alone.

A blender whirred in the distance. Soon a tall, rail-thin young Black man came toward her carrying a tall glass on a circular tray.

"Welcome! I'm Clark, the bartender here." He set the drink in front of her with a big smile. He had a charming silver tooth, which drew her smile in return. Hope turned her attention to the frozen concoction.

"This is a Painkiller," Clark said. "It's the official drink of the Virgin Islands, and I make the best one on St. Croix, if I do say so myself." He winked one brown eye at her. "It's made with Cruzan rum, which is distilled right here in St. Croix. You enjoy now."

She took a deep drink. Clark had been liberal with the rum.

Painkiller—exactly what I need right now. As she sipped the pineapple, coconut, and orange juice mixture, Hope kept reminding herself to relax her shoulders. She'd had a knot in her stomach since arriving, and it didn't show any signs of abating. Charlotte soon brought the blackened fish sandwich and fries she had ordered, and Hope was impressed. The flavors of the fish were both bright and fiery. It was flaky and cooked to perfection.

Guests trickled in after getting cleaned up from their morning adventures. Several were from the dive boat, but there were others too. The divers traded banter back and forth as they discussed the morning's dives. Hope was surprised they were excited to have seen sharks. That would be the *last* thing she'd want to see underwater. Once she finished her lunch, it was time to investigate her bungalow.

Hope stepped onto the beach. Four wooden bungalows were spread out along the sand. Taking a deep breath to calm her nerves, she had to admit the resort was even prettier in person. To her right, a sandy path wound into the foliage behind the beach. Hope followed that, meandering away from the restaurant with a canopy of jungle trees and colorful shrubs all around. The Painkiller hadn't managed to remove the ball of dread sitting in her gut.

Have I just made the biggest mistake of my life?

Soon, another path branched off to the left with a red and yellow sign and an arrow reading "Hibiscus," opening up to a weathered bungalow with a grouping of its colorful namesake flowers planted around it. The pink and yellow flowers contrasted the worn gray wooden structure. There was a screen of vegetation carefully groomed between this bungalow and the next, giving the area a spacious yet very private feel.

Hope climbed the stairs leading up to a screened-in porch directly on the beach. Sitting in front of the interior door were her two suitcases with the room key on top. She gazed at the white sand and turquoise water with the pier jutting out to her left, but feeling only shock and emptiness.

Hope unlocked the door and entered the large open room of the bungalow. A king-size bed with a mosquito net above sat on one side, facing the water. The bedspread mirrored the ocean outside with its muted blue shades. On the other side of the room were a dark-blue couch and loveseat with a coffee table in front. Hope was impressed. It could do with some updating, but most guests would be thrilled to be in this room. *I'm definitely not thrilled right now.*

The furnishings were colorful, though a bit worn, and the room was spotless. She dragged her suitcases inside but didn't have the energy to unpack yet. Pouring herself a glass of water from the pitcher sitting on the coffee table, she turned on the air-conditioning unit before sitting on the couch on the front porch while she let the bungalow cool off.

Waves lapped gently onto the shore. The view was beautiful, and she tried to absorb it and not think about anything else. It didn't work, as the first tear fell down her face. Her breath hitched, and the tears built until she sobbed, bent over with her face in both hands. It had been a long time since she'd let go so completely.

Eventually the tears subsided, and she sat back up, watching the tranquil scene in front of her. She was overwhelmed and alone in the world, even as the palm trees whispered with the breeze.

Without thinking about it, she lay down and fell into a deep sleep.

THE NEXT MORNING, Hope used the pod-style coffee maker in her bungalow and went out onto her porch. It was 6:30, and soft light filtered over the scene in front of her. The resort faced due west, so she'd been treated to a spectacular sunset the previous evening and had done her best to appreciate it. Now, as dawn broke, the sun rose above the steep mountains to the east, the line of shadow creeping across the beach toward Hope as the sun progressed.

After a good night's sleep, she felt slightly better about her situation, but Steve's sudden departure had badly shaken her. She let her gaze drift to the ocean and someone freestyle swimming with confident strokes toward the pier. Hope admired the form of the swimmer. She'd been an All-State swimmer in high school and could recognize an expert. *Maybe one of the guests?*

The swimmer climbed the ladder located at the end of the pier and walked toward the resort. Hope sat up, focusing closely. Appraising the athletic form and sandy hair, it must have been Alex, the dive guide. She was impressed he got here so early to start his day. Hope was further surprised when he climbed a set of stairs at the side of the building and entered a room.

Wait, does he live here?

She winced. Hope had been so shocked yesterday that there was no way she'd made a positive impression, which wasn't good at a resort that prioritized scuba diving. The last thing she wanted was for either Tommy or Alex to view her as a pathetic female who didn't stand a chance of being successful there.

Her frown deepened further as she remembered the first impression Alex had made on her. She hadn't liked how assertive he'd been when he found out about Steve. The one type of man she could *not* abide was an aggressive alpha male who bullied his way through life, wrecking everything and everyone in his path. Though, to be fair, she'd overheard several conversations at lunch yesterday about how fun Alex was to be around on the boat.

She went back inside and returned her empty cup to the table. Her still-packed suitcases taunted her. "If Steve's gone, there's no reason for me to stay in this bungalow."

Hope took a shower and attempted to rein in her unruly chestnut hair. Usually the wave in her hair naturally fell in soft layers, but the humidity turned it into a frizzy mess. Finally giving up, she tied it back in a ponytail and called it good.

She entered the restaurant and Patti walked toward her with a big smile. Her ebony skin already glowed from the humidity. "Good mornin'. I trust you slept well? Gonna be a hot one today."

"I slept like a rock. I was pretty worn out." Hope inhaled deeply. "Breakfast smells great. Looks like you serve it buffet-style?"

"Yes. Breakfast is a buffet, and lunch and dinner are both served plated by menu." Patti turned toward the buffet. "We like to be a little more casual at breakfast. I'll introduce you to our chef, Gerold, later. We're proud to have him. He went to culinary school in Tortola and is very talented. He could easily work at one of the bigger resorts here, but he likes the quiet west side of St. Croix."

"I can't wait to meet him. I loved the meals I had yesterday." Hope got a plate at the head of the buffet and poured some guava juice. "Patti, would you show me where the owner's house is located? I'd like to see it first thing this morning. There's no sense in my using a guest bungalow when the house is empty."

"Of course. Come find me in the office behind the front desk when you're through eating."

Hope inspected the lavish buffet with a sinking feeling. With its French toast, pancakes, bacon, sausage, and more pastries than she could count, she would need to be selective if these were going to be her daily choices.

She took her hard-boiled eggs, fresh fruit, and yogurt to her corner table. There were already several groups of guests eating, excited about what adventures the day would bring. She ate her breakfast, then chatted with some of the guests to discover what they had planned and what they were enjoying about the resort.

Hope was determined to make a productive start to her new life.

CHAPTER 12

*a*lex took a quick shower after his morning swim and made his way to the back of the restaurant and into the kitchen for breakfast. Opening the door, he was greeted with the smell of frying bacon and cinnamon from the French toast. It was a brightly lit, neat area, and the employee table he sat at was spotless, as was the rest of the kitchen. Gerold's standards and work habits were very high, something he and Alex shared.

Gerold nodded. "Hey, man. You want your usual oatmeal and fresh fruit?"

"Sounds good." Alex poured a cup of coffee and sat down.

"You meet the new boss?" Gerold spoke in a soft Caribbean accent as he deftly flipped six slices of French toast. Thirty years old, he was a St. Croix native with closely cropped black hair. "She hasn't made it back here yet."

"Yeah, I met her yesterday. She looked pretty shaken up. You heard about Steve, right?"

Gerold gestured with his spatula. "I still can't believe it. He hasn't been the same since Susan died. Patti said he couldn't bear to stay on any longer. Poor bastard."

"This definitely throws a monkey wrench into everything,"

Alex said as he accepted the bowl of oatmeal. "He'd promised the new owner he would stay on for six months to help her with the transition."

Patti entered the kitchen and turned to Alex. "Can you come see me in the office for a few minutes when you're done eatin'? I need to talk to you."

"Sure."

She nodded, grabbing a banana before leaving.

"I can understand Steve wantin' to get out of here. He misses his kids and grandkids." Gerold was now frying hash browns and cooking a huge pan of scrambled eggs simultaneously. "I wish him the best."

Alex snorted. "Then you're a better man than I am. I'm pissed at him." He finished his coffee, becoming serious as he gathered his dishes. "You don't just leave people behind. If he comes back any time soon, I'll probably toss him off the pier." He got up. "I'd better go see what Patti wants."

Alex nodded to Martine as he went behind the front desk and into the office.

"Shut the door, if you please," Patti said.

He did and sat down in front of her desk, hardly noticing the framed pictures of the staff on the walls or the other desk in the room that sat empty now. "Let me guess. This about Steve?"

"Yes. I told you yesterday I found the letter when I went to his home." Patti spoke with a lilting accent. "There was also one for Hope, by the way. She was here a few minutes ago askin' where his house is, so I gave her the keys and sent her to investigate on her own." She picked up a piece of paper from the desk. "But the letter I found was actually addressed to both you and me, so I wanted you to read it too." She passed him the letter scrawled in Steve's unruly handwriting.

DEAR ALEX AND PATTI,

I've decided to leave tonight. I'm terribly sorry to do this to you both—you deserve better from me. I'm only taking my most important things with me. The rest you can get rid of. I won't need it anymore.

I can't do this. That's what it all boils down to. Susan and I worked all our lives to build this place, and I can't bear to turn it over to someone else. I know that's unfair to Hope, and I'm sure she will do a fine job with the resort. She seems smart and willing to work hard.

I know I don't have the right to ask you two for any favors, but could you help her out? This is an awful thing to do to her—and to you guys as well. She's going to need a guiding hand here at first, and you two are the obvious choices.

Please don't try to track me down. I really need some time to decompress and start over. I'll be in contact if and when I'm ready. I know I owe everyone at Half Moon Bay an apology.

You've been like a son and a daughter to me, and I love you both.

-Steve

"Wow," Alex said, sitting back in his chair. "I was almost wondering if he got kidnapped in the middle of the night or something. I guess this letter settles that."

"I'll keep up a good front for everyone else, but I don't mind tellin' you that I'm totally stunned here." Patti reached up to fiddle with her bead necklace. "After all we've done for him, he just leaves us like this? Especially you and me?"

"I know. But we'll find a way to make this work." Alex sighed, frowning. He didn't want to let Patti know how angry and deeply hurt he was.

Like a son to you, huh? Yet you bolt in the middle of the night, you son of a bitch. Even worse, you're a coward.

"What a mess."

"We'll survive this, Patti. We're a good team here, and that can make all the difference."

She straightened and took a deep breath. "Yes, it can. This is a great place, and I love my job. Hope seems very nice, so we'll just have to take her under our wings and show her the ropes."

Alex hunched in his seat. "I don't know why you or Steve think I should be involved in this. I'm only the dive guide. What am I supposed to show her?"

"Oh, stop it. You're the dive operations manager. At a dive resort. Of course she's gonna have to know somethin' about that." A small smile crept onto her face. "She'll probably want to learn to dive at some point too."

"Says who? You never have."

Patti laughed. "I can't even swim! No, I'll keep my feet nice and dry, thank you very much." She pointed to him. "And quit tryin' to change the subject. You're goin' to have to interact with her, like it or not. It could be worse, you know."

Alex grinned. "How? If the whole place burned down?"

"No! I mean Hope. She didn't fall to pieces or blow up yesterday. And when I saw her this morning, she was focused and determined to make Steve's house her own. I'd say it was the best possible start under the circumstances."

He shrugged, then narrowed his eyes as a full smile spread over Patti's face. "What?"

"You know, she's not so bad looking either." She was clearly trying not to laugh now.

"Oh, no you don't." Alex tensed, sitting up straight. "That is the absolute last thing I need in my life right now, and probably the last thing she needs too. Jeez, what else could go wrong?"

～

HOPE DESCENDED the same stairs outside the lobby she'd climbed yesterday morning. She followed the road Patti had indicated, and after a quarter mile, it opened onto the front facade of a lovely single-story house painted white with green shutters. Several stairs led to a small deck in front of the dark-red front door. Like the guest bungalows, it was raised on two-foot cement blocks. A garage/shop sat at a ninety-degree angle to the cottage, painted to match, and a grassy lawn surrounded the house until it met the sandy beach.

Hope stood there, blinking.

She'd never lived in a detached house before. Living in Chicago had meant a series of apartments, and growing up, the closest she had come was her family living in an attached townhouse for several years.

I live here—this is mine.

There was such a jumble of emotions inside her that she couldn't untangle them. Pride, joy, fear, and uncertainty all competed for supremacy. After climbing to the landing, she used the key to open the front door and stepped inside.

The house had an empty, forlorn aura about it. She inhaled—there was a humid, stale odor. *I'll have to see what I can do to breathe some life back into it.*

The front door entered into a hallway with an office on her left and an open kitchen and great room to the right. A cozy side table sat inside the door, an envelope with her name on it on top. Hope left that alone for the moment, entering the office. The top of the desk was bare except for some empty desk trays and a pencil organizer. Several file cabinets sat along the wall. Not wanting to face that yet either, she continued her tour.

The kitchen was clean and modern, sporting a large granite island with barstools on the far side. The great room contained a typical layout, with a tan couch and loveseat, a couple of bright blue accent chairs, and a flat-screen TV on the wall.

Hope continued into the spacious master bedroom at the back of the house, which was dominated by a wall of floor to ceiling windows showcasing the ocean view. Passing a king-size bed, she moved into the attached bathroom and opened the closet to find it stuffed with clothing and the various accumulations of life. Sadly, all of Susan's clothing still seemed to be present as well.

Hope sat on the bed and sighed. How would she tackle this?

I can't just throw out all of Steve's things. What if he comes back for them?

She decided to investigate the prospects of the garage out front for storage. Nearing the front door, the envelope on the front table called out to her. "Ok, I guess it's time for you now." She picked up the letter and sat down on the couch to read it.

DEAR HOPE,

I'm sure you're furious with me right now, and I don't blame you. It might not mean anything to you, but I'm very sorry to leave you alone like this. I'd like to explain. My wife and I moved to St. Croix and started Half Moon Bay Resort in 1994. We poured our heart and soul into this place and raised our two children here. After growing up, they left St. Croix and moved back to the mainland. After Susan passed last year, all I could see around me were memories of happier times.

That's when I decided to retire and move closer to my kids and grandkids. The lottery seemed like a great way to leave on a high note, knowing I helped someone out. I hope you at least feel the same way about that.

I fully expected to stay on and teach you everything you need to know about the resort to keep it the success that it is. In the last week or so, I've found it harder and harder to think about staying here and drawing all of this out.

To put it bluntly, I can't do it.

I ask your forgiveness. Patti can teach you almost as much as I about the resort operations, and Alex knows the dive op better than anyone. Lean on them—they won't let you down. They are both stellar people.

I've written down some things Patti or Alex might not know, such as bank information and the names of some professionals I use (lawyer, accountant, etc.) I hope it's helpful.

Again, I'm sorry for leaving like this. With your hotel experience and work ethic, I have no doubt you will be a great success and lead Half Moon Bay into its next phase.

Best regards,
Steve Jackson

HOPE SIGHED and rubbed her eyes before turning to the other sheet of paper. Listed were bank account numbers, though she had completed the account transfers when she and her lawyer had signed the documents Steve's attorney had sent. But the accountant and insurance agent information would come in handy. Steve also noted a wall safe behind a painting in the office and the combination. She looked around the bedroom with new steel in her spine.

You're goddamn right I'm going to be successful. No thanks to you.

Hope returned the envelope to the entry table and left the house to investigate the garage and shop. She was relieved the Jeep Wrangler was inside, as she'd already taken the title to it.

Gathering an armful of boxes she found in the garage, Hope headed back to the house and started her battle in the master closet, boxing up everything until the closet was an empty shell. That took the rest of the morning. Sealing up someone's intimate details, even though they were strangers, left her drained and miserable.

Hope made a brief stop for lunch, and by late afternoon she had removed all of Steve's and Susan's personal effects from the house, leaving it furnished like a general vacation rental. The office took the most time, as she had to separate the business items she might need from their personal documents, which she boxed up. Hope opened the wall safe, not even sure what she expected or wanted to find, but it was empty.

She returned to the main area of the house and soaked in her surroundings. It no longer felt like someone else's house, but it wasn't hers yet either. Maybe some new artwork, throw rugs, and pillows would help, and definitely new linens.

Satisfaction washed over her. She'd accomplished a lot today. Hope let her gaze drift to the sun nearing the horizon.

"I think a celebratory drink is in order," she said to the empty room.

CHAPTER 13

*L*eaving through the rear porch's sliding glass door, Hope walked along the beach. Her cleaning had left her thoroughly dirty, so after a shower, she'd changed into a pair of skinny jeans and a white tank top. Carrying her flip-flops in one hand, she let the waves wash over her feet, then on impulse turned and walked to the end of the pier.

For several minutes she stood still, looking out at the ocean as the water lapped against the wooden pilings below her feet. Resolve filled her as she watched the horizon. It was a strange mixture of peace and determination. She was finally able to soak in the serenity and beauty around her and relax. Tipping her head back, she closed her eyes and let the breeze wash over her, soaking it all in.

With a small smile, Hope turned around and continued to the bar, a double-sided wooden structure with stools along one side and submerged swim-up stools along the other. Scattered around were several tables, some on the tile floor under the thatch roof and some on the sand. Lilting island music played from speakers suspended from the bar ceiling as Clark worked the bar. Hope sat on a stool in front of him.

"How's it going today, Clark?"

"Always a good day! What're you in the mood for?" He grinned, his silver tooth glimmering.

"Well, I've been cleaning Steve's things out of the house all day, so I'm pretty thirsty. What kind of beer do you have?"

"We got Red Stripe, our local craft beer made by Leatherback, and some crappy American stuff."

She laughed and ordered a Leatherback, which tasted cool and delicious after working in the stuffy house all day. A soft breeze blew past, and she was relieved to finally be unwinding.

"I see you have good taste in beer," said a voice behind her. She turned around as Alex walked up to the bar, and she looked at him closely, trying not to react.

How did I not notice yesterday how good looking he is?

Fit and tall, he was over six feet. "I'll take one too, Clark." He turned to her and smiled politely. "May I join you?" Alex spoke in a deep, confident voice.

"Of course, please."

Alex sat next to her. He had vivid blue eyes, short light hair, and a strong chin.

It would be inaccurate to say alarm bells went off in her head. It was more like klaxons, air-raid sirens, and multiple searchlights.

Oh, Hope. You need to keep this guy far away.

Still, she would be seeing him nearly every day. Taking a deep breath, she would strive for friendly but aloof.

He tilted his beer toward hers, and they clinked together. "I hope you're having a better day than yesterday."

"Well, that wouldn't be too hard. I spent today getting settled in the house." She took a drink. "How was the diving today?"

"Pretty decent." He was serious now. "No one died, so that was good."

As her eyes grew larger, a wide smile crossed Alex's face. "I'm kidding. The conditions have been perfect lately. This is why people come to the Caribbean." His eyes sparkled, and she withdrew, moving further away on her barstool. He cooled a bit at that.

Hope searched for something to say. "So, did I see you swimming this morning?"

"Guilty as charged. I swim most mornings before I start work."

"You start early." Hope rubbed her brow. "I'm a little confused. Do you live here at the resort?"

"Oh! I guess there's no way you would know, huh? Yeah, I live in an apartment on the pier right over the dive shop."

She turned to Clark. "What about you?"

Wiping a wineglass, he shook his head. "No, you and Alex are the only ones who live on site." Then he smiled at Alex. "He earns his keep. Every once in a while, we get his help with a rowdy guest."

"Sometimes someone drinks a little too much. I, uh, *encourage* them to go back to their bungalow. Well, him. It's always a guy." Alex pointed a finger at Hope. "And it's almost never a diver, I'll have you know. You should come out on the boat with us. Are you certified?"

Hope shook her head, trying to ignore how at ease he made her feel.

I can see why he's popular with guests. Not gonna work on me though, buddy.

"No. I went snorkeling once in Jamaica. It's really beautiful down there. The fish are so colorful." She spun a coaster on the bar as she tried to avoid looking at him. "I don't think diving is for me, though. It sounds scary. A lot could go wrong."

"You can't own a dive resort and not dive," Alex teased, relaxed and confident as he leaned on one elbow before becoming animated. "Open water certification is more than just breathing off a regulator. I'd make sure you were comfortable with all the skills you need to learn. During the class, you learn how to respond if anything goes wrong. And, if it makes you feel better, equipment failure is extremely rare. I maintain our scuba equipment myself, so I can vouch for all of it." He turned to Clark. "Maybe you and Clark can take the course together. I've been trying to get him to dive for a year now."

With wide eyes, Clark shook his head. "No way, man. I'm not afraid of the water, but I'm not goin' near no sharks. Uh-uh."

Alex's smile grew. "Clark, I've done thousands of dives, and I have yet to be bitten by a shark. You need to come up with a new excuse."

"I'll work on one then," Clark said.

"The idea makes me pretty nervous too," Hope said. "Not only the sharks—all of it. But I've got enough to worry about right now just figuring things out. Sorry, Alex. Not interested."

His smile faded, and a neutral mask fell over his face. "No problem. It's your choice."

She looked at him. *Was I a little too cool?* "Maybe I could ride along with you guys sometime? I'd like to see how it all works."

He finished his beer and stood, one corner of his mouth raised. "Whenever you want. You own the place, after all."

ALEX WALKED AWAY from the bar, a confusion of emotions rushing over him.

What are you doing?

He had no answer to that. He'd been sitting on his porch and enjoying the late-afternoon sunshine when Hope had appeared at the end of the pier below him.

At first, she had a closed, guarded look on her face, and his stomach clenched in sympathy. That was a visage he'd seen on his own face. Hope hadn't made much of an impression on him yesterday when they'd met on the pier. Alex hadn't really even looked at her.

But he was looking now.

Her tight jeans and white tank top showed every curve, but he saw much more than that as she tipped her head back with her eyes closed. She stood like a woman trying to face the entire world alone. Alex was a protective man by nature, and it drew him like a magnet to steel.

Hope turned and walked away with a faint smile as Alex sat, staring at the empty place where she'd stood. "She's your boss— nothing more." He closed his eyes and pressed his palms into the wooden surface of the table. Then, before he knew what was happening, he had trotted down the stairs to join her at the bar.

Now, he walked back down the pier, his flip-flops thwacking on the wooden boards as he muttered to himself, "And you positively *flirted* with her, Monroe. Good thing she shut you down fast. You do *not* need this in your life." Alex automatically rubbed his right hip before ripping his hand away.

As he walked into his apartment, he tore off his shirt and started his weight routine, determined to do something productive to work off his frustration at himself.

 *pril* ...

A SOFT BREEZE rustled the palm trees as Hope entered the lobby and exchanged greetings with Martine, the front-desk clerk. She was a beautiful twenty-two-year-old with caramel skin, multiple thin braids in her long black hair, and a warm, infectious smile. Behind her, Hope walked into the office, where Patti sat behind one of two desks.

It was a plain white box of a room, with framed staff pictures on two opposite sides. Group photos were on one side of the room and individual ones on the other, but Hope's attention was drawn to the empty desk, which sat in front of a panel of three windows.

Patti smiled and waved an arm at it. "This will be your desk. Steve wasn't the neatest person in the world, so you might take some time to arrange things more to your likin'. Next, I can give you an introduction to the types of things Steve worked on, as well as my duties."

Hope nodded, making her way over to it.

It was worse than she'd thought. A disorganized jumble of papers, some crumpled and torn, sat on the desk. Messy writing was scrawled over several of them. Hope opened the drawers to find solace and instead found veritable chaos within. As a neat and organized person, Hope was made acutely uncomfortable by Steve's desk. "Ok, Patti, I need to get this desk situation straightened out first. And it looks like it might take a while."

"Yes, I know. I'm so sorry. I can only imagine what you went through in his house yesterday."

The two broke into laughter. "Well, I guess it's a good thing organization is one of my strengths."

By late morning, Hope had three enormous stacks of papers on her desk—one that could be thrown away, one she wasn't sure of, and one that needed to be kept and filed accurately. This third pile was already a foot high, and she wasn't done yet. For the last half hour, a gnawing feeling had been growing in her gut that threatened to become panic.

You can do this. Keep concentrating.

Her stomach gave an angry growl that Patti overheard.

"Hope, why don't you take the afternoon off and get settled in? You've been at that for hours now. You don't have to tackle everythin' immediately, you know."

"You might be right. I feel pretty brain dead right now. I think I'll go have lunch, but I'll come back this afternoon and shadow Martine at the front desk."

Patti turned her warm gaze to Hope. "Don't work yourself too hard, child. I can't even imagine how overwhelmin' this must feel right now."

"Thanks, Patti. I've never been afraid of hard work." Hope gave her a smile as she stood up. "But I know when to take a break too. See you this afternoon."

~

AFTER A COUPLE OF WEEKS, Hope was a little less panic-stricken. She'd settled into a routine of spending mornings with Patti in the office, learning the details of operations, and afternoons on her own in other areas of the resort. She'd learned most of the chaos of paperwork on her desk was financial in nature.

Patti had nodded when she'd commented on it. "Yes, I tend to handle the front desk, restaurant, and housekeepin' areas, and Steve handled all the financial aspects. I also tried to comment on guest surveys, but I've fallen off on that with all my other duties. Steve didn't like to work on computers much."

Hope turned her head sharply. "Well, I think responding to guest surveys is extremely important, so I'll take that over from you right now. Steve should have kept up on that, not dumped it on you. The guests are the whole reason we're here."

Now she was settled enough to discover more about the resort's other major area of operation. After finishing her breakfast, she approached a family who'd been there a week. "You guys are having a nice, long vacation. Good for you!"

"We're going diving again today." The boy, Noah, looked about fifteen. "This is the third time on this trip."

"I'll see you on the boat then," Hope said. "I'm riding along today. I feel like a little fresh air." She went back to her house to change into a swimsuit. Over it, she pulled on some board shorts and a staff T-shirt she'd had Patti hunt down.

Putting on a sunhat, Hope made her way down to the pier for the 9 a.m. departure. She passed through a tunnel of sorts with the compressor and gear storage room on one side and the dive shop/scuba classroom on the other. Alex's apartment was overhead. On one wall was a whiteboard where divers signed up for the two-tank morning trip.

Hope continued down to the end of the pier, where a thatched palapa provided shade. Underneath it were several wooden benches. Tommy and Alex were busy preparing the boat for the morning, so she made her way over to the side of the pier near the ladder into the water. The turquoise sea was crystal clear with ripples of white sand visible on the ocean bottom. A myriad of colorful tropical fish darted about.

"Come on aboard, Hope!" Tommy called out, beckoning to her.

She smiled as he helped her into the boat. "I picked a good morning to join you. Looks like a beautiful day. How many divers do we have today?"

"Only two guys and the family of three," Tommy responded. "Should be a nice mornin'." She made her way to the covered bow area of the boat next to him and set her bag down on a broad shelf above the dashboard to keep it dry. Tommy, who looked to be in his mid-thirties, had ebony skin and tightly curled black hair. Behind her was a long row of white plastic half-cylinders that held the scuba tanks. Alex nodded at her from the stern where he was setting up someone's gear.

She approached him. "Ok, Alex. What is all this stuff?"

"I'll give you the brief version." He took hold of the mouth-piece. "This is the primary regulator, and you breathe through this, the second stage." He pressed the purge button on the mouthpiece, causing a hissing sound. Then he moved his hand up the black hose to the top of the tank. "It's connected to the first stage, which attaches to the tank. This," he put his hand on a vest attached to the tank, "is a Buoyancy Compensation Device, but everyone just calls it a BCD. It's also attached to the tank, and you add or remove air to it during the dive to keep yourself neutrally buoyant."

Hope held her hands up, laughing. "Whoa. That was the brief version?"

He shrugged a shoulder. "It becomes second nature after a while."

"Well, I think I'm happy to stick with snorkeling for now."

She shifted her gaze to his. Alex watched her with a small

smile, his blue eyes sparkling. Her breath quickened, and a flutter tickled through her abdomen.

Where did that come from? Hope, stop it!

"It's your call." He spoke softly. "But you're missing out on the best part, you know. Being able to breathe underwater is a pretty unique experience. It's kind of a superpower." She gave him a quick, polite smile in return before hurrying back to her spot on the bow.

She waved to the family as they boarded. The two other divers came aboard shortly after, and then they were ready.

"Good mornin', everyone!" Tommy said with a smile. "I'm pleased to announce we have a special guest on the boat today. This is Hope Collins, the new owner of Half Moon Bay Resort." Hope smiled as everyone greeted her. "Since you've all been aboard *Deep Diver* before, you can relax and enjoy the scenery while I go over the boat briefin' with Hope." Tommy proceeded to tell her about the safety features of the boat, including where life jackets and fire extinguishers were located. It was clearly a speech he made regularly, but she was pleased with his professionalism.

Alex untied the lines from the dock, and they started to idle away from the resort. "Where are we goin' this morning, Alex?" Tommy asked.

"Anyone have any requests for dive sites?" Alex scanned the group, who all shrugged or shook their heads. "Ok, Tommy, let's head for Turtle Gardens." He turned back to the group. "It's less than a ten-minute trip, so you guys might want to start getting into your wetsuits."

Tommy throttled up, heading north. Hope took a deep breath of the fresh, salty air and removed her floppy sunhat, looking out over the flat ocean and feeling exhilarated. The warm sun on the stern section looked inviting, but she opted to stay out of the way of all the divers busy pulling on their wetsuits and preparing their dive gear.

Despite Alex's explanation, it still looked very intimidating to her. He stood next to Tommy, chatting with him as he pulled his wetsuit over his board shorts. He peeled off his shirt and tossed it on the console in front of Tommy so it would stay dry. Tanned skin complemented his muscular chest and shoulders.

Hope immediately averted her eyes. After turning back, she was relieved he had the wetsuit all the way on and was zipping up the back, pulling the zipper leash over his head. He grinned at something Tommy said, and Hope could see he wasn't trying to impress her—this was simply part of his daily routine.

After several minutes, Tommy throttled down, and Alex put on a dive mask. He made his way to the bow of the boat, grabbing a coiled rope. Putting on a pair of fins, he dove into the water with the rope and disappeared.

"What's he doing?" Hope asked Tommy.

"The dive sites have submerged moorin' buoys. They're at about fifteen feet, so he has to dive down to tie off the boat."

"Huh? How do you know where the buoys are if they're submerged?"

Tommy laughed. "We have GPS, of course, but I don't use it. After doin' this for a while, you learn where everythin' is by lookin' at the landmarks on shore. See the green house and white house next to each other?" She nodded. "I know the moorin' ball is between them and the bottom is about twenty feet." He pointed at the depth gauge.

"Wow. That's impressive."

Alex surfaced at the side of the boat, making eye contact with Tommy and bumping the top of his head twice with a fist. Tommy shut off the engine, and Alex swam to the stern and climbed back aboard.

"All right guys, I know you're eager to get going, but listen up while I go over the dive," Alex said, wiping the seawater from his face. Hope and the other divers immediately turned to listen as he described the topography of the site, how they were going to dive it, and what kinds of life they might see.

Alex had a natural authority and was one of those people who drew the eye. People broke off conversations as he entered the restaurant, though he seemed unaware. His commanding presence was just part of his makeup.

He continued the briefing. "There's usually some really big groupers here, so keep an eye out. They're pretty friendly. It's about forty-five feet to the bottom here, so take your time descending. That's about it. Everyone gear up!"

Most of the divers were already in their BCDs and had their fins and masks on. Tommy made his way to the stern, helping them walk to the platform by holding onto their tank valves to steady them as the boat rocked in the gentle waves. Then they jumped into the water with an enormous splash and popped back up.

Alex got into his dive gear, helping the last person into the water before jumping in himself. The whole group exchange ok signs and disappeared beneath the waves as Hope stared at the surface, surprised to feel a pang that she wasn't with them.

CHAPTER 15

*T*he boat was now quiet and serene after all the frenzied activity. A soft breeze rippled the ocean as the sun warmed Hope's back. She made her way to Tommy, who was still at the stern platform. "That was some production. How long do they stay down?"

"Oh, it's easy on a day like this. Wait till we have to do it in rough weather, then it's a different story. The first ones will pop back up after forty-five minutes or so, but we have a sixty-minute maximum for each dive. Now is the relaxin' time for me." With a big smile, Tommy went back to the wheel.

Hope dangled her feet in the water and smiled as a silvery fish darted back and forth around them. Every now and then there was a flash of color from one of the diver's fins. *What would it be like to be down there with them?* With a happy sigh, she turned to lie down on her back and dozed as the sun warmed her.

She awoke to a sound similar to gently boiling water and turned her head as a large group of bubbles broke on the surface off the stern of the boat. She sat up and looked at her watch, surprised that fifty minutes had passed.

"They'll be comin' back up soon. I need to put the ladder down, if you don't mind," Tommy said.

Embarrassed she'd fallen asleep, Hope returned to her place at the bow. Soon, Tommy was helping the streaming wet divers back on board, with Alex last to appear.

"That grouper was as big as me!" Noah grinned, his dark hair flopping over his forehead. "And he came right up next to me. So cool."

Alex smiled at him. "That guy has been around here a long time. His name's Bubba."

"I've never even seen a turtle before. I can't believe I got to see four. I can see why you call it Turtle Gardens," said Noah's mother, Amy, pulling her wetsuit down to the waist.

Tommy pointed to a cooler. "We've got soft drinks and bottled water. Drink up! Divin' makes you dehydrated. Also, fresh fruit and Chef Gerold's famous cookies."

Hope took a bottle of water and ate a cookie, looking around the group. Alex came up to Tommy as everyone helped themselves to the snacks. "Let's head toward Pillar Coral for the second dive." Tommy put the boat in gear and motored south, slowly this time.

Alex grabbed a bottle of water and drank the whole thing before turning to Hope as he pulled his wetsuit down to the waist. She made sure to keep her eyes on his face.

"The second site we're going to is a shallow reef that's great for snorkeling," Alex said. "I put a mask, fins, and snorkel on board for you. Feel free to check out the reef while we're doing the second dive if you'd like."

"Thanks. I think I will." She smiled at him, pleased he'd thought of it. "Can't let you guys have all the fun."

He nodded, then went back to the stern area and started swapping the divers' gear over to fresh tanks for the second dive. She turned to Tommy. "How come you're going so slowly? Is something wrong with the boat?"

"Oh no, she's great today. The divers need about an hour between dives. It's called a surface interval—clears out the nitrogen that builds up durin' the dive. Goin' slowly kills time, plus it's easier to eat the snacks!" He grinned and popped a cookie in his mouth.

"Great today? Does that mean the boat isn't great on other days?"

"Nah. She's older, so I have to show her the proper respect, you know." He smiled again, then got serious. "We have some problems with the bilge pump, but nothin' major. Every boat's got somethin'."

Before long, they were at the second site and the whole process was repeated. Hope put on the mask, fins, and snorkel Alex had handed her before jumping in the water himself. She eased herself off the platform.

Alex wasn't exaggerating.

At first, she floated on the surface as fish of every shape and color darted and flitted about over corals of red, purple, and even green. Hope smiled as a school of small blue fish came to investigate her, then went back to the reef and chased off a much bigger fish. She lost herself watching the thriving reef below her, jack-knifing her body to dive for a closer look before needing to surface for a breath.

Looking over, Hope was surprised two divers were heading back to the boat. It was time to get back on board herself. Watching the remaining group of four divers, she tried to distinguish them—they were in similar wetsuits and tanks. But after a moment, there was a clear difference in one of them.

That was Alex.

The other divers moved with somewhat clumsy fin kicks and one moved like he was riding a bicycle. Alex flowed over the reef, up and down but never touching it, his fins an extension of his body. Hope stared until he waved at her, making her stomach lurch. Waving back, she turned back to the boat, climbing aboard.

She made her way to the bow to wrap a towel around herself before venturing into the sunshine to enjoy the warmth. Soon after, Alex came back with the family of three. Noah looked apprehensive.

"Dad, something doesn't feel right. I felt lopsided all of a sudden while I was waiting to get back on the boat."

Alex hurried over. "You're missing a weight pouch. That's the problem with these weight-integrated BCDs that only use Velcro to close. The pouches fall out easily."

Noah's father scowled. "Noah! I told you. You have to be careful with your gear—looks like your diving's done for this trip."

"I'm sorry!" Noah was stricken. "I didn't mean to lose it."

"It's ok, Noah. It happens." Alex leveled a steady gaze at Noah's father and turned back to the boy. "This isn't your fault. You said you noticed it at the end of the dive when you were waiting to get back on the boat?" Noah nodded. "Well, it's probably right underneath the boat somewhere. I'll dive down and look for it."

"Could you do that?"

"No promises, but I'll give it a shot." Alex went to a storage area in the bow and removed a pair of very long fins and a weight belt. He went to the platform, donning his mask and fins before slipping into the water and holding onto the side of the platform as he became still and quiet. Finally, he took a deep breath and slipped beneath the water.

Hope frowned. "Is that safe? How deep is the water?"

James, one of the two single divers, answered, "The bottom is over forty feet down, so that's a pretty decent free dive."

"How come he didn't just put his scuba tank back on?"

"It's a hassle," Tommy replied. "I'm guessin' he thinks it's right underneath the boat and he can get it right away. That guy loves to free dive." He peered at Hope over his sunglasses. "Besides, my man Alex has *skills*."

Hope joined the rest of the group at the stern of the boat,

pulling on her staff T-shirt. She crossed her arms, fingers tapping on her biceps.

The group waited . . . and waited . . .

Noah's forehead wrinkled. "How long has he been down there?"

James checked his dive watch. "Close to four minutes. When should we start to worry, Tommy?"

"I've seen him dive longer than that. Don't you guys be concerned. One time, we were on the north—"

Alex surfaced ten feet behind the boat. He raised his right arm out of the water and held up the weight pouch, triumphant. "Got it!" That broke the tension, and loud cheering ensued as he swam back to the boat.

James stopped his watch. "Four minutes, twenty-one seconds. That's pretty impressive."

After stowing his fins and weight belt, Alex replaced the weight pouch back in Noah's BCD. "There you go. Now you're all set for tomorrow."

"Thanks! Can you teach me that?"

Alex shook his head, peeling his wetsuit off. "I only free dive for fun. You need to get a certification to learn it properly. I can teach scuba, but not free diving."

With that, they headed back to the resort. Alex retrieved another bottle of water as his board shorts dripped on the fiber-glass deck.

Hope approached him, smiling. "You made that young man very happy."

"Weight pouches are expensive to replace." He reached over and put his staff T-shirt back on, then added in a lower voice, "Besides, I didn't like the way his dad talked to him. That could've just as easily have happened to the dad as Noah. They have the same BCD."

Hope smiled again as she and Alex now wore matching T-shirts. "You can hold your breath a long time. Wouldn't it have been easier to use your scuba gear?"

Alex shrugged. "Maybe. But I don't get that many chances to free dive. It's like anything—you have to practice it to keep your skills up. I couldn't have stayed down much longer. His weight pouch was further away than I thought it would be." He reached for a towel to wipe his face. "I used to be better at it. Getting lazy in my old age, I guess."

"Old age, huh? You don't look it."

"I just turned forty. But I'll thank you for the compliment, Boss Lady."

THE SUN APPROACHED the horizon and pink, wispy clouds streaked across the sky as Hope studied the bar menu, indecisive. Iced tea was her typical choice, but she didn't want to be typical. Not anymore.

"You know," Clark said. "You are standin' in the presence of one of St. Croix's greatest mixologists. Or at least I hope to be." He laughed. "Every year at The Buccaneer Resort, they hold the St. Croix Mixologist Contest. I am goin' to win that—mark my words."

She rested her chin in her hand, smiling at him fondly. "I would never doubt you, Clark."

"I come up with a special cocktail every day. Often, it's my own recipe. Today it's the Half Moon Breeze. It's light rum, Midori, pineapple juice, and 7UP, all blended to perfection. Can I get you one of those?"

"Sold. As long as it's cold, I'm in. I'll be at that corner table over there." Hope sat down, glancing at the dive boat tied to the pier, which reminded her of the great time she'd had on it. She rode along again this morning, repeating her solo snorkeling while the rest of the boat dived. She was impressed after watching Tommy and Alex in action. It was obvious they'd worked together for a while. They had the easy rapport that came from long-time friendship.

Hope leaned back in her chair as Alex approached. After ignoring the jolt in her gut at making eye contact with him, she beckoned him to join her.

Have to be friendly, after all. But remember the aloof part.

"Looked like you enjoyed yourself this morning," he said. "I saw you snorkeling during the second dive." Clark brought over her cocktail, and Alex ordered a beer.

"It was fun, and it really is beautiful down there." She frowned. "I didn't realize you were watching me."

"Don't worry, I wasn't stalking you." He sat back in his chair and laughed, then his smile fell. "What?"

Hope took a quick drink of her cocktail to cover her reaction. "Huh? Oh, nothing. I was just thinking about the snorkeling." Alex's laugh transformed his face, making him appear much younger.

Don't even think about it. He might be good looking, but he works for you. Not to mention you have no idea why a forty-year-old guy is being a beach bum on a Caribbean island.

"I try to keep an eye on anyone who's in the water. You looked plenty comfortable. You sure you don't want to learn to dive?"

"I don't know." Hope stared out at the ocean. The sun had set, and there was a faint orange glow in the west. "The thought of it used to terrify me. You know, running out of air and drowning. But now I'm getting used to the idea a bit more." She turned back to Alex. "If I decide to go ahead with it, you'll be the first to know."

CHAPTER 16

*a*lex sat at his workbench in the gear room, inspecting the regulator in front of him. Finally, he gave up with a sigh. He was getting frustrated, and that frame of mind while working on intricate equipment never ended well—for him or the gear. He sat up and rubbed his eyes.

The dive trip that morning had taken some skill on his part, both in terms of diving and guest relations. Most of the time, leading his dive trips was a piece of cake. Alex snorted.

Especially compared to what I used to do.

He bit back the thought, returning his mind firmly to the dive.

A brother and sister duo had been diving with him for several days. The sister, Jade, was newly certified and a bundle of nerves. They'd been at the deepest part of the dive this morning when Alex had looked over to see her sinking rapidly as she wildly stabbed the inflator button on her BCD to add air and stop her descent.

But from the amount of air being released into the water, she was pressing the wrong button and venting more air out instead of adding it, making her sink even faster. Jade was spiraling into panic—her fins kicking hard as a frantic burst of bubbles appeared with each rapid exhale. Alex recognized the trouble signs immediately and rushed to her, quickly inflating her BCD before placing her finger on the button to show her the correct one.

Jade stopped sinking and relaxed a bit as Alex smiled at her around his regulator, nodding as he squeezed her shoulder. A comforting touch did wonders to calm scared divers. He kept a hand on her until she returned his ok signal, then he turned around to lead again. Jade had clung to Alex like a limpet for the rest of the dive, her brother forgotten, though he reasserted himself once back on the boat.

Tim was several years older than his sister and had just logged his hundredth dive, which was a big accomplishment. Unfortunately, he was also an asshole who paraded around the boat making sure everyone knew about his milestone while oblivious to Jade's distress, which irritated Alex to no end. But he'd maintained his professional demeanor, shaking Tim's hand and congratulating him.

Alex had done his best to reassure Jade, giving friendly encouragement while maintaining a professional distance, especially when she'd stroked a finger down his arm as she thanked him. That had made him back away in a hurry.

He never got personally involved with female guests. Plus, she'd recently graduated from college, and young girls didn't interest him in the slightest. At least the second dive had gone better, though Jade still hadn't let him get far away from her.

Alex flushed. He hadn't been involved with any woman, guest or not, for a long time now.

Doesn't matter. This is how it has to be now.

But did it? Was he going to remain celibate forever? Casual flings weren't his style and never had been. But he'd made exactly zero effort to seek out a relationship with any woman living on the island. It was too complicated, and not something he was ready for.

Several fans blew cooling air around the room, half of it dominated by the large air compressor. Its whip hoses were attached to a large open trough filled with water, used to fill tanks with air. The other half of the room was neatly arranged by him to store scuba gear. Both the rental equipment the resort provided and any guest's personal equipment, which Alex stored for them after each day's diving.

He was returning to the regulator on his workbench when the doorway darkened as someone entered. Alex worked to keep a friendly expression as Jade sauntered toward him, dressed in a skin-tight top and very skimpy shorts. Her blond hair hung in curled ringlets and she wore heavy makeup. She looked like a Barbie doll, putting Alex off even further.

"Hi," she said. "I wanted to come back and say thank you again." She stopped in front of him, pressing her leg against his. Alex scooted his chair back a little.

"It's ok. You handled it fine. And you liked the second dive, didn't you?"

She took another step forward. Her breasts were at his eye level. Alex began trying to find ways to extricate himself with some semblance of grace. He was getting ready to rise when Jade grasped his face in both hands and kissed him full on the lips, trying to stuff her tongue into his mouth.

Alex clamped his lips shut and rocketed to his feet, nearly tipping over his chair as he broke off the kiss. His heart pounded.

"What's wrong?" Jade widened her eyes, but she took yet another step toward him.

"I'm sorry, but I never get involved with guests."

Her expression softened. "Well, we're fine then. I'm not looking for involvement, just a little fun."

Time to pull out the heavy artillery. "I can't. You're a beautiful woman, but I'm involved with someone. Seriously involved." This was completely untrue, and Alex hated to say it, but he found himself in this situation from time to time, and it was the best way to gracefully refuse without creating waves with the female guests. And so far, the little white lie hadn't failed him.

"Oh. Well, that's too bad." Jade stopped with a pout, one hand on her hip. "It's your loss, though. I don't mind sharing. If you change your mind, Tim and I are staying in the Orchid bungalow. I can send him out for a walk on the beach easily enough to give us some privacy."

"See you on the dive boat tomorrow, Jade."

She finally took the hint and turned, shooting him a sultry smile as she ambled out the door. Alex sagged with a sigh. The room was stifling hot, even though both fans still oscillated on their stands.

He marched out and stood in the tunnel of the pier as the breeze cooled the sweat that had broken out over his face, relief pouring over him. He rubbed the back of one hand across his lips, glad to see no trace of lipstick as he grimaced.

Voices drew his attention to the left, where Tim, the asshole brother, talked to Hope. Alex focused his gaze on her.

This must be my day for perplexing women.

He still didn't know what to make of his new boss. Over the past month, they'd interacted many times. She worked incredibly hard, which had impressed him from the start, and she would show glimmers of a warm sense of humor once in a while. Alex normally had an easy, relaxed manner with people, as long as they respected his boundaries and kept things from becoming personal.

But Hope had pulled back from him several times, her demeanor cooling, and he couldn't figure out why. *Does it matter? Not like you're looking to get closer to her than you need to.* Yet curiously, the coolness was reserved only for him. He'd seen her with Gerold and Clark—she was warm and funny with both.

Alex couldn't help but be concerned seeing her alone with

Tim now. He had hit on a couple of women on the dive boat, trying to get them to celebrate his diving milestone with him, but didn't get any takers.

Was he trying now with Hope?

Tim took a step forward as Hope retreated. She stood squarely and leaned away. Alex narrowed his eyes as he evaluated the tension in her posture, Jade completely forgotten.

He moved toward the pair.

As he neared, the smarmy grin on Tim's face made him want to deck the guy. Hope probably wouldn't appreciate him doing that to a guest, though, so Alex made sure his voice sounded friendly. "Beautiful afternoon, isn't it?"

Both turned toward him. Hope showed relief for a moment before being replaced with a cool anger, surprising him.

Tim showed straight belligerence. "Yes, it is. Hope and I were having a private conversation."

Alex flashed a smile, but let his eyes become cold as he straightened and crossed his arms. Tim took two steps back. Alex had years of experience putting overconfident men back in their places without even opening his mouth. But he still had to interact with the guy—couldn't take it too far. "Really sorry to interrupt you, Tim. But I've got some new scuba equipment I need to show Hope. I'll catch you on the boat tomorrow, though."

"Oh, ok. I'll let you guys get to work then. See you later, Hope." Tim scurried away as Alex stared lasers into his back. When Tim was well away, he returned his usual pleasant expression to his face as he shifted back to Hope.

She glared at him with her lips pressed tightly together. "Really? You have some scuba equipment to show me all of a sudden?"

Taken aback by her ferocity, Alex blinked several times. "No, but I've been around that guy the last couple of days. He's a jerk, and you didn't look really happy being around him." *Though you sure looked relieved when I first showed up.*

Hope thawed slightly, turning to look at the turquoise ocean. She wore a long blue sundress with thin straps. He narrowed his gaze at the tattoo on her shoulder.

It was a cocoon with a black line leading to a butterfly, very colorful and not too big or flashy. For some reason, he couldn't take his eyes off it.

What would it feel like if I stroked a finger across it?

Alex wrenched his eyes away, making sure his expression was neutral as Hope turned back to him with a cool, professional look on her face. "Thank you for your concern," she said. "But I can assure you that I'm quite capable of taking care of myself. I don't need a man to do it for me." With that she stalked away, her sandals slapping against the wooden boards as Alex tried to keep his eyes off that tattoo.

He frowned, not able to figure her out. "What did I do?" he asked the empty pier. As expected, he got no response and turned to trudge up to his apartment.

CHAPTER 17

*H*ope set down the empty coffee cup with a thump on her porch coffee table. Another morning was dawning, and she *still* hadn't been swimming yet. In the distance, Alex walked down the pier with a towel over his shoulders.

Unfortunately, that reminded her of his little intervention the other day. She'd avoided him since, but that couldn't last forever. Nor was it very mature or professional. Hope needed to face him and prove to herself that she was *not* attracted to him, despite his gorgeous blue eyes and chest to die for. The truth was, she had been very reassured to see him approach and chase off Tim. At least until that had made her feel weak and helpless.

Hope shook her head and groaned. "You like being around a guy who's strong and protective, then hate that you feel that way. Hope, you're a mess."

None of which was Alex's fault, either.

And a small part of her couldn't help but glow a little at how easily Alex had handled the situation, and without ever raising his voice. Good thing she wasn't attracted to him. If she kept repeating it, maybe it would sink in. Still, she might owe him an apology. But being a man, he'd probably forgotten about the whole thing.

She returned her gaze to the distant pier as Alex dove off and began his swim. *I was a top swimmer in high school, for God's sake. I should never have stopped swimming in college.*

There was no time like the present.

She hadn't brought any sensible, one-piece swimsuits with her to St. Croix, so she changed into her sportiest bikini, threw on a cover-up, and headed out the door. At the pier, Hope tossed the cover-up on the bench and shucked off her flip-flops. She stood near the edge opposite of the side Alex had dove off, watching the water shimmer in the morning light, hesitant now.

How would it feel to swim after so many years? Nothing for it but to dive right in.

She smiled at the cliché, donning her goggles and entering the water with a perfect dive.

Surfacing quickly, Hope swam in a sure, steady freestyle, breathing to either side every third stroke. The motions came back to her quickly, and she felt fluid and relaxed. After twenty minutes, she pulled up to tread water, breathing heavily but satisfied as she rested. Looking back at the shore, she lingered on the four northern bungalows spread along the beach. Soon, she took a deep breath and turned around to head back, enjoying every moment.

The fatigue hit halfway back. By the time she neared the ladder, her arms burned, and she was out of breath. As she climbed back onto the dock, the sound of clanging caused her to look over. Alex was loading scuba tanks onto a cart.

He smiled when he saw her. "I wondered who that was. Good morning."

Hope quickly replaced her cover-up, flustered in her bikini. It didn't escape her notice that he hadn't put his shirt back on after his swim—his chest was nearly hairless, and water beaded on his skin. "I was on the swim team in high school but stopped after I graduated. This seems like the perfect place to take it up again. I'd forgotten how much I love it."

"I swim just about every morning. Feel free to join me if you'd like."

"Thanks," Hope said. "Maybe after I build up my stamina a little. Don't think I'm ready to try keeping up with you yet."

Alex looked at the wooden planks and stubbed a bare toe into it, then looked at her from under his brows. "Can I talk to you for a minute?"

"Sure." Her heart sped up as she took a seat on the bench. *Is he about to unload on me for how I acted the other day?*

"I feel like you and I got off on the wrong foot, and I'm not sure why. I've been wondering if you've been avoiding me the last few days."

Warmth crept up her face. She hadn't thought about Kyle in months, but couldn't help it now. He'd avoided uncomfortable discussions and had been almost passive-aggressive about insisting everything was fine—until he broke up with her out of the blue. Yet here was Alex, a man she wasn't even involved with, initiating a conversation because he knew something was off.

"I'm sorry," Hope said. "I got off to a really rough start here, and it has made me defensive." Hope met his gaze to find eyes full of concern. The first stones of the wall around her began to crumble. "Thanks for your help the other day. You were right—that guy was an asshole, and he made me uncomfortable. That's not a position I handle very well, and I lashed out at you."

His eyes softened. "It's ok. You've really gotten up to speed here quickly. I know it's been a whirlwind."

"That's no excuse." She lifted the corner of her mouth. "And that wasn't a nice way to treat one of the most important people working here. I'll try to refrain from biting your head off for no reason."

Alex broke into a dazzling smile. "Thank you. I much prefer to have a good reason for getting my head bit off."

"Something tells me that has happened a time or two."

He affected an innocent, hurt look. "Of course not! I'm all sunshine and rainbows. Perfectly behaved—always."

A smile spread across her face, which Alex returned. Their gazes held until Hope spied movement behind him and Tommy walked by.

"Man, you haven't even started loadin' stuff yet." Tommy shook his head, grinning as he kept walking. "Hope, you need to get on this guy. He's the laziest dive guide on the island. Doesn't do a damn thing."

"Hey!" Alex called. "It's not even eight yet. And I was trying to have a conversation here."

"Yeah, yeah. I'm sure she wants you to shut up and get to work. And you can start by puttin' on a shirt, you degenerate."

Hope laughed and stood from the bench. "I think that's my cue to let you start your day. I'll see you later." She stepped away, a little lighter now.

Two female guests walked along the pier toward her. Hope had met them yesterday and learned they were long-time friends on a getaway without their families. "What's on the agenda for today?" she asked.

"We'd like to go snorkeling this morning and were hoping to get equipment from the dive shop. Is it open yet?" asked Denise, a short, round woman in a flamboyant cover-up.

"Of course. Let me give you a hand." Hope turned back toward the boat. "Hey, Alex, these ladies wanted to get some snorkeling equipment."

"Sure, just a sec." He finished putting the last tank in the holder before climbing out of the boat and headed toward the dive shop, now wearing his blue staff shirt. He beckoned toward them as he proceeded through the compressor room and over to the dive gear storage area. On the other side of the room, the scuba gear was neatly arranged. After determining their shoe size, Alex handed the two guests fins, then grabbed masks and snorkels. "What about you, Hope?"

"Oh, no, it's just—"

"That's a great idea! Why don't you join us?" said Terri, a thirty-something brunette, as Denise nodded.

Hope paused. Patti had practically forced her to take today off, but mingling with guests was never a bad idea. And snorkeling was hardly work. "Why not? It sounds like fun."

Alex set her up with the equipment. "The far end of the beach has a nice reef close to shore. If you don't feel like walking down there, it's also pretty good right here underneath the pier. Have fun." After giving them a professional smile, he went back to the boat.

"Let's go to the end of the beach. I want to see the natural reef," Denise said.

They put their fins on at the shoreline, then duck-walked into the ocean, trying not to fall. Laughing, Hope said, "I can't help but think there's an easier way to do this."

Before submerging, Terri turned to Hope. "I can't believe you don't dive, living here. How come?"

"Everyone keeps asking me that." Hope laughed. "Alex says he'll teach me anytime I want, and I'm starting to come around. This is fun." She turned to Terri. "You don't dive?"

"No way. All that equipment scares the crap out of me. Snorkeling is easy, and it doesn't take any special training."

Nodding, Hope put her face in the water to watch the vibrant reef below. Every fish was a different color and shape—yellow and blue and even one that was half black and half yellow. Another angelfish, gray with bright yellow margins around its scales, came close, and she stopped to watch it gracefully swim away.

They continued slowly snorkeling toward the end of the reef. Soon Hope looked up as Denise sputtered and spit.

"I can never get the hang of spitting the water out of my snorkel." She decided to stay on the surface.

After nearly an hour, they were ready to head back. Hope started finning toward shore, but the current was now against them. "Ok, ladies," Hope said. "We're going to get a bit of a workout on the way back."

Terri nodded and started back. Denise tried to keep up with her, but her movements were slow and erratic. After a few more kicks, she stopped and said, "I need a rest for a few minutes." Hope swam over to her, treading water nearby in case Denise needed help.

After a brief rest, Denise nodded and continued. Hope became more concerned with her as she started to sputter and breathe hard. Grasping her arm, she helped her along, eventually doing more of the work and kicked hard herself to propel Denise, who kept wanting to rest.

"We can't," Hope said. "We lose ground each time we stop. Relax. I'll do the kicking." Denise inhaled some water and coughed, clutching Hope with wide eyes. Terri seemed to be doing better, but was clearly also tired. By the time they made it back to shore, all three were breathing hard and glad to be on solid land once again.

Terri lay on the sand while Denise stood, leaning over with her elbows on her knees as she inhaled quick lungfuls of air.

"Take deep breaths, Denise. We made it back ok." Hope tried to keep up a steady stream of encouragement. She was tired too, but in a lot better shape than the other two. When they had recovered, Hope walked them to their bungalow, then waved goodbye.

She walked along the beach toward her house. Maybe some

formal training wasn't such a bad idea. She was never in any danger, but Denise could have gotten into real trouble if Hope hadn't helped her to shore. *Maybe it's time to talk to Alex about this diving thing. That class might have helped me with Denise.*

She turned her gaze toward the pier.

CHAPTER 18

*a*lex stepped out of the dive shop into the late afternoon sunshine, absorbing his peaceful surroundings with a smile. He had tomorrow off and looked forward to some solo diving. As of now, he was officially off duty.

He walked to the end of the pier to make sure nothing was left behind. A woman sat on a bench. This area was prime real estate on the resort, so it wasn't unusual to find someone sitting there, but he didn't feel like conversation with guests and almost turned around before discovering it was Hope.

Probably all the more reason to turn around.

Alex had spent much of the day trying *not* to think about how good she had looked in her bikini this morning after her swim. Her swimsuit hadn't been overly revealing, but what it had revealed was spectacular. No, he was content with his simple, uncomplicated life.

Yeah, keep telling yourself that.

He was not altogether pleased with his growing attraction to her or the complications it might bring. As he remembered the tattoo on her right shoulder, his pulse increased.

She turned her head and saw him standing there like an idiot. "Hey, you."

Alex was moving before he knew it. He sat down next to her with a smile, relieved after their conversation this morning. Her explanation didn't explain everything, though. *Could her cool attitude be because she might be trying to deny an attraction to me?* Maybe that was why she treated him differently than Gerold or Clark. "What are you doing out here at the edge of land?"

Hope sighed. "Feeling guilty. I gave myself a day off today, but I feel like I should be working. I've barely made a dent in anything." Her voice was low pitched and had a sexy as hell huskiness. "I finally got Steve's paperwork organized, and now Patti is showing me the booking software and front-desk policies."

"You know what they say about all work and no play," he teased.

She barked out a laugh, then got serious. "Believe me, I'm well aware."

He sensed an undercurrent there, but didn't want to push her away when they were finally on good footing. "And how was the snorkeling adventure?"

She turned her head to him. Her eyes were almost golden in the sunlight. Normally they were greenish brown, but now there were flecks of gold in them. "Interesting. The reef was beautiful. You were right about that. But the current picked up, and we had a hard time getting back to shore. I had to almost tow Denise back—she was wiped out. It was a bit scary."

Alex raised his eyebrows. "Really? The current is usually mild there, though there is a new moon right now—that can increase the currents. Just goes to show that you always have to keep your wits about you where the ocean is concerned."

She nodded, one leg swinging back and forth below her. "It got me to thinking some formal training might not be a bad idea. Does the scuba course go over situations where you have to help someone?"

"Yeah. You learn different ways of towing tired divers." Alex poked her with his elbow, trying to ignore the warmth spreading inside his chest. "You thinking about getting certified?"

"Maybe." She turned to him, and her smile grew. "But how do I know you're a decent instructor?"

Alex grinned as his gaze zeroed in on her mouth. He quickly returned it to her face. "Want references, do you? Ask Tommy. I certified him a few years ago—took him through open water and advanced."

Her eyes softened. "No, I'm just teasing. I've heard from plenty of guests how lucky we are to have you. What exactly is involved?"

"There are two classroom sessions, each followed by a pool session. Both sessions will be several hours, by the way. Then there's two days of open water training at the end. I'm sure we could knock it out in less than two weeks."

Her brow smoothed out. "That's more extensive than I thought. It's reassuring, though. How long have you worked here, anyway?"

Alex hesitated. "About five years."

"Did you come here from another resort?"

"No. I was in the military." His jaw tightened.

"And?"

"I'd been diving for a long time and had my instructor license. When I got out, Steve offered me a job. I've been here ever since." He shrugged, aware his voice became flat like it did anytime he talked about that time in his life.

And that is all the reason you need not to get more interested in her.

Hope smiled. "You don't like to talk about yourself, do you?"

"Not much to say. I'm pretty boring."

Her eyes grew warmer as she looked at him. "Well, I'm not sure I believe *that*, but I do believe I'm ready to learn to scuba dive. I work with Patti most mornings, and you've got the dive trips. Could we do it in the afternoons? I'm sure I could carve some time out."

Alex relaxed, back in safe territory once again. "Works for me. We can juggle it around if any guests want to do an afternoon dive trip. Most only want to do the morning trip, but once in a while we get some hard-core divers who want to dive all day. And I don't have any other classes scheduled for the next couple of weeks." He sat up straighter. "I'm off tomorrow, but we could start in a few days if you'd like. I'll get you the materials."

"Yes, I would like that. Let's go ahead."

Alex nodded and held her gaze once again until he turned. As he walked back to his apartment, he was conflicted. Despite wanting to keep things purely professional, he couldn't deny he felt more than friendly toward her. That was a change for him, for sure. But after their conversation, he was more convinced Hope was trying to deny the same sort of feelings—that she wanted to avoid it as much as he did.

So why is that only drawing you more toward her?

SEVERAL DAYS LATER, Hope enjoyed an afternoon drink on her porch as she thumbed through the scuba textbook Alex had handed her earlier. She smiled, remembering their conversation.

"Wait a minute," she'd said. "You never said anything about homework."

Alex raised a brow. "I said there were classroom sessions—that implies homework. Read the first three chapters and complete the quizzes at the end. You need to understand the concepts for the first classroom session before we meet, Ms. Collins. I have high expectations of you."

She saluted him. "Aye aye, captain."

Hope set the book aside with a smile before taking another sip of wine, thinking about Alex. Despite her best intentions, it was more difficult to remain aloof as she got to know him better. He had a charming, confident manner that was hard to resist, and though he'd gotten defensive about his past, Hope had known extended family members who had been in the military and weren't eager to discuss their experiences. She was curious about him but didn't want to pry.

She returned her attention to the scuba textbook and read over something called Boyle's Law. Catching movement out of the corner of her eye, Hope looked to her left. A medium-sized, thin yellow dog stood at the edge of the jungle. It stood there silently, tail straight behind and on alert. "Well, hello there. I haven't seen you before."

The dog cocked its head at her. She slowly rose and made her way to the stairs. "Come here, boy . . . girl . . . ok, boy." When she reached the top step, the dog huffed and bolted back into the jungle. "Hmm, fine. Be that way."

She frowned and returned to the couch. "I guess there's no escaping Boyle's Law." She picked up the textbook and read.

CHAPTER 19

*H*ope sat in the lobby office, staring at an invoice. Her fingers grew whiter as she clenched it. She darted her gaze back and forth between the invoice she held and a nearly identical one on the desktop before her.

Both were from F.P. Walker, Fishmonger.

She had received his latest invoice earlier that day for February's seafood deliveries. On the table was January's. She had also dug out the previous six months of invoices just to confirm her suspicions. His prices had held steady and unchanged—until this invoice, after she'd arrived, when the price for every variety of seafood he delivered to the resort increased, some nearly doubling.

Mouth pressed in a grim line, she picked up the phone and dialed a nearby resort, speaking with Constance, their food and beverage manager. After exchanging pleasantries, Hope asked who delivered their seafood.

"Oh, we've used Central Seafood Supply in Frederiksted for years." Constance nearly sang the words in her lilting accent.

"Did you notice any sudden increases in price on your February invoices?"

"No, the prices are exactly the same as they've always been."

Hope closed her eyes. "I'm curious, how much do you pay for wahoo?"

"Hmm, oh, here. $9.99 per pound. Everythin' ok, Hope?"

"Yes. I just wanted to verify whether our pricing was correct. Thanks for your help." Hope glared at her own invoices. Wahoo in January and the previous months was $9.50 per pound. In February, it was $16.99 per pound.

She gathered up the invoices and opened her lower desk drawer, now perfectly organized with separate folders in hanging files. She placed all the invoices in the correct file before rising. Hope walked through the lobby and entered the kitchen, eyes blinking at the blinding cleanliness of Gerold's domain.

He was chopping carrots and looking a bit harried. "Everything ok, Gerold?"

He smiled at her and kept chopping, his dark hands moving like lightning. "Yes, thanks. Lucinda called in sick, so I don't have any prep help tonight." He waved his knife absently, making Hope step back. "Don't worry, I'll be fine. The extra exercise will do me good." Gerold was an avid cyclist and rode his bike to and from work every day, saying it kept him trim.

"I may not be a chef of your quality, Gerold, but I'm perfectly capable of chopping some vegetables. What can I do to help?"

He gave her a big smile. "You really want to?"

Hope laughed, reaching for an apron hanging on the wall. "Yes! Put me to work."

Gerold pointed to an enormous bowl of freshly washed zucchini. "You can start by slicin' those—half an inch thick."

She grabbed a chef's knife and began deftly chopping the zucchini into equal sections. "Oh, ho!" Gerold laughed. "Look at that. She's got skills!"

Hope couldn't help grinning. "Like I said, I'm not a practiced chef, but I took six months of culinary classes a few years ago. It was a lot of fun. I'd love to help you out when you need it."

Gerold watched her for a moment. "You got yourself a job. Congratulations."

Hope kept chopping. "By the way, when does our seafood get delivered?"

"Frank's here every mornin', real early. Usually between six and seven. Everything ok?"

"Yes. I was just curious."

SLIGHTLY BEFORE SIX the next morning, Hope stood in the receiving area of the parking lot, just outside the restaurant. She had a hoodie pulled over her staff T-shirt to ward off the early chill and wore a tailored khaki skirt and dressy flats, her hair pulled into a slick low bun. She held the incriminating invoice in one hand as she sipped a travel mug of coffee and leaned against the building.

At six-fifteen, an old van rumbled down the road toward her. Hope removed her hoodie, setting the coffee down and standing straight. The van stopped in front of the restaurant. Painted on the sides in large print read *F.P. Walker, Fishmonger—Always Your Best Seafood Choice!* Hope snorted at that. A large, middle-aged Black man poured out of the driver's side door, lifting his baseball hat to scratch his head as he appraised her.

"Mr. Frank Walker, I presume?" Hope asked in her most friendly, professional voice.

"Yeah, that's me. What can I do for you?" He stood still, eyes narrowed in wariness.

Hope walked forward, holding her hand out to shake. "Good morning. I'm Hope Collins, the new owner of Half Moon Bay. I wanted to introduce myself so we could get to know each other better."

He smiled politely and shook her hand.

"I'm afraid we might have a misunderstanding regarding my

February invoice, and I wanted to get it cleared up as soon as possible. When I was scrutinizing the invoice yesterday, I couldn't help but notice the alarming increase in prices compared to January."

Frank shifted from foot to foot and scratched his head again.

"I didn't want to jump to any wrong conclusions, so I called over to Constance at Serenity Cove. They use one of your main competitors and didn't experience a single increase in prices last month."

She narrowed her eyes at him but kept the same tone of voice. "Now, it seems to me I have two choices here. I can either change to Central Seafood Supply to receive their lower prices—"

Walker's eyes became enormous, and he held both hands out to her, taking a breath to speak.

"Or—" Hope hardened her voice and tore up the invoice in her hands, taking several steps toward him. "You can correct this . . . erroneous invoice and submit a new one to me, this time with the right prices. Which would you prefer, Mr. Walker?"

"I'm so sorry, ma'am!" He took deep, panicky breaths. "I've got a new person doin' my invoices. She musta screwed up. I'll get you the correct invoice right away. I promise it won't happen again!"

A new person screwed up. Right.

Hope stopped in front of him and glared. "I appreciate that, Mr. Walker. I may be new to the island, but I'm not new to this business. You would do well to remember that." She nodded to him. "Have a good day now."

Hope and Patti sat in companionable silence late the following morning, both working, though Patti had been furious when Hope had told her about the incident with the fishmonger.

"Frank is my second cousin's son! I can't believe he'd do this to us. Oh, you better believe I'm gonna call his mama and tell her all about this."

Hope said sardonically, "Well, to be fair, he did it to *me*—he would never have tried that on you. Everyone has to try to take advantage of the new guy, especially when he's not a guy." Patti only snorted.

As it neared noon, Hope's stomach growled. "You want to join me for lunch?"

Patti smiled. "That sounds wonderful. Besides, I'm at a good stoppin' point. You go on ahead, and I'll join you after I get things straightened up in here."

Hope made her way to the restaurant and to her usual table. Patti had been indispensable so far. She'd explained to Hope that Steve and Susan had turned more and more of the resort operations over to her as they got older and semi-retired, but especially after Susan had gotten sick. Patti managed the resort with skill and a lot of hard work. The employees loved her, though she could be fierce when the situation called for it.

After they ordered, Clark brought over their iced teas from the bar. "Did you get in that batch of lemons you were expectin', Clark?" Patti asked.

"Yes, Auntie. The ones in your glasses are fresh as can be." He returned to the bar.

"Did he just call you auntie?" Hope asked.

Patti smiled and said, "Yes, Clark is my nephew. He's my sister's boy, God rest her soul. I got him the job here two years ago after he had a minor scrape with the law. It's been a good change for him. He has a wife and son, so it's high time he started actin' like a man and takin' his responsibilities seriously."

"I've really enjoyed being around him." Hope leaned forward. "I can tell he takes great pride in his job. He told me all about the contest he wants to win for bartending."

"Oh, yes. That would be wonderful. It's an excellent goal for him, and free publicity for us at the resort too." She took a sip of iced tea. "When are you startin' your scuba class?"

"In a few days. Alex wants to make sure I've had enough time to do my homework before our classroom session. He said he expects me to be fully prepared."

Patti laughed. "Uh-huh. That sounds like him."

Hope looked around the restaurant, making sure they had privacy. "I'm pretty nervous about the whole thing, to be honest." She stared at Patti and took a breath. "I can trust Alex, can't I?"

Patti snapped her head up at Hope's question, then smiled. "Hope, I would trust Alex with my life. He's like a brother to me. And I can assure you, his skills are first rate. He has rescued several people since he's been here, both divers and swimmers at our beach. If you're feelin' nervous, make sure you tell him. He's got a wonderful manner with people, and I'm sure he can put your fears to rest."

Oh, Patti. If only it were that easy. Trusting a man is the whole problem. It hasn't exactly worked out for me in the past. Why should Alex be any different?

After lunch, Hope returned to the office, once again glaring at the fishmonger bill, her good mood evaporating before sorting the day's mail. She thumbed through until she discovered an invoice from Emerald Isle Scuba. Her brows flew up—$1200 for five new scuba tanks. "Why would Alex need more tanks? He has plenty." With a sigh, she got up and marched toward the pier.

She found him in the stuffy equipment room, sitting at his workbench with one of the vest BCD things spread open before him, and took a deep breath. "Hey, Alex, I was going through the bills. How come you needed five new tanks?"

He looked up from the bench. "Well, hello to you too."

Embarrassment caused her to flush.

"The tanks failed hydro."

She pursed her lips, on the defensive now. "I don't know what that means."

Alex sighed and opened a drawer next to him. Inside were well-organized hanging file folders, much like her own desk. He opened one and took out a piece of paper, handing it to her. "Scuba tanks have to undergo a hydrostatic pressure test every five years to make sure they're structurally sound." The word *failed* had been highlighted. "Some of our tanks are getting pretty old, so I wasn't surprised five didn't pass and needed to be replaced." He raised an eyebrow. "Or maybe you'd prefer your guests diving with compressed air bombs on their backs that could explode at any moment?"

Hope sagged, raising a hand to her forehead. "Oh crap, I'm sorry. I shouldn't have jumped to conclusions."

"I can check all expenses with you before I order anything if you'd prefer."

"God, no! That's the last thing I want. I've got enough to work on. Damn fishmonger."

Alex cocked his head at her. "That your new nickname for me?"

She couldn't help laughing. "I found out that our seafood delivery guy was trying to rip me off and confronted him yesterday. I've been assuming the worst of humanity ever since." She leaned against the air compressor. "I'm sorry."

His smile grew during her explanation before falling off his face. "Wait. Don't we get that delivery early in the morning?"

"Yes, it was around six."

"Was anyone else even there that early?"

Her brow furrowed. "Not outside. They had just gotten started in the kitchen, so I was by myself. Why?"

"You met a complete stranger in the parking lot? Alone?"

"I think I can judge whether he was dangerous, you know. And he seemed pretty harmless." She scowled. "Wait a minute. Are you saying I'm just a weak woman and can't take care of myself?"

"No!" Alex took a breath, then continued in a calmer tone. "All I'm saying is that an attractive woman needs to worry about things a man doesn't. You're going to face situations here Steve never had to be concerned with." He paused. "You have my cell phone number, right?"

"Yes, I have everyone's." Hope was doing her best to ignore the glowing feeling in her stomach. His outburst had been out of concern and not chauvinism. Not to mention he'd called her attractive.

"If you ever get in a situation where you need help, call me. I can be there in seconds."

A smile crept across her face. "I'll do that. Thanks. And I'm sorry about earlier."

He nudged her foot, his face serious. "You know, this whole teaching you scuba thing will be a lot easier if you trust me."

Her smile fell. "I don't trust easily. But I'm working on it."

"Well then, it's a good thing trust is something I take pretty seriously."

Their gazes held for a long moment before Hope turned.

She left Alex to his work and headed back to her house. Their conversation had brought home that she was possibly putting her life in Alex's hands. She was still nervous about learning to dive, but couldn't deny feeling completely at ease whenever in his presence.

It also hadn't escaped her notice that twice now she'd gotten angry at him for no reason, and he'd reacted calmly and wanted to discuss the problem. That reassured her. Alex didn't seem like the type to run when things got tough.

Are you finally ready to trust someone again?

"Maybe," Hope said to no one as the warm waves splashed over her feet. She smiled, looking forward to her adventure.

CHAPTER 20

*H*ope breathed through her regulator as she knelt at the bottom of the pool, watching Alex carefully. He closed his eyes, grasped the top of his mask, and cracked it open, filling it with water. Next he tilted his head back, pressed against the top of the mask between his eyes, and gently blew through his nose, replacing the water inside the mask with air. Alex accomplished this in a single, effortless motion. Opening his eyes, he pointed to her.

Ok, that looks easy enough . . .

Hope gave him the ok and closed her eyes. Inhaling deeply, she cracked the edge of her mask like he did, and it filled with water. Her heart raced as the water hit her closed eyes, but she fought through it. Instead of Alex's steady exhale, she blew the air out in a series of frantic snorts. Then she inhaled through her nose, got a noseful of water, and began coughing and snorting before quickly swimming toward the surface.

Hope ripped off her mask and held on to the edge of the pool while she coughed. "Oh God! How did you do that so easily?"

Alex laughed as she continued to hack, snot dripping from her nose. "I've done it a time or two."

"Hasn't anyone told you it's rude to laugh at your students?"

That only made him smile more. "You're doing fine. Don't try to rush it. Get used to the water in your mask and take a couple of breaths through your reg before you clear the water out. Remember, it's bad to breathe through your nose underwater." He laughed again. "Come on, let's try again."

They descended once more, and after a few more tries, Hope was able to clear the water from her mask more successfully. Alex applauded her, and she forgave him for laughing at her.

She was proud of herself and, above all, impressed at the depth and comprehensiveness of the certification. Hope was also pleased Alex let nothing slide. He made her perform every skill until she was comfortable with it. And when she fumbled with something, he was right there to help. She was still somewhat apprehensive about the whole thing, but gaining confidence with every minute they spent together.

STILL FRESH FROM her shower after the pool session, Hope sat in her home office with her laptop open. She frowned at the resort website. Each page was a different color, and there wasn't any brand consistency. She wanted to do a complete brand and website overhaul, but that would be a big, expensive project.

Her phone buzzed with a text.

Sara: You drunk on strawberry margaritas yet?
Hope: Nope, sorry to disappoint you.
Sara: Where you're concerned, I'm used to it. You're not working right now, are you?
Hope: A little
Sara: It's like being pregnant. A yes or no question.
Hope: Then yes

Hope: Working, not pregnant!

Sara: lol. You had me worried for a second. I don't like to be kept in the dark. Please tell me you're doing something fun there besides working.

Hope: Yes! I'm taking scuba lessons. It's been a lot of fun.

Sara: Well, that sounds promising. Is your instructor devastatingly handsome, I hope?

Hope winced at that. "Oh, Sara. I'm not about to let you in on that little detail. I know you too well."

Hope: Hardly. He's only a guy who works here. Sorry to disappoint you.

Sara: You're no fun.

∾

HOPE STOOD ON THE BEACH, the warm sand scrunching beneath her toes as she held the compass. Nearly two weeks had passed since she started her scuba class, and she was almost finished. But at the moment, her head might explode. "Wait, you want me to do what?"

"A reciprocal pattern," Alex said.

Hope narrowed her eyes, one hand on her hips.

"An out and back." He grinned and held his compass next to hers. "We're on a heading of zero degrees right now, due north, so we'll walk twenty paces, turn around 180 degrees, and walk another twenty paces at that heading, which is due south, to get back where we started."

She gaped at him. "And I'm supposed to do this underwater? Without being able to talk about it if I screw up?"

"That's why we're practicing now, before we get in the water." He paused for a moment. "Let me get behind you, and we'll march in lockstep, so you can see what I'm talking about." Putting his compass back in the pocket of his shorts, Alex stood right behind her. "Hold your compass out again." She did, and he put his arms around her and placed his hands over hers. He pivoted them to the right. "See how the heading changes depending on our direction? Straight up the beach is a zero-degree heading because we're going straight north."

Hope tried to listen to his explanation, but she was hyper-conscious of his nearness and the feel of his arms around her. He had showered after the morning dive trip and had a fresh, clean scent.

Get your head in the game, for God's sake.

She took a deep breath and tried to concentrate. "Ok, so twenty steps, right?"

"You got it. Go ahead."

Hope walked in measured paces, with Alex immediately behind. After ten steps, she started laughing.

There was a smile in his voice when he asked, "You're laughing? You think we look ridiculous or something? Come on, let's turn around 180 degrees."

Alex spun her around in the opposite direction, and like a lightbulb going off, she understood the heading at 180 degrees and walked back the way they had come. This time Alex let her walk alone and trailed a little behind.

"Try it again, only go out at a 10-degree heading and come back."

She finished the pattern in front of him with a broad smile. "Ta-da! I think I've got it now."

He laughed. "Me too. Let's get changed into our wetsuits." They walked toward a pile of neoprene and scuba equipment sitting next to the pier.

"It's hard to believe I'm already on my second ocean session."

"After this, you'll be an open water diver." Alex winked at her, and her breathing quickened.

They had spent a considerable amount of time together over the previous twelve days and developed an easy banter back and forth, though he evaded any personal questions. Alex had been calm and professional throughout her course, but also kept things light and fun, which prompted her feelings even more.

On top of that, she was pretty sure he felt the same way, though Hope was still trying her best not to encourage him. And that was getting harder when she couldn't take her eyes off him.

As they got ready to enter the ocean, he peeled off his shirt and started tugging on his wetsuit.

Yep, definitely a swimmer's body. Look at those shoulders.

"I'm surprised you wear a wetsuit on every dive. Don't you build up a tolerance or something?"

"Just the opposite, actually," he said. "The water is warm, but it's still a lot cooler than our bodies. When you dive every day, your core temperature decreases, and you get cold easier. The water gets warm enough in the summer that I go without a wetsuit sometimes, but not now."

"Then I thank you for taking the time to brave these frigid waters to help little old me."

He grinned and held her gaze. His eyes were extraordinary, a mixture of crystal blue ocean with darker indigo flecks. "You're welcome, Boss Lady. It's the high point of my day."

Hope took a deep breath, turning to tug her BCD over the tank and attaching the regulator to the tank valve. The first time Alex had gone over the equipment, she'd been overwhelmed at the complexity of it. But after several sessions, she was much more confident.

Alex was ready to go with his mask around his neck. After closing all the straps and buckles, Hope stood up, already feeling the heavy weight on her back and shoulders. She put her mask on her forehead and started to grab her fins when Alex stopped her.

"I always tell my students not to put your mask on your forehead. It's a sign of a diver in trouble, so you don't want someone thinking that if it's not true. Also, it's really easy for a big wave to knock it off—and they're expensive. Or it marks you as a newbie who was never told that. I never say anything to the divers I'm leading, but it's best to pull your mask down around your neck."

After some tugging to get the mask over her hair, she had it in place. "Satisfied now? Let's go—this is heavy."

When she got to thigh-deep water, Hope crossed one ankle over the other knee and put her fin on, then did the same with the other. She grinned and shook her head, remembering the snorkeling trip where she walked into the ocean with fins on—yes, this was definitely a better way to do that.

"Ready?" Alex asked. "We'll do the navigation and a few other skills that are left, and next I'll take you over to the reef to do a little tour." He pointed to the area where she'd been snorkeling. "Then we're done."

She gave him the ok signal, and they slipped beneath the surface.

Hope swam beside Alex an hour later, pride swelling through her. She had passed the required skills with no major difficulty, even the navigation and mask removal. After the last exercise, Alex applauded her and held his hand out. As Hope shook it and grinned around her regulator, her heart fluttered when he ran his thumb over the top of her hand. Next, they headed to where she had been snorkeling previously. Once again, there was the beautiful large gray fish with brilliant yellow accents.

As they headed toward shore, Alex pointed. She didn't see anything until he waved his hand over the sand, and a perfectly camouflaged flounder swam away, delighting Hope. Smiling, she turned to Alex, whose eyes twinkled. They kept swimming until they were in a few feet of water and stood up together.

"Great job. You did it!" Alex held up both hands for a high ten, which she slapped enthusiastically. They removed their fins and walked toward the beach.

She squeezed his arm. "Thank you. That was a lot of fun, and not nearly as scary as I thought it would be." She stopped. "Oh, I saw the most beautiful fish. I think it's an angelfish. Really big, about a foot across. It was gray with beautiful yellow margins around its scales."

His eyes lingered on hers, drawing her in. "French angelfish. Only one? Or a pair?"

"You're right, there were two."

"Yeah, they like to pair up. You usually see them together." They locked eyes for a long moment. Finally, Alex's softened. "You did a great job, Hope. Congratulations."

She grinned at the praise. "Well, I can't take all the credit. I had an excellent instructor."

As they turned toward the beach, a line of people headed toward them. Patti and Clark approached along with Gerold, who held a cake with a scuba diver on top. They were all applauding.

"Congratulations, Hope!" Patti gave her a distant hug, trying to stay dry.

"Come on, you two!" Gerold said. "We've got some cake to eat."

"And I have champagne on ice!" Clark added, leaning in.

"Absolutely," Alex said. "We'll just dump our tanks and wetsuits first."

After replacing their shirts and shorts, Hope and Alex were still wet, so the group went to the pool bar, where the furniture was designed for wet guests. They settled around one of the tables, and Clark produced five champagne flutes and opened the bottle, filling each one halfway.

He passed them around to everyone before holding his glass up. "To Hope!"

Alex, seated next to her, turned with a smile. "To the best student I've had all week."

Hope laughed as they all clinked glasses and drank while Gerold cut the cake and gave a piece to everyone. Alex's knee had been pressed against hers under the table for quite some time, and she hadn't moved away.

As she sat there, looking around at her new circle of family, tears sprang to Hope's eyes. She may have left everything behind in Chicago, but right now she felt like she had gained even more.

 *ay* …

ALEX DESCENDED his stairs to the pier after showering. A week had passed since certifying Hope, and they had been busy. He'd led several afternoon dives and a night dive too. As he looked toward the palapa, he wasn't surprised Tommy was kneeling on the deck of *Deep Diver,* the two large fiberglass panels lying on the pier while he worked on the boat.

Alex climbed aboard. "Let me guess. Bilge pump?"

Tommy sat up, wiping his hands on a rag. "Yeah."

"I noticed she was running heavy this morning."

"You could tell that?"

Alex leveled a stare at him. "I have been on this boat for a while now, you know."

"So you say. I'm still scared to let you drive, though. You'd probably run her aground somewhere. I love this boat."

Alex grinned. "Well, if you want a day off once in a while, you don't have much choice, do you?"

"Don't remind me."

Alex approached the hole in the deck of the boat. "How's the repair coming?"

"Gonna be a late day. After I finish this, I have to fix the plumbin' in the Flame Tree bungalow. I swear that shower's possessed."

Tommy had originally started at Half Moon Bay as the resort electrician and handyman, but had been around boats his whole life. Steve had seen his potential and paid for Tommy to get his Coast Guard captain's license before Alex arrived. He was still their first thought when anything in the resort needed fixing.

Alex sighed. "I still think we need to dry-dock this damn boat."

"Nah, she's fine. We do need a new bilge pump at some point, but I can keep it goin' a while longer yet."

"Steve didn't want to listen to me, and the expense of a drydock is the last thing Hope needs right now. She's got enough on her plate." Alex ignored Tommy's grin. Apparently, the whole resort staff noticed the time they were spending together. "Besides, we're in the middle of the busy summer season. When it slows down later this fall, I'm going to make sure we get this boat out of the water and inspected with a fine-tooth comb. I already warned Hope."

Tommy looked up at him, squinting in the sun. "Anybody ever tell you that you worry too much?"

Alex refused to smile at him. "There are some things I won't compromise on. Safety is one."

"Hey, man. I'm not gonna argue with you. If you want to make Hope pay a whole lot of change to dry-dock this boat, knock yourself out."

Alex hunkered down next to him. "I can take over here. You go on and get to work on that bungalow."

Tommy turned to him with a frown. "What if you screw it up? Then I'll just have to fix it again, anyway."

"God, you're an asshole. Get out of here."

Tommy laughed and clapped Alex on the shoulder as he stood. "Thanks, man. I'll see you tomorrow."

Alex pulled his shirt off, enjoying the warm sun on his shoulders as he got to work on the bilge pump. He was reasonably sure they could nurse the boat along until October or November, but he was serious about getting her thoroughly inspected.

He raised the corner of his mouth—not so upset with Steve for leaving anymore. Alex still thought raffling off the resort had been a hell of a gamble, but perhaps it had paid off. Maybe a new owner wasn't such a bad thing.

Especially this owner.

His life had been shaken up for sure, but maybe it was high time he stopped coasting. Maybe Hope was what they had all needed.

He smiled, thinking about her scuba class. He didn't get the chance to teach full open water classes very often. Most guests didn't have the time it took—and Alex did it right. It had been an enjoyable change for him, something different from his day-to-day routine.

And it had been interesting to see a different side of Hope too. Instead of the self-assured, cool resort owner, he'd seen a feisty, determined woman with a great sense of humor. And she'd been a terrific student. She'd been prepared for each session and faced every challenge head-on.

Alex sat up with a sigh. "You're in trouble here, you know that, don't you?"

The reply was obvious, so he didn't answer himself. The thought of being intimate with a woman pushed him embarrassingly close to panicking, but Hope was moving him ever closer in that direction.

You can't avoid dealing with it forever.

Alex closed his eyes and took a deep breath, fighting back the emotions surging inside him.

Hope didn't seem in any rush to jump into anything, either. Alex was good at reading people and had a strong suspicion her reluctance stemmed from a bad relationship at some point. And he certainly didn't want to finally take that leap and have her pull away because she wasn't interested.

Alex turned back to the bilge pump, now able to concentrate on his task, and soon had it operational again.

He pointed at the offending part. "Now hold together, ok?"

Alex replaced the fiberglass panels and hosed off the boat before returning to his apartment, ready to start his weight routine.

He and Hope were in a good place. Alex was definitely interested in spending more time with her and might suggest a couple of private dives to get her skills and confidence up. But he didn't mind holding off on the romantic overtures—well, mostly.

A SOFT TROPICAL morning dawned as Hope sat on her porch, responding to the latest guest review, full of praise for Alex and Tommy. Since taking over the reviews, the only consistent criticism she'd seen was the lack of a spa facility. Of course, a spa was an impossibility at the moment, having neither the money nor the facilities for one. Hope sighed and filed the idea away for later.

Soon there was an impatient huff from her left. She looked over to Cruz sitting on the sand. He lifted a paw and brought it down on the side of the bowl in front of him, tipping it completely over. "Oh, I'm sorry. Am I ignoring you, Cruz? How rude of me."

Hope padded down the stairs toward the dog. When he'd made a second appearance, she gave him a bowl of water but held the line at feeding him. He was thin, but no ribs were showing. Either he was very good at fending for himself, or someone else was feeding him. And by his third visit, he had earned a name, and so he'd been Cruz ever since.

As Hope approached, he scurried away and stood at the edge of the foliage. "Relax, I'm not going to hurt you. Only getting you some water."

She retrieved the bowl and used the spigot on the side of the house to fill it. She set it down and retreated to the porch steps. The dog slowly crept forward to drink. Cruz still wouldn't approach if she was anywhere near, but they were making progress. As he lapped up the water, she slowly ascended the stairs.

The ocean was flat calm this morning, with no breeze yet. *Perfect morning for a swim before work.* She had gone into town and bought a couple of more appropriate one-piece swimsuits, as well as some high-quality swim goggles.

Hope had developed a habit of swimming most mornings, and Alex swam nearly always, but she didn't see him in the water yet. After diving off the pier, she started slowly, letting her heart rate rise without spiking, and it took a few hundred yards to get warmed up. Breathing to her left, she was surprised when Alex pulled up next to her. Though they both swam often, they didn't necessarily swim together.

Smiling, Hope picked up her pace and pulled ahead. She swam with regular, rapid strokes, confident and assured now. Then Alex was once again beside her.

She accelerated again.

He matched her.

After weeks of regular swimming, Hope was in excellent form. Her technique had come back as her stamina had improved.

Ok, you asked for it.

She kicked into her top gear and took off. This was a pace she could now hold for several hundred yards. Hope looked for him every time she took a breath to the left. Nope, nope, nope . . . He appeared and caught her, matching her as they churned the water around them. But she was determined to beat him.

They were swimming north, with bare land to her right and the resort far behind now. Hope increased her pace again, refusing to slow. Her heart hammered, and she couldn't keep the pace up much longer.

She was close to giving up when Alex stopped and shouted, "Ok, uncle!"

Hope stopped to tread water, pleased he was breathing as hard as she.

"What got into you this morning, or are you punishing me for no reason?"

"Oh, I'm sorry. Was that too much for you? I'll remember to hold myself back next time." She laughed as he splashed her. "I'm heading back."

"You go ahead," he said. "I'll just wait here for Tommy to pick me up."

"My scuba instructor gave me excellent advice on how to help a tired diver. I'm sure the same principles apply to swimmers." She was still breathing hard and trying not to laugh. "Perhaps you need some help getting back to the pier?"

Alex's grin widened as he treaded water. "That might be a good idea. Better stay close to me on the way back in case I need to be rescued."

She got back to the pier first. As she finished dressing, Alex climbed the ladder behind her. She walked down the pier, tossing behind her, "Have a good day, Mr. Monroe."

AFTER A SHOWER AND BREAKFAST, Hope made her way into the kitchen, widening her eyes at the aroma. Gerold was at the range, standing over an enormous stockpot. "That smells incredible! What's cooking, Gerold?"

He turned and saluted her with a large spoon. "I'm startin' the stock for the lobster bisque. The longer it simmers, the better."

"Oh, I love lobster bisque! Hey, I had an idea—can you listen and stir at the same time?"

"Hit me."

"What do you think about the idea of you teaching a weekly cooking class for the guests?"

Gerold dropped his spoon and whirled toward her. "I would *love* to teach a cookin' class!" He said it quietly and reverently.

Hope laughed, holding a hand to her mouth. "No, tell me how you really feel."

He wiped his hands on a towel and went back to stirring his stock. "I talked to Steve several times about doin' a cookin' class. It's just about standard at any resort destination, but he wasn't interested. Said he didn't think the guests would care."

"Well, I disagree. I think any of our guests would be lucky to attend any class you taught."

He gave her a smile. "Thanks. Did you have somethin' specific in mind?"

"Not really. I'll leave the details for you. This is your wheelhouse, after all. My only suggestion would be a weekly class—mid-afternoon would be a good time. The kitchen isn't too busy then, and that way the divers could also attend." She came up to the pot and inhaled the savory aroma. "And I agree with you one-hundred percent about needing to start one. You'll run an incredible class."

"I can't wait! I'll let you know what I come up with."

She met his eyes. "And Gerold, if you have any other suggestions or ideas, please come to me. I'll always listen to what you have to say." Hope turned around and pushed through the double doors, pleased the resort was running so well.

Everything's going great. I've finally got my footing here and hopefully the obstacles are behind me now.

CHAPTER 22

*H*ope closed her eyes as Alex moved the throttle to full, the breeze caressing her face. The afternoon was balmy, but the seas were calm and inviting. He'd surprised her by showing up at her office door at noon and asking if she wanted to go on a private dive with him that afternoon.

Hope couldn't deny being pleased at the prospect.

"I'd really like to go back and take a closer look. It was the end of the dive and I had people low on air, but I think I saw two seahorses on this morning's dive." Alex radiated excitement.

The dive site wasn't far from the resort, and he soon slowed the boat before putting it in neutral. Turning to Hope, he said, "Keep her here in neutral while I dive down to moor us to the buoy."

Hope's heart sped up. "What? I don't know how to drive a boat!"

"You're not driving it—you're basically babysitting. Just keep the throttle in neutral. You never engage the propellers when someone's in the water. Don't worry, I'll be right back."

With that, he put on his mask and fins and dove off the bow. And true to his word, he was back on the surface a short time later. "Turn the key to shut the engine off." She did, and he soon climbed back on board.

Quickly going over the dive briefing with her, Alex said, "I hope I can find the seahorses. We don't see them often, especially more than one, and they're really cool. One of my favorite things to see."

Soon they were in the water, and Alex sank like a stone. Hope descended more slowly, still getting the hang of diving, then checked her dive computer. They were in twenty-five feet of water and her ears were well adjusted to the depth. She returned Alex's ok signal, and he beckoned her to follow.

They slipped over a ledge and descended further. Hope added too much air into her BCD and began to float up before quickly dumping the excess air and continuing after Alex, who of course, looked effortless. He hovered close to the reef but never touched it, and hardly appeared to breathe. *Goals, Hope. Goals.*

Alex approached a coral outcropping and stopped, tilting his head this way and that. Hope came up beside him as he let out a triumphant, "Ha!"

Hope startled, not realizing she could hear so well underwater. He turned to her, smiling around his regulator, and beckoned her closer. Alex gestured for her to hold on to his arm to steady herself and pointed.

Right in front of her was a bright yellow seahorse about three inches tall, its tail curled around a purple sea fan. Next to it was another, this one with brown and white stripes, its body waving back and forth gently in the surge.

Alex looked at her as she excitedly held up two fingers. He shook his head and held up four, eyes crinkling. Hope frowned, studying the reef. There! A purple one clung off to the side, so she held up a third finger. But she couldn't see any more. She turned to him and shrugged. *Is he seeing things, or what?*

Alex pointed directly in front of her, and the beautifully camouflaged seahorse appeared. It was nearly the same shade as the coral it clung to, a brownish red, and its tail curled around a clump of coral. Hope stared, fascinated.

He waited until she was done and gestured to continue. Though Hope had joined a couple of morning group trips, having Alex to herself was a different experience altogether. It was as if he knew every inch of the reef. The two swam slowly on, a school of creole wrasse splitting around them in a cloud of blue iridescence. Hope craned her neck, enchanted by the sight, and Alex stilled, smiling back at her, then held her gaze longer than strictly necessary.

He soon asked how much air she had left, and she replied with two fingers on the lower arm of her wetsuit as he'd taught—2000 psi. Alex nodded and turned back around to lead.

Out of the corner of her eye, Hope spied a turtle resting in a crevice and turned for a closer look. It watched her, slowly blinking. About three feet long, it was mottled brownish-green with a sharpened beak for a mouth. Excited, she whirled around to get Alex's attention.

Her face collided with his fin.

Hope's mask was knocked completely off, and the regulator dislodged from her mouth. The world became an amorphous scene with no clarity. She tightly closed her eyes, and by reflex tried to take a breath, only getting seawater. Her brain immediately short-circuited as her survival reflex took over.

I have to get to air NOW.

Hope wanted to scream, but some primitive part of her brain prevented that as she started to bolt for the surface. Eyes screwed shut, she was flailing upwards when two powerful hands grabbed her arms and held her in place.

She thrashed against the restraint, desperate to breathe.

I'm drowning!

The hands let go, which was somehow even more frightening. Then her regulator suddenly appeared in her mouth, and she took a long shuddering breath of cool, incredible air as her nostrils were gently pinched closed. Her eyes were still clamped shut.

Hope sucked in the clean air, taking great, panicky gasps. Her body was desperate for the life-giving air. Every muscle clenched as she opened and closed her hands. There was a gentle pressure against her forehead, followed by another soft pressure on one cheek.

At last, Hope opened her eyes, and through the fuzzy water-induced panic found Alex leaning his forehead against hers, one hand resting against her cheek as the other held her nose closed. She leaned into him, into his strength, but she was still taking shuddering breaths, her heart exploding in her chest. She reached out and gripped his arms, shaking badly but desperate for the contact to ground her.

He withdrew his head slightly, removing the hand holding her nose to point at her and gave her a fuzzy-looking ok signal. She whipped her head back and forth. He shook his and pointed at her again forcefully, once again giving her the ok.

He's not asking if I'm ok—he's telling *me I'm ok.*

Looking through the blurred scene before her, Alex held her mask in his hand. He gently placed it against her face and gestured for her to clear it, and she nodded. She closed her eyes and began performing the task. It took her several panicky breaths, and her hands trembled so badly she had a hard time keeping hold of the mask. The world became sharp again as she gazed up.

Hope's heart still pounded, and she tried to fight against the instinct to rush to the surface *now*. Her panic had subsided enough to know a bolt to the surface could be very dangerous. Forcing herself to focus, she pulled the mask strap behind her head and shut her eyes again, still taking great, gasping breaths. At last, she opened her eyes to find herself staring at Alex in sharp focus now.

He gazed at her—steady, calm, and in control—and she started to relax.

Still holding on to her arm with one hand, Alex waved his other hand gently in front of his mouth, matching his slow inhales and exhales, and gesturing for her to copy him. She tried to do so, still taking large, choking gasps. Some of her breaths were sobs as her eyes leaked a steady stream of tears.

Alex's gaze never left her, and she fixated on his crystal blue eyes—they were her lifeline.

Once again, he leaned his forehead against hers and cupped her face in his hands as she tried to match his slow, steady breaths. Hope concentrated on the gentle pressure of his hands, and, an eternity later, her breathing calmed. He pulled back from her, then gave her the thumbs-up signal.

They began slowly ascending as they held each other's arms, their eyes locked together, faces only inches apart.

As they broke the surface and inflated their BCDs, Hope pulled her mask up with shaking hands and cried in earnest. Alex drew her into a clumsy embrace—scuba equipment wasn't made for intimate moments.

"You're fine, Hope. You did great. I am so proud of you." He pulled away to grasp her arms, keeping eye contact with her.

"Oh my God. Alex, I was too close to you. I . . . I turned around and ran right into your fins. I couldn't see anything, and my reg got knocked out. I . . . I . . ."

She was so grateful to be breathing the fresh air and that the experience was over.

"It's ok. You're going to be fine." He pulled her to him again, stroking the back of her neck and repeating soft, soothing words. After a few minutes, her sobs receded and her shaking decreased somewhat.

Finally, Hope sniffled and said, "I'm doing better now. Thanks for not nagging me about my mask on my forehead."

"Yes, you are doing better." He placed his fingers under her chin and tilted her head toward his. "Hope, we're going to have to go back down and finish—"

"No, no, no." Her voice rose. "Alex, I can't. I just *can't*."

He put his hands on either side of her face and gently ran his thumbs over her cheeks. "I *promise* I won't let anything happen to you. But you have to go back down right now."

His eyes bore into hers. Her shaking increased, and her heart hammered in her ears.

"What happened was a fluke, and I'm sure you'll never let it happen again. But you *have* to go back down right now, or you never will."

Hope's lips trembled. "I almost drowned."

He stroked her cheek again, wiping away the tears. "No one drowns on my watch. I'll keep you safe. We'll only go to thirty feet max and only for a few minutes."

His eyes pierced straight into her. "You have to trust me. Right now. Hope, I keep my promises."

CHAPTER 23

*a*lex gripped Hope's arms tightly, trying to get through to her.

She stared at him with those huge, vulnerable eyes and whispered, "Ok."

The single word and the trust it contained tore through the center of him.

Alex took hold of her shaking hand and tucked it into his arm as they descended once again. He took deep, slow breaths to get himself under control again and kept her immediately next to him, glued to his arm.

He quickly assessed her posture. Her eyes were still enlarged, but her breathing was steadier. *Looks like we're both more relaxed now.* They reached the reef below the boat, which was at about twenty feet. That was plenty deep.

Earlier, he had spun around immediately when she collided with his fins. Realizing he had a major emergency on his hands, it was a pure stroke of luck he caught her mask with one hand before grabbing her arm to prevent her bolting for the surface. His actions had been automatic as he purged the water from her regulator before placing it in her mouth.

Hope had deeply impressed him with how quickly she'd overcome complete panic. He'd seen far more experienced divers completely lose it when they got a mask kicked off or their regulator dislodged, let alone both of them at the same time. She had responded far better than most others would have. He squeezed her hand and winked when she turned to him as they swam along the reef top. Her death grip on his arm relaxed to a gentle hold.

A turtle appeared, gliding slowly over the wall toward them.

Alex stopped swimming, and Hope followed suit. They hovered, trying not to move as the turtle approached. It seemed to regard him first, then Hope, before continuing toward her. It slowed as it closed in, finally stopping in front of her mask, blinking at her.

Alex hardly dared to breathe. Hope let go of his arm and hovered, transfixed as she and the turtle regarded each other. After several seconds, the turtle reached out its neck and softly tapped her mask twice with its beak, then turned sideways and swam away.

Alex's heart soared as Hope turned to look at him, a tear spilling from one eye.

Thank you, Mr. Turtle. Your timing was impeccable.

He signaled to begin their three-minute safety stop. It wasn't really necessary, but he wanted this to be as routine as possible. The turtle encounter had put her at ease. She turned and gave him the ok signal and his stomach clenched.

You're more than ok. You're incredible, Hope.

Back on the boat, they were both quiet as they removed their tanks and peeled off their wetsuits. Alex tried to think of something clever and uplifting to say, but kept coming up blank. He'd rescued plenty of divers, but none made him feel like this. He was relieved to see his hands were steady, even though he was a mess of strong emotion on the inside. Before today, Alex hadn't thought anything could rattle him underwater.

He looked at Hope and knew different now.

Alex secured his tank with the bungee cord around the valve and turned around toward her. The next thing he knew, she was crushed against his chest with her arms around him. The force of her embrace made him stagger back a step.

"Thank you, Alex," she murmured into his chest, shaking.

The heat from their warm skin touching seared through him, immediately causing a physical response. He wrapped his arms around her and almost kissed the top of her head, but caught himself.

Don't be an ass. It's not her fault you've lived like a damn monk for years. Besides, she's the very definition of vulnerable right now.

He took a deep breath, heart racing, as he stepped back and cupped her face in his hands. "Hey, everything's ok. You did great down there." The fear and vulnerability in her eyes kindled something inside him he didn't think was still there. He'd been dead inside for so long now.

Needing to put some distance between them, Alex led her back to her tank and sat her down before sitting next to her. "Listen to me. I have seen very experienced divers lose it much worse than you did today. You overcame that incredibly quickly."

She shook her head, eyes pinned to the deck. "Now that I'm safe, it almost feels like some awful nightmare. But I really did feel like I was drowning." She turned to him with haunted eyes. "Thank you."

Swallowing hard, Alex touched her hand, then withdrew. "Don't thank me—that was all you." He reached out and stroked her foot with his, which felt safer. "Then you faced your fear and went down again. I'm so proud of you. You did an amazing job. And the last part of the dive was pretty special, wasn't it?"

A smile spread across her face, her golden eyes still wet. "That turtle was magical."

He nodded. "Encounters like that are the best thing about diving. That turtle didn't care about me at all—he only had eyes for you."

"The thing is . . ." Hope buried her face in her hands. "No. You'll think I'm even stupider than you do now."

Alex's stomach twisted again. Heart still pounding, he nudged her foot once more. "The last thing I think you are is stupid. What?"

She wiped her face dry and turned her gaze to him. "I'm pretty sure that was the same turtle that started the whole thing. I noticed it in a crevice and wanted to show you. That's when I collided with your fins. I think that when that turtle saw me again, coming right up to me and touching my mask, it was letting me know everything was going to be all right. It was reassuring me I was ok." She shook her head. "That's ridiculous, isn't it?"

Alex looked back at her, saying words he hadn't in a long time. "Ever since I was a kid, I would turn to the ocean to help me deal with anything that upset me. A few years ago, I was going through . . . a tough time. To get away from everything, I went free diving. There's a serenity I get from that I haven't found in anything else." He watched the horizon, but couldn't stop his gaze from turning back to hers.

"This dolphin came up to me. Dolphins are very curious and often swim by, but they rarely hang around. Hope, that dolphin stayed with me for over thirty minutes. When I surfaced to breathe, so did he. We swam alongside each other over and over again. I've never had another experience like it, before or since. I believe that dolphin came to—I don't know—encourage me that day. To give me solace."

He paused for a moment. "No, I don't think you're being ridiculous at all. I know exactly what you felt down there."

~

THE HOT STEAM swirled around Hope as she wiped her mirror after showering. She was still trying to come to grips with what had happened that afternoon. If she'd been diving with anyone other than Alex, she might be dead right now. He had been calm and confident the entire time, completely in charge. Her recollection of the event was fuzzy at best—really just sensations of utter terror and choking.

The one clear memory she had after replacing her mask was of Alex's eyes, anchoring and steadying her.

She groaned, glaring at her reflection as an embarrassed flush rose over her face. "And you *literally* threw yourself at him. Hope, you are a colossal idiot. He probably deals with stuff like that all the time. It didn't even affect him."

Feeling better after berating herself, she got dressed. She'd been in bad situations before, but never like this, and made a determined attempt to find a positive in the situation. Smiling at the memory of the turtle, she was proud of herself for continuing the dive.

He's right—it was an accident.

Hope was at war with herself, in constant flux with conflicting emotions. Embarrassment that after trying for months to remain aloof from Alex, she had collapsed into his arms. Utter gratitude that he'd been there for her that afternoon. Relief that her trust in him had been fulfilled to the highest degree possible. And something much deeper—she'd given him the perfect opportunity to act when her defenses had been laid bare, and he hadn't. What that said about his character.

And how incredibly *safe* she'd felt in his arms.

Given her state of mind, Hope didn't feel like going to the restaurant to eat. Making a sandwich, she sat down in her great room and turned on the television. She took one bite before putting it down, feeling nauseated.

The resort had satellite TV, but she gave up watching after flipping through several channels, slamming the remote down on the coffee table. She was as restless as a caged wolf but didn't know what to do with herself. Hope paced around her living room for a while, taking deep breaths to calm herself, then threw a pillow against the wall as she tried not to scream.

A walk along the beach would help, so she headed out into the night air. There was a cool breeze blowing off the ocean, and a three-quarters moon supplied plenty of light.

It even smells different at night.

Cleaner, crisper—as if the sun's disappearance allowed the breeze to clear out all traces of the day. Holding out her arms, Hope closed her eyes and let the soft wind whisper over her.

That's what I need. To let the breeze wash away the bad parts of today and leave the good ones.

Because there had been good parts—the seahorses, her friendly turtle, and throughout all of it, Alex.

She continued walking along the beach, conversation and laughter emanating from the restaurant, but feeling apart from all of it, numb now. The beach loungers were all stacked up for the night, and she stopped to pull one off and dragged it toward the shore. She adjusted the back to an upright position and sat down with a sigh to watch the moon.

Hope wrapped her hoodie tighter around her, feeling the deep emotions start to rise and taking deep breaths to calm herself, determined to overcome the whole experience. Like a magnet, she was drawn to the lights in Alex's apartment. Knowing he was up there right then, sensations of warmth and relaxation washed over her at last.

Closing her eyes, she slept.

CHAPTER 24

*H*ope awoke the next morning with a terrible, gnawing kink in her neck from sleeping upright in the lounger.

"Oh God. Ouch. Oh, *hell*."

"Did you sleep there all night?" Alex walked up the beach toward her.

Surprised, she darted her eyes to him, causing her neck to spasm again. "Ow—goddammit! Yes, apparently. Though I didn't mean to." She rolled her neck, and it began to loosen up. Pale pink streaked the sky to the east and a soft light grew around them.

"I woke up early and was heading into the dive shop when I noticed someone in the chair, so I came over to make sure everything was ok." He stopped in front of her. "Is everything ok?"

"Except for my broken neck, yes." She was still rubbing it.

"I can come back later if you'd prefer. When you're not cussing at me."

He was smiling, and she couldn't help but return it. "I can't believe I slept all night like this."

"I can. You must have been exhausted after yesterday."

That brought it all back, and she turned to sit sideways on the lounger. "I'm sorry I bolted off the boat when we returned to the dock—that wasn't fair to you. I needed some time alone."

Alex sat down next to her and pressed his leg against hers. Her stomach tightened, and she shifted her eyes to him, but there was no sign of teasing or flirting. He was simply offering comfort. Hope relaxed and leaned against him as Alex put his arm around her shoulders.

"Don't apologize," he said. "Sometimes I need to go off by myself too. And I meant what I said yesterday—you did great down there."

A warm light spread inside her at his closeness. "Thank you. I'm determined not to let this beat me."

"No one would expect you to get over something like that in a day, but I've got an idea. There's an afternoon trip scheduled for today, but why don't we dive the house reef here tomorrow afternoon? Just you and me. You had a great time when we dove it on your check-out."

Hope drank in his face. His morning stubble was much darker than the hair on his head. She focused on his chin—there was gray mixed in, too. Alex wasn't some boy pretending to be a man. He was so different. "I'd like that."

"Good. I'll keep you safe." He pressed his leg tighter against hers. "Do you trust me?"

"Yes."

Their eyes locked and held, and Hope became aware of everywhere their bodies touched, even more so than when they were on the boat yesterday. She dropped her gaze to his mouth. His lips were full and slightly parted as he moved them toward her. Time seemed to slow as she leaned toward him, their lips only inches apart. He'd closed his eyes, his breathing much deeper.

Then it was as if someone poured ice-cold water over her head. How incredibly different it was this time with this man. Yesterday, they'd shared an experience like very few others and come out the far side. Together. A roaring sound thrummed in her ears as her heart pounded and she wrenched herself back, standing on shaky legs.

"No! I can't do this, Alex. I'm sorry!" She turned and started running back to her house.

"Hope! Don't go."

Tears flowed as she ran. How could she tell him he hadn't done anything wrong? That he'd been everything she'd ever wanted since she met him? Which completely terrified her. The depth of emotion that came over her as they nearly kissed had rattled her to the core.

Everything could come crashing down.

She couldn't face it. Alex was a very different man, but it was too big of a risk—for herself and for everything she'd fought so hard to accomplish in her new life.

ALEX SET both BCDs down on the steps of the pier, inspecting everything to ensure all was ready for his dive with Hope. Yesterday morning had shaken him badly. He hadn't meant to lean in to kiss her—it'd just happened. She stared at him with those big golden eyes and he couldn't stop himself. And he felt terrible about it.

Hope wasn't as vulnerable as she'd been on the boat, but he had no business moving in on her like that. Thank God she stopped it before it happened, though her reaction hadn't exactly been normal.

And he was even more baffled that he'd felt so natural doing it. After years of enduring sweaty palms even thinking about being with a woman again, he'd come very close to jumping in with both feet yesterday. Gooseflesh rose on his arms. He wasn't ready for this yet. Hope had done him a big favor, even if she didn't know it. And he didn't want her to know it.

He hadn't seen her since she'd left him on the beach. When he'd come up to the resort after the morning dives yesterday and again last evening, she'd been nowhere to be found. Finally, this morning he'd texted her, asking if she still wanted to dive like they'd planned. She'd surprised him by answering yes. He admired her grit.

Regardless of what had almost happened yesterday, he still had a job to do. Alex was damn good at what he did, and was determined to help Hope overcome her accident. She'd said point blank she wanted that.

There was a steady case of fluttering in his stomach, and he couldn't help smirking at the thought of him being nervous before a dive. Of course, it wasn't the diving he was worried about.

Hope walked down the beach from her house, dressed in a tank top and long board shorts, her hair in a ponytail. No makeup. Then again, Hope didn't need it.

Knock it off, Monroe.

Normally Hope moved with a graceful, confident stride, but now she walked slowly with short steps, as if she wanted to disappear into the sand. Alex bent down, fiddling with his BCD so it didn't look like he stood there waiting for her. Two feet sporting dark-pink nail polish and flip-flops appeared in front of him.

"Do you ever wish you could get a do-over?" she asked.

You can't even imagine.

"Sometimes." He straightened. "How are you?"

Hope rubbed the back of her neck. "Embarrassed. Ashamed I ran away like a ten-year-old girl instead of talking about it like an adult."

"Maybe we got a little carried away in the moment. Maybe I did. I'm sorry."

"Me too. I'm not looking to get into a tropical romance down here. Can we just forget it happened?"

"What?" He gave her a small smile, even as he experienced a pang at what she'd said. "I don't remember anything."

Hope returned the smile, but it faded as she shifted from foot to foot, shaking her hands out. "I have to admit, I'm pretty nervous about diving again."

"Don't be. It was an accident. You'll do fine."

"That's what I keep telling myself. Now I have to prove it."

Alex had known plenty of divers who had flat-out refused to get back in the water after less traumatic events than what she'd faced. He just needed to build her confidence back up. "After a couple dives, you'll probably be showing me how to do it."

She turned warm eyes to him, and Alex completely relaxed.

"Maybe I've got my next goal then," she said. "See if I can knock you down a few pegs."

"You can start giving me classes."

She looked down and frowned as she placed a hand on her hip. "Maybe we'll start by not setting equipment in the sand when there's perfectly good wood planking available, Mr. Monroe. It makes a mess everywhere."

Alex grinned. "Sand generally comes off pretty easily in the water."

"Already arguing with me. I see how it is. Let's get going—I don't have all day, you know."

"Yes, ma'am."

They began tugging on their wetsuits. Hope stripped off her tank top, revealing a sporty one-piece swimsuit. Her tattoo drew his eye. A caterpillar becoming a butterfly was a pretty symbolic emblem, and he wanted to know the story behind it. But he didn't want to disturb the tenuous balance they'd regained, so he kept quiet. Alex was a patient man.

It wasn't the most exciting dive in the world, but routine was exactly what Hope needed. Had he been with anyone else, Alex would have been bored out of his mind, but watching Hope kept him focused and alert. She was nervous to start, as he'd seen on the beach. Her hands shook as she clipped her BCD closed.

As they entered the water and began the dive, Alex stayed

close to her, offering solid support but without holding her arm like he had immediately after her accident. It didn't take long for Hope to regain her confidence. He enjoyed watching her explore, though she kept a close eye on him, needing his reassurance.

Alex hovered a few feet behind her as she studied a large lobster. She looked up and didn't see him next to her, spinning to her other side before finally whirling around and spotting him immediately. He waved to her, and her eyes filled with relief at finding him again.

Feels kind of nice to be wanted ...

The rest of the dive passed uneventfully, and by the end Hope was relaxed and at ease in the water again.

They'd accomplished something important.

After exiting the water, Alex tossed his fins on the pier near the stairs. "Just set your tank on the planks. I'll take it to the gear room."

Hope unbuckled her BCD and redressed, turning to him with a smile. "Thank you, Alex. That helped a lot."

He returned her smile, riveted to her eyes. "You're welcome. You were great down there, Hope."

LATER THAT NIGHT, Alex took a big pull of his beer and sat down on his deck with a relaxed sigh, watching the black sky above. He was relieved to end the day in a much better frame of mind than when he'd started it.

After getting cleaned up from the dive, Alex had gone to the kitchen for dinner and done something unusual, sitting down with Patti and Clark. He'd mostly kept to himself since his arrival at the resort, but lately had found himself seeking people out more. The three of them had a great time, with Gerold joining in when he wasn't cooking for guests.

Alex stretched his shoulders, feeling the pleasant ache after his workout. He'd performed a ninety-minute weight routine every other day since January. He was pleased to see some of his old muscle tone returning.

Physically, he was getting back. Mentally, he was still working on it.

It was fully dark now, and he finished his beer but made no move to get up and get another one. He was experiencing a strange sensation, and it wasn't the beer. After thinking a minute, Alex was surprised to discover it was happiness.

He actually looked forward to getting up in the morning now. He enjoyed his job more, and the people around him . . . It had been a long time since he could remember being anything but numb. Hope had a lot to do with that.

Alex set the bottle down and leaned his chair back on its two rear legs, gazing toward the shore. The water shimmered as it lapped upon the beach in front of the restaurant and the lights reflected in the water. Putting his feet up on the table in front of him, Alex leaned back, watching the stars above. A meteor streaked across the sky and he smiled, appreciating the beauty of it.

CHAPTER 25

*H*ope walked down the wooden pier toward the palapa, enjoying the early morning sunshine. Swim goggles in hand, she tossed her towel over her shoulder. Alex was already there, getting ready for his swim. Their initial encounters after her accident had been somewhat strained as they tiptoed around each other. But as the days turned into weeks, they fell back into their easy banter, though both of them avoided the precipice they'd reached the morning after her accident.

Being around Alex was one of the highlights of her day. She'd never been this at ease with a man, but was too scared to risk anything further, though she still couldn't figure out her reaction to him. She'd never run away from Kyle when he'd tried to kiss her—and she wasn't some dewy virgin who'd never been around a man.

Why does Alex inspire these reactions in me?

It seemed a moot point, anyway. Alex was friendly and caring, but didn't make any romantic gestures toward her, only friendly teasing. It was what she wanted, so why did that fill her with regret?

Hope tossed her towel on the bench next to his with a smile, ready to enjoy the morning.

"You joining me today?" he asked.

"Sure, but I'm thinking about swimming longer, maybe an hour. You have enough time?"

"Plenty of time. I haven't swum long in a while. It'll be good for me."

"Ok, but I don't want you to strain anything trying to keep up with me. I need to keep my dive guide healthy."

Alex looked at her, eyes lighting up. "If I get into trouble, I'll call for help. Or you can just tow me back to the pier."

"Or maybe I'll leave you to your own devices and let you suffer the consequences of biting off more than you can chew."

"I'll take the risk." With that, he dove in with no goggles.

Hope finished adjusting hers and followed. Setting off at a measured pace, she enjoyed the powerful movement her body produced, catching up to Alex quickly. They swam side by side as she checked her watch periodically. The ocean floor steadily slipped by beneath them, occasional black spiky orbs scattered on the sand. She pulled up at the thirty-minute mark and called out, "Halfway."

They treaded water and caught their breath. "How come you don't wear goggles most of the time? Doesn't the saltwater sting your eyes?"

"I'm used to it, I guess. I wear goggles sometimes, but I like the feel of the water on my face."

She grinned. "You know, it's been a while since one of our friendly competitions. How about we race back to the pier?"

"Deal!" He immediately took off.

"Hey! No fair—" It was a long way back to the dock, so she tried to equal his pace, moving up to his shoulder and staying there. She had plenty left in the tank today. Alex increased his speed and pulled ahead. Hope pulled up alongside him, staying even with his shoulder again for several minutes. Then she tired of the game and increased her arm turnover, taking the lead, but she wasn't able to drop him.

Is he gaining on me again? Oh, this cannot stand.

Hope surged forward, once again ahead of him, heart beating strong and body moving powerfully through the water. After a few breaths, he was next to her before drawing ahead. *Not today, you're not.* She found more speed, arms churning faster and breath heaving, pulling even with him again.

Hope matched him stroke for stroke, their arms turning over in unison.

She sighted quickly—they were nearing the dock. With arms flying and feet kicking hard, she moved into her top speed, giving it everything. The water was a white froth around her, and Alex's head was now even with her shoulder.

She touched the dock just before he did.

"Yes!" she yelled to the sky.

Alex held on to the ladder, breathing hard. "Damn, woman. Maybe you should try out for the Olympics or something."

She laughed, flush with victory. "I wish. But next time I might let you win to help your poor bruised ego."

"Thanks. It needs all the help it can get."

They climbed out and toweled off. Hope had seen more of the circular spiky black objects on the way back, and now they were scattered all around the shore area on both sides of the pier. They were large, some a foot across. "What are those black things?"

"Black sea urchins." Alex frowned, inspecting the area. "They sometimes migrate in this time of year. This is a lot. I don't remember seeing this many before. You should warn the guests to look out for them. Stepping on one is no fun."

"I'll do that." She looked out at the inviting ocean. "Great morning for a dive."

"You want to come with us? There's room on the boat."

"No, I've got too much going on this morning. Another time." She started to walk away but turned back. "Oh. I need to check some permits and licenses for the dive operation. After you get back, can you show me the paperwork?"

He smirked at her. "Never a dull moment with you, Boss Lady. Just come find me after we're back."

AFTER BREAKFAST, Hope strolled into the lobby office. "It's another beautiful day, Patti."

"What has you so happy this mornin'?"

Hope didn't realize it was so obvious, making her self-conscious. "Oh. Things are going really well right now. Everything seems to be firing on all cylinders." She couldn't resist. "And to top it off, Alex and I went swimming this morning. We raced back to the dock, and I beat him! I was a pretty decent swimmer in high school, and it makes me feel great to know I've still got it."

Patti smiled, biting her bottom lip. "Well, that is quite the accomplishment! Congratulations. You're right—we're havin' a wonderful month, for sure. Our reservations are up ten percent this month over last year, and I've never seen such positive reviews."

Patti regarded Hope with a gleam in her eye. "You know, there's been quite an attitude shift in the staff since you got here. And I've *definitely* noticed a change in Alex."

On the wall next to Patti were several rows of eight-by-ten staff photos. They were of each person from head to mid-chest, set against a white background. Patti laughed, pointing to the photo of Alex, who stared at the camera more like a drill sergeant than a dive guide. "He used to look like that all the time, except on the dive boat. And I'm enjoyin' my job more these days too. I only wish you'd take it a little easier. You work too hard."

Hope was touched. "Thank you. That means a lot to me."

Another thought had been percolating in her head for a while now and this seemed like a good time to broach it. "Patti, with the success of Gerold's cooking class, I've got another idea. What do you think about starting a weekly manager's reception? We could hold it every Wednesday, the hour before dinner. We'll have free beer and wine, and because it's only an hour, we don't need to worry about the drinking getting out of hand."

"What did I just say about you workin' too hard? You don't have to change everythin' at once, you know."

"I thought it would be another opportunity to increase interaction between staff and guests. Of course, you could come in later on those days to make up for staying late."

"Oh, I don't mind the extra hour." Patti frowned, though.

"Tell you what. Let's try it out for one week. If no one shows, or it turns out to be a disaster, we can forget about it." Hope turned to the wall clock. "It's after twelve o'clock. I need to get down to the pier and talk to Alex. It's time to renew their captains' licenses."

HOPE STROLLED DOWN THE PIER, waving at several people splashing in the shallows before stopping in front of the dive shop. Tommy hosed off the boat as Alex walked toward her.

She waited by the dive shop as he neared and held up her hands. "Look, I know paperwork isn't the most exciting thing in the world, but let's get—"

"OW! OH SHIIITTTT!" shrieked a man from behind her.

She whirled around to see a guest in the water, arms flailing as he slipped under the surface.

Hearing movement behind her, Hope turned as Alex stripped off his shirt and sprinted to the side of the pier, diving in barefoot. She ran as fast as she could down the pier toward the beachfront, her stomach clenched with dread.

As she ran, Alex *flew* toward the man. She'd known he was a powerful swimmer, but this was a whole different level.

God, he's so fast!

She got to the beach and waded in. By that time, Alex had the man's arm around his shoulder and was helping him toward shore. Hope got on the other side, and together they helped him to the beach as he limped along on one leg.

"I stepped on one of those urchins you warned us about at lunch," he told Hope. "Oh my God, it hurts! I thought I was safely away from them. I didn't know they could move."

Hope bit back a sharp retort as they sat him down on the steps leading up to the pier. Patti and several other employees rushed out to help.

Alex kneeled on the sand, examining the foot. It was bleeding steadily, drops soaking into the sand as black needles protruded from the skin. "Yeah, you've got quite a few spines in there." He noticed the case Patti carried. "Good, you brought the first aid kit. I'll pull the spines out with tweezers, but we should send you to the medical clinic to get it checked out in case any of the spines break off and lodge in your foot." Alex opened the case, pulling out some latex gloves and getting to work.

With the excitement of the emergency over, the gathered crowd dispersed and within fifteen minutes, Alex had done what he could with the wound. He stood up and peeled off the gloves.

"I'll take him to the clinic in the van. You can come too, of course," Patti said to the man's wife. With Clark on one side of him and Patti on the other, they helped the man off the beach and toward the lobby.

"Well, I'm glad that wasn't more serious," Hope said, the ball of dread draining away. When she turned, Alex was already walking back toward the dive shop, and a great surge of irritation rose in its place.

～

ALEX WALKED DOWN THE PIER, relieved the man's injury hadn't been more serious. *No matter how much you warn them, some people have to experience things for themselves. I guess now it's back to the paperw—*

"Hey! I wasn't done with you yet." Hope marched up the stairs toward him, fists clenched and her entire body transmitting furious indignation.

Well, this is interesting. . . Looks like the feisty is back.

"You," she said, poking him in the center of the chest with her finger, "have been holding out on me."

"What did I do?" He started backing up as she advanced toward him.

"I saw you swimming to rescue that man. Were you planning on just keeping this from me forever?"

"Hope, what are you talking about?"

"You've been letting me win!" A stamp of her foot actually accompanied the last word.

He couldn't help the slow smile that crept across his face, enraging her further, much to his delight. "Not competitive at all, are you? Look, it was adrenaline. I was rushing to reach the guy."

"Oh, bullshit." Hope stood square, both hands on her hips. "You could probably beat me with one hand tied behind your back. Literally!"

"Come on, you're an extremely strong swimmer. Believe me, you push me hard." He couldn't stop smiling. She was like an adorable spitting cat jumping around with her tail puffed out. And he wasn't lying—Hope was a fantastic swimmer.

"Stop patronizing me!" She deflated a little. "I thought I really beat you."

Now he wasn't sure how to respond. "What kind of man would I be if I just raced ahead and left you behind?"

"Oh, I don't know, maybe an honest one?"

His smile fell and he winced.

Hope slumped and gave a wince of her own. Looking contrite, she said, "I'm sorry, that was a low blow. I didn't mean it. I was just really proud of myself for beating you."

Then she looked at him with those eyes, and he melted.

As they continued walking down the pier, the butterfly on her shoulder peeked out from under the strap of her tank top.

What would it be like to touch it?

"Of course you should be proud of yourself," he said. "You told me you hadn't swum in years until you moved down here. I've been swimming nearly every day for longer than I can remember. I can't believe how much progress you've made. And, you know, I am taller than you. Also, there is a slim possibility," he held up his hands, "*maybe*, that I'm a little stronger. Though I'm sure you'd be willing to arm wrestle me over that."

Success! That earned him a small smile. "Perhaps."

He nudged her with his elbow. "How would you suggest we move forward from this crisis?"

They had reached the end of the pier, and Hope sat down on one of the benches with a big sigh. "With my admitting I'm being a bitch. I'm sorry."

Alex smiled at her. "It's ok. I'll live."

Gazing out at the ocean, Hope shook her head. "I seem to be apologizing to you a lot. I don't mean to be hard on you."

That made him grin more. "Meh, I don't scare off that easily. And I'm swimming tomorrow morning if you feel like joining me." His smile faded. "But don't expect me to leave you behind. That's not going to happen."

With that, he turned toward the dive shop, smiling at her over his shoulder. "Besides, you shouldn't apologize. I kind of like this feisty side of you."

A FEW NIGHTS LATER, Hope looked around critically at the patio outside the restaurant, fully recovered from yet another embarrassing outburst at Alex as she smoothed her light-colored floral sundress. A flush wanted to heat her cheeks, but she concentrated on the scene before her instead. The patio looked lovely, over-looking the ocean and next to the pool. Recently installed brick pavers were set in a herringbone pattern, alternating light and dark-gray bricks.

Tonight was their first manager's reception, and it was a resounding success. Patti talked to a couple who were repeat guests as Clark circulated through the crowd with a bottle of white wine in one hand and red in the other. A large steel trough was filled with ice and bottles of beer, water, and soft drinks.

There were fourteen guests at the resort presently, and they had all come to the reception. Hope had mingled with them, and they seemed genuinely happy to spend more time with her and Patti. She spoke with one older couple who were on their eighth trip to the resort, both noting the new energy around the resort.

"Thank you." Hope's toes curled with happiness. "You can't imagine how much that means to me. I have a lot of plans for this place. You'll have to come back next year to find out what has changed."

Patti finished her conversation and approached Hope. "All right. I have to admit you've got a great idea here. Let's start makin' it a weekly occurrence. I have a few ideas that might make it even better . . ."

A wash of satisfaction rippled through Hope.

CHAPTER 26

J une . . .

HOPE SET the housekeeping schedule down on the porch sofa next to her, idly swinging one foot back and forth as the ocean waves splashed on the shore. Cruz was sleeping, stretched out in the late afternoon sun as he snored. He still wouldn't let her approach him, but lately he had taken to hanging around her porch if she was outside.

Hope frowned, remembering her blow-up at Alex over the swimming. She was starting to regret stopping that kiss, unable to deny the attraction any longer. Maybe she was trying to scare him off with her tendency to snap at him, though it seemed to be having the opposite effect.

Her phone interrupted her musing. Sara's name appeared on the display.

"How's life in paradise?"

Hope smiled and tucked her legs next to her. "It's going great, actually. Well, apart from me acting like a bitch sometimes."

"Oh? Something special, or just your usual level of bitchiness?"

Hope laughed. "Nothing. A disagreement I had with someone, and I kind of blew up. Long story."

"That sounds like you." Sara paused, and Hope could practically hear the wheels turning. "So does the 'going great' part have anything to do with your mysterious Alex?"

"Jeez, Sara, would you drop it?" Hope sighed and shifted positions. "I've told you, he's only a guy who works here. There's nothing more to it than that. He isn't even remotely good looking."

"So you keep saying. Just an average guy you get private scuba lessons from and go swimming with all the time." Sara paused. "If you won't satisfy my curiosity on that front, let's get to the reason I'm calling. I have some vacation time I need to use. How would you feel about a sisterly visit? I could come down there in a couple of weeks."

Hope beamed. "I'd love to see you! It's been too long. We're pretty booked up, but I have extra bedrooms in the house so you can stay with me."

Maybe I can send Alex on vacation or something and replace him with some mean old guy.

"All right, then. I'll let you know when I've worked out the details."

TWO WEEKS LATER, Hope stood in the arrivals area of St. Croix airport, bouncing on the balls of her feet to see better. The flight arrival was announced, and Sara texted that she was there. Finally, her dark head popped up amid the surrounding crowd, and Hope waved frantically to get her attention.

Sara caught sight of her and ran up, the two of them embracing. "Do you need to pick up a suitcase at the carousel?" Hope asked.

"Nah, I'm only here four days, so I just brought a carry-on. Bring on the strawberry margaritas!"

After arriving at the house, Hope showed her to the guest bedroom, where Sara dumped her suitcase on the bed. Her long dark-brown hair still in perfect curls despite the long trip, Sara wore a long blue and green tie-dyed sundress. Multiple long necklaces with pendants complemented the outfit. *How did she get through security with all those necklaces?*

"Come on! I can't wait to show you around." Hope opened the sliding glass door and led them onto her porch, but the view stopped Sara cold.

She stood there, focused on the ocean as the breeze blew her hair back. "My God, Hope. This is incredible. I can't believe you get to look at this every day."

Hope hugged herself. "I know!" She was still concerned Sara would make trouble with Alex, but maybe she'd be too distracted.

Or maybe I'm the only one who thinks he's gorgeous and she won't even notice him.

They went to the restaurant and pushed through the double doors into the kitchen. "Gerold, here she is! This is my sister Sara."

Sara turned around the kitchen in full circles, blinking like an owl. She shook Gerold's hand. "Well, I can already tell I'm going to enjoy eating here. Your kitchen is very bright and clean." She waved an index finger at him. "And I always say you can judge the quality of the food by the cleanliness of the kitchen the chef maintains." Gerold beamed. Hope managed to refrain from rolling her eyes as she steered Sara toward the bar.

Clark opened two beers, and Hope and Sara moved to one of the tables in the sand. "Hope, this is fantastic. You are so lucky to have me in your life to make you do the things you'd rather avoid." They both laughed, and Sara pointed to the end of the pier with its covered palapa. "Let's head out there. That looks great."

"Sure. The dive boat should be back any minute. We might need to stay out of the way when it does. It's a little hectic for a while right after the dive."

Sure enough, as they left the bar area, Hope spied the boat returning. They made their way onto the wooden planking. "Let's stay out of the way for a bit." Hope led Sara to the side of the pier in front of the dive shop.

"Everyone on the boat seems happy," Sara said. The guests chatted with each other as they walked by.

"They usually are. We run a good operation here." Hope turned around to face the beach, enjoying the sunshine on her face as several guests played in the sand.

Sara lowered her sunglasses and peered above them. "Oh. My. God. Who is *that?*"

Hope closed her eyes and sighed. Even without looking, she knew exactly who it was. She turned back around and said as casually as possible, "Oh, that's Alex. And behind him is Tom—"

Sara interrupted with a loud belly laugh, clutching her stomach. "*That* is Alex? That guy is Mr. Average Nobody? Oh, Hope. You are such a huge, dirty liar."

"Sara, don't embarrass me! There's nothing between us. We just work together."

"Yeah, right."

Alex walked toward them, wearing a brilliant smile.

Well, at least he has his shirt on.

Hope introduced the two of them. Alex shook Sara's hand and said, "It's great to meet you. Don't believe anything Hope has told you about me. None of it's true."

"Yes, I see that," Sara replied sweetly.

Alex's face went blank, and Hope hurried in. "I'm showing Sara around the resort. We'd better be moving on. I know you're really busy after the dive, and we—"

"I'm starving," Sara interrupted, and turned to Hope. "You said they were serving lunch now. Alex, why don't you join the two of us?"

"I'd love to. You can tell me all of Hope's dirty laundry. Let me shower and change and I'll join you in a few minutes." He trotted up the stairs.

"Wait a minute," Sara said to Hope. "He lives here too?"

Hope grabbed her arm and steered her down the pier. "Yes, he does. Sara, I don't need you meddling in things. I mean it. We're just friends and nothing more. He works for me for God's sake."

"You really haven't slept with him?"

"No! Of course not."

"Would you slow down? I'm shorter than you—I can't walk that fast." Sara shook her arm free. "Hope, have you suddenly switched teams? Because I can't see any other reason—"

"God, you're impossible. This is exactly why I didn't tell you he was good looking. I knew you wouldn't believe that a man and a woman can have a perfectly platonic relation—"

"Oh, save it. I need another beer."

Hope guided them into the restaurant and to the most secluded private table in case there were any fireworks.

They verbally sparred for a few more minutes as Hope tried to set some ground rules. Clark appeared with two more beers. "You might as well bring Alex one too," Hope said. *He's gonna need it.*

Alex appeared at the edge of the restaurant and headed their way, wearing dressier shorts than normal and a light-blue button-up shirt that perfectly matched his eyes. *That doesn't help. Couldn't you have worn earth tones or something?*

His short sandy hair was neat, and he smelled like a breath of fresh air.

"I ordered you a beer." Hope pointed to it.

"Thanks, but I'm teaching a refresher this afternoon so I'll pass." Charlotte brought over three menus and a pitcher of water with three glasses. Alex filled all three, then drank his in one shot.

"You can have my water if you want," said Sara.

Alex smiled at her as he refilled his glass. "Diving dehydrates you, especially when you dive every day. I wouldn't dream of taking yours."

"Well, I can see you're a gentleman," Sara said. She took a drink of beer before setting the bottle down with formality. "Alex, I wanted to let you know that even though Hope is my big sister, I take it as my responsibility to watch out for her. This is especially important since she's been known to make very poor decisions and has terrible taste in men."

Hope choked on her beer. She looked up and Alex was smiling widely at her. A flush crept up her neck.

Sara held out her hand toward Alex. "I know. Don't tell me. Hope has made it crystal clear the two of you have a very proper employer-employee relationship and only that. However, the fact remains you are an important part of the operation of this resort, and if I'm going to get any sleep, I must get to know you better."

"I'll help however I can," he said gravely. He was clearly biting the inside of his cheek to keep from laughing.

Sara folded her hands together on the table. "Hope tells me you were in the military. We have several family members who are part of the armed forces, so Hope and I hold the military in high esteem. What branch did you serve in?"

"Navy." He wasn't biting his cheek anymore.

"Our uncle was in the Navy. What did you do?"

"I was a Navy diver." His jaw tightened, and his words were clipped.

Sara brightened. "Oh! Like in the movie?"

"What movie?"

"You know, the one with the guy with the big metal . . ." Sara twirled her index finger in circles around her head. "The metal thing on his head and the big suit and boots."

A flush ignited Hope's face, and she closed her eyes. When

she opened them, Alex was watching her with an enormous grin on his face.

She sent him her most lethal mock glare.

"What? Why are you giving me the stink eye? I'm the one in the hot seat here." He turned back to Sara. "It's called a diving helmet, and I never used one. Only scuba most of the time."

"Oh? Did you lead people around on tours?"

"Not exactly. Mostly salvage." He rubbed the back of his neck. "I did a lot of picking up things that other people lost. It was pretty boring, actually."

Sara took another long drink. Hope kicked her under the table. "Alex, I know you're the one who taught Hope how to dive. I was hoping you could enlighten me about something."

"As I said before, whatever I can do to help." He still wore a slight smile.

"Thank you. You're very gallant. Hope has mentioned an . . . unpleasant dive she had, but she won't elaborate. I'd like to know I can entrust her to your care, but I can't get her to open up much about the incident. Was it serious?"

Alex's demeanor changed like a light switch being flipped. The smile and teasing were gone, replaced with a solemn expression, and his shoulders tensed. The change made Sara sit back in her chair. He darted his eyes to Hope and raised an eyebrow. She gave him a small nod in return.

"Yes, very serious. I'm not surprised she doesn't want to talk about it. She probably wants to put it behind her." The intensity of his stare made Sara squirm.

Good, let someone else feel the effects of those eyes for once!

But being the older sister, Hope came to her rescue. "It's ok, Alex. I don't mind talking about it. And I have put it behind me." *Well, mostly.* "I've gone on plenty of dives since."

Sara looked at Alex, motioning for him to continue.

"She had an out-of-air emergency. Her regulator got knocked

out of her mouth so she couldn't breathe, and she lost her mask too. You should be very proud of your sister."

His words were directed at Sara, but he watched Hope. "With little experience, Hope reacted to a really dangerous situation better than most divers I've ever known. I can't imagine any new diver handling that situation better than she did. Within minutes, she was breathing calmly and had put her mask back on."

It was as if she and Alex were the only two people left in the world—the rest faded away. He leaned more toward Hope. "She went through a very scary and dangerous experience. But it didn't stop her from going again immediately afterward. That's the definition of courage in my book."

He stopped talking, and the two of them sat there with their eyes locked together. Hope's heart pounded in her chest. The throbbing pulse in his neck told her he felt the same. Finally, Alex leaned back in his chair and took a drink of water, the spell broken. Sara sat there, looking back and forth between the two of them.

"The whole thing was my fault," Hope said, taking a deep breath to steady herself. "I wasn't watching where I was going, and I collided with his fins. It was only a freak accident, so I didn't let it get the best of me. But I'm damn lucky Alex was there, or it might have ended very differently."

And then I acted like a child and ran off.

"Lots of people let one-off freak accidents rule their entire lives. But not you." He raised his glass to her and finished it. Turning to Sara, he asked, "You're not a prosecutor by any chance, are you?"

She laughed. "No. I work at a hair salon in Charleston. I just like to look after my sister."

"You missed your calling." Alex pushed back with a teasing smile. "I'd better be off. Sara, it was great meeting you, and I'm really looking forward to our next conversation. But I need to get back to work. You wouldn't believe what a hard-ass my boss is." He waved as he walked out.

"I hope you're happy," Hope hissed. "You chased him off before he even had a chance to eat!"

Sara finished her beer in several long swallows and slammed the bottle on the table. "Hope, it is high time you pulled your head out of your ass!"

"Keep your voice down! What specifically are you referring to this time?"

Sara leaned toward her, eyes fuming. "How many years have I been telling you to stop settling for these men you're not that interested in and find a man who deserves you? That—" she waved an arm in the general direction Alex had departed, "is exactly what I mean. And don't give me your bullshit about you guys just being friends. There's enough electricity between the two of you to light up Chicago! Why are you so afraid of being happy?"

She sat back in her chair, relaxing a little. "And I'm not only saying this because he is a very fine-looking man. Hope, after one conversation, I'm more impressed with him than with every other boyfriend you've ever had—combined. And don't think I didn't see that he wasn't going to tell me anything about your accident without your approval." She grabbed Alex's untouched beer and drank.

"Sara, it's complicated, even without . . . the rest." Hope picked at her fingernails. "What if it didn't work out? He works for me—it would be sexual harassment or something. If we broke up, then I'd have to find a new divemaster—forget about an instructor—and good ones aren't that easy to find. It could really affect the resort."

Sara sighed and counted on her fingers. "One, it's only harassment if it's *unwelcome*. I recently had to take my annual training on this, so I know all about it." She snorted. "Trust me, the way that man looked at you, unwelcome is the last thing you need to worry about. And two, we're on a tropical island. You could probably throw a rock and hit three divemasters. A good *man* isn't easy to find, and you've got one right in front of your nose."

When Hope said nothing, Sara reached out and squeezed her hand. "Hope, I get it. I know you better than anyone. But you can't go through the rest of your life being afraid to get close to anyone. There *are* still good men out there. Sweetie, you need to lead with your heart on this one. Your head has gotten you nowhere."

CHAPTER 27

*S*ara was still sleeping as Hope walked down the sand road from her house toward the resort. The sun peeked over the mountains to the east when she leaped out of Gerold's way as he barreled by on his bike. "Whoa! Sorry 'bout that!" He grinned as he pedaled past.

"Slow down!" Hope laughed, continuing toward the pier. She sat down on a bench to wait for Alex. Before too long, he trotted down his stairs with a towel around his neck.

He took in the T-shirt and shorts she wore. "No swim this morning?"

"No, I'm sitting this one out today." She took a breath. "I wanted to apologize to you for Sara. She means well, but once she gets going, she's like a force of nature. You just have to hold on and let her blow herself out. If she gets too personal, tell her to be quiet. I mean it."

"It's fine." Alex sat next to her. "She didn't cross any lines. And I get a kick out of watching you two together. She's a pistol, that's for sure." He nudged her knee with his. "Besides, I have a little sister, too. I know how they can be."

Hope raised a brow at him. "I do believe that's the first personal detail you've ever volunteered."

"She's married with two kids and lives in Baltimore."

"Well, maybe she'll come and visit us some day." He shrugged, staring at the deck, and Hope relented. "Sara and I are going into Frederiksted this morning to look around, but she said she'd like to go snorkeling this afternoon. She's expecting a fully guided tour."

"Of course she is." Alex smiled, now back in familiar territory. "I'm at your service."

"Could you lead us around the house reef?"

"I can do better than that." He put his arm around her and squeezed before letting go. Hope took that as an apology of sorts. "Let's take the boat. I'll take you guys to a great spot." He frowned. "Assuming the boat behaves herself, of course."

"You think we can wait until fall to do repairs?"

He shrugged. "It's pretty normal. Boats are temperamental." He turned to her with a smile. "I don't think it's going to sink if that's what you're worried about. Sara's perfectly safe."

She returned his smile. "Thanks. I'm sure she's terribly worried." The smile fell as Hope rose from the bench. "And prepare yourself, Alex. I'm not sure Sara's done with you yet."

"If she tries to swallow me whole, I'll count on you to save me." He stood up, throwing his towel on the bench before diving in.

IT WAS STARTING to get warm as Hope and Sara walked along the Frederiksted pier. No cruise ships were in port today, so it was nearly deserted along its one-third mile length, especially at 10 a.m. A main feature of the town, the dark wooden pier jutted far out into the turquoise water.

"It's so pretty here. I expected some seedy sections," Sara said.

"There are some parts that are a little sketchy, but overall, it's an amazing island."

Sara sighed. "Listen, I'm not going to beat a dead horse here."

"She says as she gets out her baseball bat and starts looking for equines."

"Fair enough. But how many years are you going to go on punishing yourself for something that wasn't your fault?"

"I'm not anymore. I know it wasn't my fault. But old habits are hard to change, you know?" They stopped and leaned with their forearms against the railing, the warm breeze blowing against their faces.

"Has Alex given you any indication he can't be trusted, or worse?"

"No. Just the opposite, actually." Hope sighed. "Though he really hates personal questions. The man does *not* like to talk about his past."

Sara threw back her head and laughed. "Oh my God—you two are made for each other!"

Hope had to laugh, too. "Maybe. But whatever his issue is, it's also holding him back."

"Give it time. Doesn't seem like either of you is going anywhere."

"I know. It seemed so much easier with Kyle. And I know why."

Sara turned toward her with a raised brow.

"Because I care about Alex. A lot. God, emotions are coming up in me that send me into a tailspin. It's ridiculous. We almost kissed a while ago, and I ran off like a schoolgirl. I'm amazed he's still speaking to me." She shook her head. "Sometimes I feel like I need a huge sign held up for me: *Hope, this is worth the risk*. I've got so much to lose now."

"Sounds to me like you've got a lot to gain too. Not all men desert the people they love, you know."

"Yes, wise sister, I'm aware. But I'm the one who had to clean up Dad's colossal mess for years. It didn't make a good impression on me."

"I know. And I know you went from bad to worse. But it's also not something you should punish every man on earth for. Men can be fun, you know. I'm thinking about a particular dive guide right now." Sara snuck her a sideways glance that made Hope sigh with dread. "A nice roll in the hay would do you a world of good, you know."

"Oh, come on. Sex just complicates things. It's not that great."

Sara turned to her, mouth open. "Oh my God! Hope, have you even had B sex?"

"I'm scared to even ask, Sara. What, pray tell, is B sex?"

"Above average. Don't you know anything?" She frowned. "Ok, big sister, looks like a lecture is on order. Let's forget about A— extremely rare and definitely something to hold on to if you find it. But come on! B sex is totally obtainable."

Hope scowled at her. "That is incredibly shallow."

"Oh, stop it. We're not only talking about the physical act here, you know. It's the whole thing—how he makes you feel, and therefore how you make him feel, mmm? The feelings, the chemistry, the emotion. It's love—declared or undeclared." Sara nodded wisely.

"I'm not having this conversation with you."

"I bet you've never even had above a C+, have you?"

Hope rounded on her. "And I suppose you've had A, huh?"

A dreamy smile appeared on Sara's face, and she twirled a lock of hair around her finger. "Once. During that glorious summer I spent in Berkeley." She turned to Hope. "Alas, we were incompatible."

∼

THE TWO SISTERS shared a sedate lunch in Frederiksted before heading back to the resort for their snorkeling adventure. Sara restrained herself from asking more questions about Hope's feelings for Alex.

He had everything ready on the boat so they were soon at the site, a protected bay that caught the sunshine but not the wind. Hope shut the engine off so Alex could get safely back on the boat after tying off to the mooring ball.

Sara stood there with her eyebrows raised. "Wow, you guys have this down to a science. I'm impressed."

"Thank you," Hope said. She was still sending dark glances Sara's way. Earlier, Alex had stripped off his shirt before mooring the boat, completely oblivious to his effect on the two women. Sara had leaned behind him, giving Hope a very pointed look.

Hope had glared back and mouthed, "Behave!"

But at least now Sara seemed to be used to the sight of Alex's bare torso and was inspecting her mask. No wetsuits today. Alex was clad in board shorts, Hope in one of her sporty bikinis, and Sara in a one-piece black swimsuit that clung to her curvy figure.

Alex wiped the water off his face and shook his head like a dog, sending droplets flying. "This site is great for both diving and snorkeling. The reef off to port here is shallow, and the sun hits it in the afternoon. We'll swim down the reef, then make our way back. This can be a good place to find octopuses, so keep your eyes open."

Sara reared back. "An octopus? Will it stick to my face?"

"They only do that to nosy people. Let's go."

Hope smiled as he handed them their masks, fins, and snorkels. All three made their way to the platform to don their fins, Sara in the middle, who turned to Alex. "You forgot your snorkel."

"I never use the things. Hate them."

"How are you going to breathe?"

He looked seriously at her. "Open my mouth and inhale."

Hope laughed out loud at that, and they pushed off into the

water with Sara mock glaring at Alex as she put her snorkel in her mouth.

They swam to the shallows, where they watched the fish dart about until Sara grew more comfortable in the water. Then Alex swam down as the reef top fell into a sloped wall. He wore his long free diving fins and weight belt.

Alex descended around seven or eight feet, gliding left and right as he looked for something. His movement was grace in action, effortless and controlled. A single fin kick would propel him just the right amount, and he would hover, searching for his quarry, only to float up several feet and float again without appearing to move his fins at all. Hope looked at Sara, whose eyes were wide.

Alex beckoned to them. The sisters descended clumsily, as their bodies wanted to float. Sara grasped his free arm and Hope his bare shoulder. In front of them was a four-inch damsel fish flitting back and forth in front of its eggs and periodically rushing them.

They watched the brown and white fish fiercely charging to protect its eggs until Sara let go to surface. Alex took Hope's hand and squeezed it, and as he reached out the fingers of his other hand, the damsel fish promptly began biting him. Hope laughed, then squeezed his hand back and signaled she needed to go up, so they ascended together, letting go at the surface. Sara was still catching her breath.

"Now I see why you don't use a snorkel," Sara said. "Do you breathe? How can you hold your breath so long?"

"Practice. I've been doing this for a long time. Come on, let's continue." They slowly made their way to the end of the reef before turning around to head back. Sara and Hope wanted to stay on the surface by the shallow reef top, so Alex took the opportunity to free dive.

The reef sloped down deep, and it looked like he was easily diving to sixty or seventy feet. Graceful dolphin kicks propelled him along as he stopped periodically to peer into crevices. Even Sara watched Alex more than the reef in front of her.

She pulled up and grabbed Hope's arm. "Only the resort dive guide, huh? Hope, that guy is a fish! He's amazing. Are you sure he's human?"

THEY CLIMBED BACK ON BOARD, and Hope passed out towels.

Alex pointed to the cooler. "I put water and soft drinks in there. Help yourself if you want one."

Sara put her towel down. "How thoughtful. You see, Hope? The man gives us a first-class tour *and* thinks of our needs too."

"It's standard procedure, Sara. He does that on all the trips."

"Don't be such a bitch. Would it kill you to show a little appreciation for once?"

"I make sure I always fill the cooler," Alex said. "I told you yesterday, Hope terrifies me. I don't want to think what might happen if she found it empty."

Alex's smile was back. She mock glared at him, and it got bigger. She couldn't help smiling back.

"There. You see, Hope? He's making a joke." Sara opened a water and turned to Alex. "Hope was concerned I was too hard on you yesterday. I told her you were a grown man, and you definitely look like you can take care of yourself. And I only asked you questions that respect the boundaries of any good employer-employee relationship."

"You did."

"Thank you. So where did you learn to become a scuba instructor?"

"In the Red Sea. I was stationed around the Mediterranean a lot, so the Red Sea was close." His voice was getting flatter. "I got most of my advanced certifications there."

"I don't understand," Sara said. "If you were a diver in the

Navy, why would you have to take a separate course to teach scuba? Surely the Navy has stricter requirements."

Alex frowned. "All the instructors for the scuba-certifying agency have to teach to the same standards. So your individual qualifications as an instructor don't matter as much. You still have to learn the curriculum."

"But I don't—"

"Sara, would you shut up!" Hope crossed her arms.

"Calm down! These are perfectly legitimate questions." She turned back to Alex with her most innocent smile. "Besides, if I wanted to be nosy, I'd ask you what I really want to know, which is, have you ever been married?"

"Sara!" Hope turned scarlet.

Alex gave Sara a long, measured look before answering, "Divorced. For a long time. Military life is hard on wives." His eyes flickered to Hope, then back to Sara. He stood straighter. "And turnabout's fair play. How's your love life, Sara?"

"Oh, I'm a free spirit. I float wherever the wind takes me." Sara held her arms out and twirled side to side. "I can't see myself settling down with a man, raising our two-point-five children." She dropped her arms and waved a finger at Alex. "Don't get me wrong—I'm not promiscuous. My rule is only one man at a time. Who on earth would want more than one?"

Alex looked like he was trying not to smile, much to Hope's relief. Then he turned his eyes to her. "And what about you?"

Her heart nearly stopped, but she opened her mouth to answer—

"Oh, we already established that yesterday," Sara said with a casual wave of her hand. "Hope has terrible taste in men. Alex, my sister is an amazing woman. The *only* reason she wasn't snapped up years ago is because she keeps dating these boring men who have absolutely no class. She knows this, and when they show their true colors, things fizzle out until she meets her next failure."

"Sounds like she needs to find a better man."

"That's exactly what I've been telling her!" Sara put her hands on her hips. "Thank you. I'm hoping the situation will change soon. She deserves better."

"Are you two finished?" Hope asked. "Can we stop talking about me like I'm not even here?"

"Oh, you're right. We're being extremely rude," Sara said. "I'm sorry, Hope. Apologize to her, Alex."

Alex turned to Hope, his eyes piercing hers. "I'm sorry. Sara's right—you do deserve better."

"And I thank you, Alex," Sara said. "I've never been snorkeling before, but I've talked to others who have. And comparing what I just experienced with what those people told me, I think I enjoyed something very special."

Alex visibly relaxed. "Only the best for the Collins ladies." He winked at Hope, grabbing a soda and drinking it in one shot. "I did see several octopuses on the way back, but they were hiding in the reef where it's too deep for snorkeling. I'm sorry I couldn't find any for you. They don't like the bright sunlight in the shallows."

"There you are, being a gentleman again," Sara said. "Hope, you need to give this man a raise." She turned back to Alex. "Besides, if you had found us an octopus, I probably wouldn't have my face anymore."

CHAPTER 28

"*N*o, you are *not* wearing shorts and a T-shirt to my goodbye dinner. And when was the last time you wore makeup?"

Sara stood scowling in Hope's bedroom doorway, her hands on her hips. She wore a dark-red and gold flowing dress that landed mid-shin. Her hair and makeup were perfect. She was curvy and voluptuous compared to Hope's toned and athletic, and the outfit showed her figure to full advantage.

"I didn't bring much with me, so I don't have any fancy clothing. I only brought one nice dress."

"Which one?"

Hope frowned at her closet. "Killer Black Dress."

Sara's eyes lit up. "Oh, *now* we're talking!"

Hope clenched her fists at her sides. "No. It's my sexy dress. These are my co-workers, Sara. It's inappropriate."

Sara breezed past and rifled through Hope's closet. "There's no such thing. A gorgeous woman in a black dress transcends all boundaries." She pulled out the dress, a knee-length sheath with tank straps and a low neckline. "Oh yes, this will do!"

Thirty minutes later, Sara had Hope's dress, hair, and makeup completed to her satisfaction. "We're amazing." She lifted Hope's arms out. "My God, your arms look incredible. I guess you have been swimming a lot." Then she narrowed her eyes, gazing at Hope's shoulder. "You got the color freshened up on your tattoo, didn't you?"

"I did, right before I left Chicago. I changed the green on the chrysalis and the butterfly to more of a turquoise. I was ready for a change."

"You have changed. This place has been good for you." She turned back to the mirror. "I never knew I had such a hot sister. Let's go—we have a grand entrance to make!"

Hope took a deep breath and stared at her reflection in the full-length mirror. Her chestnut hair was flat ironed, sweeping past her shoulders and with lighter highlights thanks to the tropical sun. Hope had on much more makeup than she generally wore, but she had to admit the effect was good. Her eyes glowed, her cheekbones were sharply defined, and her lips were a bright red. And she was definitely showing some cleavage. She turned sideways in the mirror. Killer Black Dress was like her Superman costume.

Time to put on your cape and fly, girl.

They walked into the restaurant, and the party was already going. Patti, Tommy, and Clark were all sitting together. Even Martine from the front desk was there, and from the loudness of the conversation, the drinks were already flowing.

Everyone at the table was dressed up from their everyday attire, and a general round of appreciation went around at the sisters' entrance. Hope took a seat next to Sara and looked around the table, but Alex was nowhere to be found.

Great. I've been having fantasies of knocking him dead with my appearance, and he's not even here.

There were several bottles of wine at the table, and Hope poured herself a glass of red. Next to her, Sara was deep in discussion with Tommy, trying to identify a fish she saw. Hope caught

Patti's eye, and they raised their glasses to each other, Patti winking at her.

Tommy seemed convinced the fish was called a Rock Beauty, and Sara was arguing. They were going back and forth. Hope smiled, knowing Tommy was hopelessly outmatched, when Alex's voice came from across the table.

"Sorry I'm late. I got held up."

Hope looked up as he took the last free seat, which was across from her. He wore a long-sleeved black shirt and khaki pants.

He actually owns pants!

The contrast between the black material and his tan skin and blue eyes made her tingle.

Alex searched around the table, skipping right past her to Sara and Tommy before he whipped his eyes back to her. He widened them and even from across the table, the blue irises allowed her to see his pupils dilating as he stared at her.

His gaze changed, and her body responded immediately. Before she knew what she was doing, Hope opened her mouth and touched the middle of her top lip with her tongue. Alex tightened his jaw and his chest expanded with a sharp inhale before a lazy smile spread across his face as their eyes held. Hope breathed hard, and Sara's knee knocked hers under the table.

As Alex poured himself a glass of red wine, there was a lull in the conversation. He raised his glass. "Here's to all the beautiful women we're lucky enough to know." Glasses clinked around the table with cheers.

Shortly after, the food came. Gerold had outdone himself with a traditional Cruzan dinner with haute cuisine touches. He served filet mignon but included a traditional roast goat for the more adventurous and even dressed up the rice and beans. Hope kept returning her gaze to Alex all evening. Each time, their eyes met. *Either we're catching each other's eyes at the same time, or he's been staring at me all night.* The thought made the tingle come back.

She overheard Sara talking to Tommy. "What, she didn't tell

you?" Sara turned to Hope with a pout. "You didn't tell these fine people I'm the reason you're here?"

"Oh my God, I completely forgot! I haven't said anything about this, have I?" Hope had the group's attention now, with blank looks all around. "It's true. I wouldn't be here without Sara. It's a funny story, but I didn't tell it when I first got here because of all the turmoil with Steve's leaving."

"Oh, Hope, be quiet. You're a ghastly storyteller." Sara made eye contact with everyone at the table. "I happen to be the recipient of all my sister's tales of woe. And tales of woe are one of Hope's specialties. This past February was particularly horrible for her. First, she goes out to a lovely dinner with her boyfriend, who dumps her out of the blue." Murmurs of sympathy followed this as Hope tried not to wince, a different flush rising.

"Anyway, a friend of mine had just returned from this lovely island, flush with information about the raffle. I suggested Hope enter it, loving sister that I am. She gave me a bunch of lame excuses and hung up. So, I went back to the lottery website and looked everything over." Sara waved a finger around the table. "Making sure this was a legitimate enterprise, you know. Next, Hope got passed over for a promotion she was easily the best person for." More exclamations of outrage at this. Sara raised her hand. "But wait! My sister isn't some meek pushover. She marched right into her boss's office and quit on the spot!"

Patti applauded. "Good for you, Hope."

Next, Sara's face broke into a wide smile. "And this is the best part! She was so sad on her birthday that I bought her three tickets as her present. And you all know what happened next. She won! How's that!" She slapped the table.

There was applause and exclamations all around.

"Sara entered you in the lottery? And you didn't even know?" Tommy's mouth was open, then transformed into a big smile.

A flush ignited Hope's face. "Yes, it's true. When I first arrived, I was so self-conscious about it. Steve deserts the place, and the crazy lady who's taking over didn't even enter the lottery to win it—her sister did."

She leaned forward, serious now. "And after I had been here a while, I forgot about it. It's so strange to hear Sara talk about it. That almost seems like a different life to me. I feel like a new woman now." Once again, her gaze was pulled toward Alex, whose eyes blazed into hers.

Finally, without taking his eyes off her, he raised his glass and said, "Here's to second chances."

After they all drank, Sara raised her glass and said, "And don't you all wish I was your sister?"

ALEX SAT at his workbench and rubbed his eyes, tired after a sleepless night. He'd been late to the goodbye dinner last night when a guest had shown up at the dive shop, panic-stricken because the mouthpiece on her regulator broke. Then, after he'd worked late to fix it, she hadn't even bothered to show up for this morning's dive.

The water had been very rough. Alex had thought about canceling the dive, but the guests insisted they could handle it. Half of them threw up the entire time, and the other half were completely out of shape, so he'd had to manhandle them all morning. His back was feeling it. He stretched, wincing at the tightness before checking his watch. It was already after three. Lunch was long past, and he was starving.

Food first.

Above all, Hope had induced his sleepless night. He'd hardly recognized her last night—she had looked spectacular. Alex was almost glad he hadn't been sitting next to her. There's no way he could have kept his eyes on her face. That dress with the plunging neckline had driven him crazy—he couldn't stop watching her. He smiled, imagining Hope marching into her boss's office to quit her job in Chicago. That sounded like her. She certainly didn't take any crap from him.

Alex cut through the restaurant to get to the kitchen. He usually avoided the dining room because he frequently got waylaid by guests. Normally he didn't mind talking with them, but today was *not* the day. But during mid-afternoon the restaurant should be deserted.

He peeked into the dining area before entering to make sure the coast was clear. Hope sat in the corner with a pencil between her teeth and both hands in her hair, which stuck up all over the place.

She might be having a worse day than me.

The entire surface of the table was strewn with accounting ledgers, a pile three inches thick off to one side.

"That looks fun," Alex said, and Hope jumped, glaring at him with the pencil still in her teeth. It was all he could do to keep a straight face. *My day's starting to look up.*

She removed the pencil with one hand and placed it over her ear. "No. Not even a little bit."

"May I join you?"

"Your choice, but consider yourself warned. I may bite, and I haven't had my shots."

He couldn't hold back the smile anymore. She was almost as much fun in a bad mood as she was in a good one.

"Whatcha got there?"

She unclenched her hands from her hair and rubbed her temples, leaving two giant tufts of hair sticking up. "Accounting ledgers. I have spent the last," she peered at her watch, "four hours trying to make sense of the system Steve used. Every time I think I have it figured out, I see something else I missed."

He frowned. "Don't we have an accounting firm that takes care of all that?"

"Trust but verify, Mr. Monroe."

He nodded, still trying not to laugh. "Excellent advice."

He'd lost her attention. She was looking at her ledgers again, and the pencil was back in her teeth. Eating didn't seem urgent anymore, so he searched for something to say. "So, did Hurricane Sara vacate the area and move off to destroy some other island?"

Hope snapped her head up, the pencil dropping to the table. There was a battle going on her face as she tried to decide whether to explode at him or laugh. Given her present mood, he gave it a fifty-fifty shot either way. He raised his eyebrows, trying to tip the scales. First, she narrowed her eyes and tightened her face, then she pursed her lips, trying to keep it in. Finally, her shoulders started to shake, and the war was won.

"Oh my God, Alex, that's the perfect analogy," she raised a hand to her mouth and laughed.

"I thought you might punch me at first, but it was kind of funny."

Her laughter was contagious, and before he knew it, he was laughing right along with her, his hilarity building on hers. As their mirth started to die down, Hope snorted and slapped her hands over her mouth, horrified.

That set him off again, which transferred to her. Tears were coming to his eyes, but he didn't care—it just felt so good. Hope had her head down on the table, her shoulders shaking. Patti stood at the kitchen entrance with her hands on her hips and the strangest expression on her face. She came over to their table.

"What on earth is going on with you two?"

"Alex made my day," Hope said. "He said, and I quote—So, did Hurricane Sara . . . vacate the area and . . . move off to destroy some other island?" Laughing, she could hardly get the words out.

Alex looked at Patti. "It was a lot funnier when I said it."

Patti's brow lowered, and she puffed herself up, standing with her hands on her hips. "Mr. Alex Monroe! I cannot believe you would say such a thing about a lady. And Ms. Sara, she was so nice to us!"

Uh-oh, now I'm in trouble.

But it only made him laugh harder. He tried to rein it in, but the whole situation kept getting funnier.

Hope tried to come to his defense. "Oh, Patti. You can say that. You weren't her target." She broke off for more hysterics, tears streaming down her face. "You have no idea how much of a gentleman he really was. I'm surprised he didn't strangle her."

"Well, I know nothing about that. You two just . . ." Patti waved her hand vaguely at them, turning around and going back into the kitchen.

He and Hope turned to each other and burst out laughing once again. Eventually, both of them had their heads down on the table. She slapped her hand down and he grabbed it in his before they slapped them down together. Her hand was soft and warm in his. But as their laughter finally died down, he let go. Wiping his eyes, Alex looked at Hope. "Oh God, thanks. I needed that. I've had an awful day."

Hope reached out and squeezed his hand, making his heart jump. "Anything I can do to help?"

"No, don't worry about it—the usual hassles. Now I need to patch things up with Patti. Wish me luck." He tightened her hand in return and stood up.

Alex walked into the kitchen, his smile still lingering. Patti, Gerold, and Clark were all standing in the corner whispering. They snapped up their heads as he entered, all wearing matching guilty expressions.

"Now who's up to no good?" Alex asked them with a laugh.

Patti cocked her head. "Who are you, and what did you do with our Alex?"

He held his hands up, surrendering. "All right. We got a little carried away in there. I'm sorry. We both needed to blow off some steam. And regarding Sara, let's just say she's incredibly protective of Hope and wasn't sure . . . I was trustworthy regarding her sister."

He looked down. "Come to think of it, I'm not sure I ever

assured her of that. A root canal would be less painful, I think."
He opened the fridge and grabbed two of the sandwiches Gerold
always had ready before waving as he left by the back door. Probably better to avoid Hope for the moment.

Alex walked along the side of the restaurant.

Avoid Hope . . .

He now knew that was impossible for him and was ready to
admit to himself he was crazy about her. It had been a very long
time since he'd felt like this, if ever. Naturally, these thoughts led
to the physical desire more difficult to deny.

Hope was attracted to him too. That was obvious last night,
despite her mixed signals. She was holding something back—
something made her scared to get closer to him. He snorted.

Like you're any different.

Alex stopped to look at the ocean, standing straight with arms
crossed. The sun had almost set, and a large cloud bank turned
the sky purple. With a sigh, he understood if he got intimate with
Hope, there'd be no putting that genie back in the bottle—everything would change.

The last thing he wanted was to take a risk like that, only to
have her run away from him again. The question was whether he
was finally ready for that step. His head was drawn back to the
restaurant, remembering the feel of her hand in his.

Hell yes, I'm ready. I just wish I knew if she was.

CHAPTER 29

July...

ALEX WAS LEADING a group of what he referred to as wanderers. No matter what he told them, the group *would not* stay together. Today he was like a sheepdog, trying to herd the eight of them around, especially one guy. They were on the second dive and running late. Usually they got back to the resort around noon, but it would be later today. Alex glided down the wall at seventy feet and turned around to check the group.

Sure enough, that one idiot was down at a hundred feet taking a picture of a turtle—the third turtle of the dive. Alex tightened his shoulders as he banged on his tank so hard he was afraid he might break his pointer.

The guy had been a problem since getting on the boat that morning, in Alex's face from the start and complaining about everything. He finally heard the clanging and looked up. Alex glared and pointed at him, signaling to him to move to shallower water with the rest of the group.

Forget a sheepdog—this is like herding cats.

As they continued, the current increased against his face, so he moved the group up to forty feet and headed over the top of the wall onto the reef top. As he moved over the lip, the flow was stronger than on the wall. Nearby purple and yellow soft corals were bent and waving in the steady stream of water.

An increasing current and a group who wouldn't stay together weren't a good combination. A strong current could scatter divers far and wide, as well as rattle the hell out of them. Alex hoped he wouldn't need to chase anyone down. He'd learned long ago to trust his instincts, and he was starting to get a bad feeling about the dive.

He checked behind him and counted only six divers. *Dammit.* Seeing bubbles coming from the wall, two other divers had never come up with the rest of the group. Alex swam hard against the current to the edge, banged his tank yet again and beckoned to them—they acknowledged and came up.

The flow of water continued to increase, and he'd need Tommy to throw out the trailing lines for the divers to use to pull themselves back to the boat. *This is gonna be some work.* The group was nearing the boat now, and he couldn't wait for the dive to be over.

Alex gazed out over the wall and froze, not believing what he saw.

At first, his brain refused to process the image.

He stared in astonishment as *Deep Diver* sank directly in front of his eyes. Still upright and trailing debris above, she looked almost graceful as she disappeared into the deep water behind the edge of the wall.

Oh my God!

Alex snapped his head up. Debris was strewn across the surface of the ocean thirty feet above him.

What about Tommy?

Heart pounding, he spun around to his group. They were scattered about, but he saw at least six of them had blank, unbelieving looks on their faces. He signaled for them to stay put while he went up. *Fat chance of that.*

Alex surfaced and shouted, "Tommy! Tommy!" He whipped left and right, his vocal cords straining.

"I'm over here, Alex."

He whirled around and spotted Tommy floating twenty feet away. Swimming hard, he neared and relaxed a little at Tommy wearing a life jacket and floating with his hands on his chest, calm.

"Are you ok?"

"Yeah. Yeah, I'm fine." Tommy took a deep, quivering breath. "A little shaken up at first, but I'm doin' better now."

"What the hell happened?" Alex clenched Tommy's life jacket, his voice tight.

"I don't know, man. I was sittin' behind the wheel and she started listin' at the stern. There was nothin' I could do. She went down so fast!" He ran a hand over his hair. "I got on the radio and called a Mayday. The Coast Guard got our position on GPS and they're sendin' someone out."

"Thank God." Alex's dive watch said it was just past noon. He evaluated the debris, already scattering in the current. "I have to get my group and bring them up." He patted Tommy's shoulders. "Stay put, Tommy."

"I ain't goin' nowhere, man."

Alex descended again. Six divers clustered in a tight group, clinging to anything they could to keep stationary in the rising current, while the other two were off to the side looking at a coral head. *At least six of them are together, and this is not the time to lecture them about damaging the coral.*

He banged his tank for attention and gave them a thumbs up, signaling they were all ascending to the surface. He had to bang several times before the two strays noticed, and he wasn't surprised to see it was Turtle Guy and his wife.

Very irritated now, Alex swam over and grasped the arms of the two strays and brought them into the main group. There were six pairs of wide, scared eyes behind masks. They knew the boat had sunk and were looking to him for help. The other two pairs were a different story. Turtle Guy looked like he was about to punch Alex, and his wife only seemed confused, looking around vaguely.

They totally missed the boat sinking! Did they even realize I was gone for a while?

After they surfaced, Alex called out, "Everyone! Inflate your BCDs fully. All the way! I want everyone to gather around in a circle and link arms with the person next to you. You too, Tommy."

As the group moved together, Turtle Guy glowered at Alex, his wild, frizzy brown hair spilling around his head. "What is your problem, man? You have been a dick since we stepped on the boat."

Alex glared back and kept a tight rein on his temper. "My problem? Notice. Anything. Missing?"

The guy's wife, Teresa, looked around, a frown forming. "Guys, where's the boat?"

One of the other divers barked out a laugh at Turtle Guy. Annual guests, his name was Ben and his wife was Mary. "You seriously didn't see the boat sink right in front of us? Are you kidding me?"

"*Enough!*" Alex yelled.

That got everyone's attention. In a lower tone, but still authoritative, he continued, "I want everyone in a circle with full BCDs and linked arms. NOW."

He waited for them to circle up, himself in the middle, slowly spinning as he addressed the group. "As most of you saw—" he shot a hard look at Turtle Guy, "—the dive boat experienced some major malfunction and sank, but Tommy is ok. He was able to get off a distress call to the Coast Guard before he had to abandon ship at twelve hundred hours. We will be just fine, but we have to stay in a group." He raised his voice, effortlessly slipping back into his familiar role. "I repeat, we will be fine as long as we stay together!"

Alex descended a few feet and swam to the outside of the circle, surfacing behind the group to ensure their tanks were tight. He tapped Mary on the shoulder. "Add more air to your BCD. You're not fully inflated."

He descended again, swimming hard to the center of the group as the sandy bottom flew by beneath. *This current has to be three knots at least, and it's taking us into deep water—away from the GPS coordinates the Coast Guard has.*

Alex surfaced again in the middle and surveyed the shore, determining how far away they were when Tommy said from behind him, "Can you swim to shore and get help?"

Alex shook his head. "This current would carry you guys too far away, and I'm not leaving you." He turned to Tommy. "Did the Coast Guard give you an ETA?"

"Yeah. They've got a ship nearby. They said 'bout thirty to sixty minutes."

This announcement resulted in loud cheering, and several people broke their arm holds with their neighbors to applaud and high five.

Alex boomed, "*Negative*! You will NOT break formation!"

The guilty ones quickly linked up again and regarded him with wide-eyed, shocked expressions.

Good. If they're scared, they'll listen to me.

Turtle Guy had linked up, so Alex continued rotating when his voice came from behind. "God, knock it off. You're scaring my wife. We're thirty minutes from rescue, so stop acting like a goddamn drill sergeant. Enjoy the sunshine or something, you prick."

Alex whirled around and glowered at him.

Oh, do not *test me today.*

His face must have scared Turtle Guy because he visibly gulped, eyes wide now.

Alex took a deep breath. "Everyone listen up! Here is the situation."

He met every pair of eyes as he turned in a circle, using his most commanding tone of voice. "We are adrift in the ocean and moving away from land in a strong and increasing current. I'd estimate we've already drifted at least one klick from where the boat went down. That means for every minute after Tommy got off the SOS, we're further from rescue."

He paused for a moment. "Listen. My responsibility is to keep you safe, and I take that damn seriously. We can enjoy the sunshine when we get back to the resort." He returned his attention to Turtle Guy. "Until that time occurs, you *will* do what I say. Copy that?"

"Yes, sir," the man said in a small voice.

Mary started to cry, and Ben reached over to stroke her dark hair. Alex swam over to her.

Ok, you played bad cop. Maybe it's time for good cop now.

He softened his voice and placed his hands on her shoulders. "It's ok, Mary. We're doing fine. This is a serious situation, and I'm trying to prevent it from becoming worse."

He let go and addressed the group again, confident and in full command. "We will be rescued. I have no doubt of that. But I can't predict when. If it's in thirty minutes, you can all join him in calling me an asshole when we get back." He tipped his head to Turtle Guy and got some laughs.

Good.

"But if it's longer than that, I plan to do everything in my power to keep us strong and safe until we get picked up. Everyone put your masks down around your necks. You don't need them on right now, but I want to make sure no one loses theirs."

Alex took a breath. His heartbeat was calm and steady now that he had the situation under control. "Ok, who has an SMB?" He received nothing but blank looks in return.

Oh, this just gets better and better . . .

"What's an SMB?" Turtle Guy asked.

Alex closed his eyes and took a deep breath before reopening them. "Surface marker buoy. A piece of equipment every diver should have to increase your visibility if you ever become lost. Anyone?"

Nine shaking heads.

"Ok. I have two." He looked around the group, evaluating them. He pointed to Ben and another man. *Definitely not Turtle Guy.* "I'm going to inflate these and give them to you two to attach to your BCDs. I need to keep my hands free and be able to move while we're waiting."

He unclipped his primary SMB, detached it from his reel, and inflated it with his regulator. As the air entered, the long red cylinder unfurled to its full six-foot length and rose straight into the air. Alex attached it to Ben's BCD. He repeated this with his backup SMB, attaching it to the other diver he'd picked. The two SMBs rose high above the group. "That will make us more visible to the rescue ship."

Alex moved back to the middle of the circle, again evaluating the group. "All right! Since we're going to be together for a while, let's do some introductions and get to know each other better. I'll start."

He raised his voice. "My name is Alex Monroe. I got certified to dive twenty-five years ago, and I served for eighteen years in the United States Navy, a *lot* of it on or under the water. I've been a recreational scuba instructor for eight years. I have logged tens of thousands of dives. I'm highly qualified to get you all through this, ok?" He paused, inspecting everyone.

Their expressions were now calmer, and their eyes not as enlarged. "Also, I love classic rock and my favorite color is blue."

He waited with a smile for the laughter to die down, then said, "Ok, Mary, you go next."

As she started, Alex again swam to the outside and circled the group to make sure everything was ok there. He checked his dive watch, having started the stopwatch as soon as he surfaced with the group.

Forty-five minutes . . .

He checked the horizon. Nothing yet. *At least it's a calm day*.

The ocean around them was deep blue. They were well away from shore now. Rolling two-foot swells lifted the group, then set them down in regular waves.

After everyone introduced themselves, he had them go around again and say where they were from and their jobs. Alex listened closely when it came to Tommy's turn.

"I was born on St. Croix. I've been the boat driver here at Half Moon Bay for seven years. It's been my dream job. I also do most of the repairs on the resort." He took a deep breath as he repeatedly ran his hand over his head. "I don't know what happened to the boat. I take care of her like she was my own, and I loved that boat. I can't believe this is happenin'."

Alex looked sharply at him. "Nobody's blaming you, Tommy. I don't know what happened today, but the one thing I'm sure of is that it's not your fault."

Mary spoke up. "Tommy, I read about dive boats sinking pretty much every month in scuba magazines. It happens sometimes." She gave a shaky laugh. "Just never thought it would happen to me."

She went on to explain she and Ben were from Atlanta, and she owned a cupcake shop. That was interesting enough to keep the conversation going for a long time—lots of flavors to discuss. Alex had no idea green-tea bacon cupcakes were a thing.

After that, the group moved on to their favorite dive destination and what they loved about it. "And it better be St. Croix," Alex said, and couldn't help laughing at his terrible joke.

He looked up and noted the full moon muted against the blue sky.

Well, that explains the strong current.

He checked his watch again. Nearing two hours . . .

Alex was like a restless shark in constant motion—inside the circle, then outside the circle, checking on everyone individually to make sure they were doing ok. Tightening BCD straps to make sure every diver's flotation was secure. He breathed hard from fighting the current as he swam around the perimeter of the circle, keeping everyone talking.

Mary grimaced at her white, pruny hands as she opened and closed them.

"Hold your neighbors' hands and everyone raise them out of the water. Let the sun warm them." Alex stopped to clear his throat. His voice was becoming hoarse. "The water's a lot cooler than your body temperature, and you don't have any exposure protection on your hands like the wetsuit for your body. Again, maintain your grip on your neighbor." He checked his watch again.

It was after 3 p.m.

Where are they?

He tightened the straps on his own BCD, making sure it was secure before going around and tightening each diver's tank band.

Teresa, Turtle Guy's wife, looked worried, her head whipping around and her eyes darting everywhere. "We've been out here forever. What if they don't come? I'm getting cold and really tired." Her breathing was escalating. "My God. What if they can't find us?"

CHAPTER 30

"*P*atti, it's a shame to keep all these staff photos inside the office," Hope said. She'd spent the morning running an idea through her head, and it was time to do something about it. The two women stood in the lobby, ceiling fans cooling the air above them.

"We have the best employees on the island," Hope said. "Let's show them off. There's this huge expanse of white space on the lobby wall—let's hang the photos here. Guests love to know who the staff is, so we should give them the opportunity."

Patti regarded the blank wall. "Hope, that's a fantastic idea. We can start now."

"Let's wait." Hope clasped her upper arm. "I'd like to get updated photos of everyone. That picture of Alex has to go—it will scare small children. He looks like he's ready to rip the arms off a gorilla."

Patti laughed. "Yes, he is rather intense in that photo." She paused, tapping her lips. "New pictures for a new start! I love it. These ones are over four years old."

"Yeah, I noticed they seemed kind of outdated. There are people in those pictures I don't even recognize."

Patti sighed. "We've been coastin' for a while now. It just took you comin' here for us to notice." She squeezed Hope's hand, then headed into the office as the phone rang. Hope continued studying the blank wall.

"Half Moon Bay Resort, Patti speakin'." She paused. "Actually, I am the manager in charge at the moment. What is this regardin', please?"

Hope turned her full attention to the office as Patti listened on the phone, her posture getting stiffer and more alarmed before she finally exclaimed, "Jesus, Mary, and Joseph! Are they all right?"

"What's wrong?"

Patti waved her off. "Yes, I understand. We'll stand by here." She hung up the phone and leaned her hands on the desk, blinking rapidly as her chest heaved.

"Patti, what is going on? Talk to me!"

She stared at Hope, trembling and wide-eyed as shock transformed her face. "That was the Coast Guard. The dive boat sank. Tommy got off an SOS, and the Coast Guard is on the way to their last-known location. But that's all they know. Hope, the boat sank!"

Hope's blood roared in her ears, and gooseflesh broke out all over. They'd had a full boat this morning—eight divers plus Alex and Tommy.

Ten people out there unaccounted for.

She lifted both hands to her mouth, tears coming to her eyes. "Are they ok? Please tell me they're ok."

Patti collapsed into her chair and stared at her, glassy-eyed. "They don't know. All the Coast Guard got was the Mayday call. They asked us to stay by the phone and said they'd call with an update as soon as they have more information."

Hope glanced at the wall clock.

It was just past noon.

"Patti, we have to let everyone here at the resort know." She tapped her fingers on her arm as she started pacing. "Family members with loved ones out there are staying here."

"Yes, I agree. I only wish we had more to tell them."

"Dammit, I can't believe we don't have cordless phones here! That means someone needs to stay by the phone at all times. You and I need to spearhead this, ok? Let's trade off every hour. Why don't you stay in here for the first hour and I'll get the guests rounded up in the restaurant, so I only have to make one announcement for updates? We can make that our central hub."

Hope stopped pacing. "We're fully booked right now with sixteen guests. Eight were on the dive boat this morning. Two went on a zip-line tour, so they won't be back for another couple of hours. Another two were the wives of two divers on the boat."

Hope closed her eyes. "Oh my God, those poor women. I'll see if I can track down the other four guests too. I'll come back in an hour and swap with you."

Martine was at the front desk, watching them with wide eyes. Hope turned back to Patti. "Can you fill Martine in? She can be our runner if we need to get communications back and forth from the office." She started running out of the office before turning back. "Oh, can you call Tommy's wife? She needs to know ASAP."

Hope ran to the kitchen and found Gerold. "We have a major emergency on our hands." She quickly explained the situation. "Can you make something quick and easy for lunch that we can set out buffet-style? Get Clark, Charlotte, and anyone else you need to help." Hope got his agreement and spun around, heading back to the front desk.

She found out which bungalows the two wives were in. Thanks to the manager's reception, she knew every guest by name and face, so she'd easily be able to identify them. Hope hurried to the pool first, where the two middle-aged women sat side by side in loungers under a shade umbrella. Daphne was a willowy redhead, and Sue was a heavy-set blonde with a bubbly personality. *Don't think she's going to be feeling real bubbly in a minute.*

Hope's fingers were ice cold as dread sent tendrils reaching through her abdomen. She took a deep breath as she approached, trying to quell the nausea. "Sue, Daphne, we've had some pretty scary news, and I wanted to let you know right away." Both of them sat up straight, asking what was wrong.

As calmly as possible, Hope explained the situation to them. "The Coast Guard has their position and is en route right now. That's the best news we could have." She grasped their hands as both women started crying. "Please come with me to the restaurant. We're all gathering there."

As soon as she walked into the restaurant with an arm around each woman, Hope dispatched Clark to the office to see if there was any update. He was back quickly, shaking his head. Hope turned and held each of their hands. "I need to find the other guests. We have a system set up to relay messages. I promise we'll keep you updated with any news we receive." She made eye contact with each woman. "It's going to be all right. Please think positive, ok?"

Hope couldn't find the other couples, who must be out sight-seeing, so she went back to the restaurant. Gerold had set up a small buffet, and both women had plates with a few items, though neither was eating. She checked in with them, then excused herself and went back to the office.

"Nothin' yet," Patti said, wringing her hands, her eyes wide with terror. Hope hugged her as both tried not to cry.

"Gerold has a buffet going. Go ahead and get some lunch, Patti."

Now Hope was alone, which was much worse than the frantic activity of the hour before.

Where are they right now? Please let them all be safe. Alex is with them—he'll keep them safe.

But who will keep Alex safe?

She tamped down hard on that last thought.

Hope jumped as the phone rang. Heart pounding, she stared

at it like it was a poisonous snake that might bite her. Finally, she picked it up.

"Hello, this is John Strickland of the *St. Croix Chronicle*. We've been hearing a lot of chatter on our scanner regarding a missing dive boat, and it seems to be yours. Do you have any comment?"

Hope's heart dropped into her stomach.

How am I supposed to handle this?

"We don't have anything to comment on yet. Just that the Coast Guard is on the way to the coordinates given in the Mayday call. That's all we know." Strickland tried a few more times to get more information out of her, but Hope told him she needed to keep the line clear and hung up. *He doesn't need to know we have multiple lines.*

She paced back and forth in front of the two desks, meeting Alex's eyes in his picture on the wall each time she paced in that direction.

Patti and Hope continued to trade off. The phone still hadn't rung, but at least the reporter hadn't called back. At 3 p.m. Patti came back to the office to relieve Hope, who was still pacing and trying not to grow more frantic with every minute with no word.

"Did you get something to eat, Patti?"

"Yes, child. I had a bite of lunch." She touched Hope's shoulder. "But I know you haven't. Please eat somethin'. You need to stay strong."

Hope sagged, leaning both hands on the desk, nauseous and dizzy. "I can't. I'd only throw it back up. I can't eat with them out there." She stood and tried to smooth her hair. It didn't calm her. "Why haven't we heard anything, Patti? It shouldn't take this long to find them—they were just offshore. It's been nearly four hours!"

Patti embraced her. "I don't know. We have to pray and wait. They have Alex with them. There's no one better to be in charge. And it's amazin' how things like this bring people together. People from all over the island are here givin' their support. We must have faith. It's all we have right now."

Hope left the office and made her way to the ladies' room. She locked the door and finally gave in, sobbing with her head on the granite vanity. A running film went through her mind of all the times she had yelled at Alex for no reason.

She closed her eyes, remembering how it had felt when he'd held her face in his hands during her accident and how he'd wiped her tears away on the boat afterward. *It can't possibly take this long. Something happened, and they don't want to call.*

What if they're gone?

Oh God. What if my Alex is gone?

"No!" Opening her eyes, Hope growled the word and stared at her tear-streaked reflection. "He'll come back to you."

Her fierce expression morphed into a stricken one. "He *has* to."

CHAPTER 31

*T*eresa stared at Alex with wide eyes, nearly panting.

Alex swam to her, maintaining eye contact as he placed his hands on her shoulders, speaking softly. "It's ok. You're doing a great job. They *are* coming for us." He backed up and addressed the group again. "We've been in a steady current, and it's a strong one. But we're gonna be fine, ok? The Coast Guard has the coordinates of where the boat sank, and they know the direction and strength of the current we're in right now."

Alex paused, looking around the circle. "Listen. I've been in worse situations than this. You guys don't need to worry until I start to. And I'm not even close yet." He cracked a small smile. "It's just taking a bit longer. You guys are doing great—keep it up."

He turned his piercing gaze back to Teresa. "You have to trust me, ok? We *will* be all right." She stared at him and nodded, drinking in his every word and needing to believe.

Alex made another swim around the outer perimeter of the circle, verifying all the tanks were still tight, then looked down at his hands. They were shredded and bleeding from being submerged for so long and wrestling with everyone's gear.

Once again, Alex checked his watch. It was 3:30.

Now he had them talking about the best and worst movie of all time. Two guys were having a spirited discussion about it.

"You're crazy. *Return of the King* was so much better. *The Two Towers* dragged, man."

Mary spoke up. "What about *Forrest Gump*?" Lots of appreciative murmurs resulted from this suggestion.

They're hanging in there. Just keep it up . . .

Alex said, "You're all wrong. The best movie ever made was clearly *Rambo*." He grinned, submerging to move to the outside of the circle again.

They had been floating in the water for nearly four hours. Alex had been watching a smudge on the horizon for the past fifteen minutes. As it got closer, the smudge became a large ship —definitely the Coast Guard vessel at last. He turned back to the group, making sure the SMBs had air. Alex had refilled them an hour ago, so they were full. He swam into the middle of the circle again.

"Ok, guys. I hate to interrupt you." Alex cleared his raw throat and turned to Ben, who was bald on top and sunburned now. "But seriously. *Notting Hill?* I might need to revoke your man card." He smiled as everyone laughed.

"Ok, listen up!" Alex continued. "I've been watching something on the horizon for a while, and I'm confident it's our rescue ship." Everyone cheered, and he had to smile when no one dropped hands. "Don't change anything you're doing. You guys are doing a great job."

He rotated in a circle, making eye contact with everyone, even Turtle Guy. "Seriously. I couldn't ask for a better group. Thank you."

Another fifteen minutes passed before the vessel approached, finally discharging a Zodiac to pick them up. As the rubber craft approached the group, a crewman called out, "Good afternoon, guys. Heard you called an Uber?"

Alex closed his eyes and heaved a big breath.

There were two crewmen in the Zodiac, so they had to make two trips to rescue the entire group. Tommy and Alex were in the second group. He made sure Tommy was safely climbing the ladder into the Zodiac before quickly swimming to the opposite side and heaving himself aboard in one single motion, smiling at the familiar action.

He and Tommy exchanged a relieved nod as Alex removed his fins. Tommy drifted his gaze down and widened his eyes. Alex also looked, knowing Tommy was staring at his water-logged, bleeding hands. He quickly hooked his thumbs around his BCD straps and looked to the horizon.

As the Zodiac made its way back to the Coast Guard vessel, Alex finally relaxed.

ALEX LOOKED AROUND THE ROOM, trying to stave off exhaustion. The dive group sat around a table in the ship's commissary. All were wearing Coast Guard T-shirts and scrub-type bottoms that had been handed out in the sick bay. Rescue and warm food had put everyone in a good mood, and they were underway back to the resort.

Alex sat off by himself and gazed down at his new flip-flops and Coast Guard shirt. The adrenaline was long gone, and now he was drained. He was on his fifth bottle of water but had no appetite for food. Taking another swallow, he tried to soothe his scratchy, sore throat. He inspected his bare hands and snorted softly. The medic in the sick bay had wanted to bandage them, but Alex had simply said, "I don't think so," and given him his best command stare.

The guy had held both arms up. "Ok, man. They aren't deep or anything, so you should be ok as long as they don't start bleeding again. Don't use your hands too much, or they'll open up again." He cleaned the wounds up and trimmed back the abraded flesh, then Alex went on his way. The medic looked happy to see him go.

An older man with captain's bars and salt-and-pepper hair entered the commissary and got their attention. "Hello folks, I'm Captain Barnes. I'd like to apologize for taking longer than we thought to get to you. That was quite a current you were in. We picked you up over ten miles out from your last-known location. Which of you is the dive leader, please?"

Alex straightened but remained seated. "I am, sir. Alex Monroe."

The captain approached and held out his hand. Alex immediately stood, and they shook hands. He ignored the pain in his hand.

"Son, I'd like to thank you for helping make this rescue a whole lot easier than it could have been."

"Thank you, sir."

Alex sat again as Barnes returned to the front of the room, moving his gaze around the group. "Finding ten people adrift in a three to four knot current in the middle of the ocean is no minor feat. Usually, people are strung out to hell and gone by the time we get there. The fact that you stayed together in a tight bunch may have made a world of difference today."

He paused, glancing at Alex before turning his attention back to the group. "Four hours is a long time to be in the water in an unknown situation. I'm sorry for that. But without the actions of Mr. Monroe, you might have been out there far longer."

"We have some bunks prepared for you to rest. It's going to be a while before we get you back to your resort, so you might as well enjoy some sleep." Barnes looked over at a man by the door, who nodded. "I'll let you all know over the PA when we are approaching your resort. Meanwhile, Private Samuel here will show you to your bunks." Barnes spun around and departed.

Several divers sent Alex haunted looks as they passed by, along with murmured thank yous. Tommy was last in line. "You comin' with us?"

"No, I'm fine. I think I'll go up on deck. Get some sleep, Tommy—you did great today."

∿

ALEX STOOD at the starboard railing, watching the waves pass. He stretched, his hip stiffening up. *That would be just perfect.* Relaxing down on the rail again, Alex checked his dive watch. Six o'clock . . .

Let this day be over.

Now that the group was safe, his thoughts returned to Hope. While in the water waiting for rescue, he'd found himself thinking about her and firmly resisted, keeping his mind and attention on the matter at hand. He'd always had a laser focus while on mission and was pleased to find that hadn't left him.

But now, he just wanted to get home and see her. To hold her in his arms.

The bulkhead door opened behind him, but he ignored it. Someone came up and leaned on the rail next to him. He turned to see it was Captain Barnes. Alex had been around many petty, awful commanding officers in his time. This guy wasn't one of those.

"Mr. Monroe, I've been looking for you. One of your divers told me you were Navy. How does it feel to be wearing a Coast Guard shirt?"

Alex gave a small smile, still staring out at the ocean. "Desperate times, sir."

Barnes laughed at that, then got serious. "I meant what I said in there. I'm sure those people have no idea how much you did out there to keep them safe."

Alex shrugged, uncomfortable with the praise. "They did as instructed. That's all that matters."

"They told me you were a Navy diver?"

Alex nodded but didn't reply.

"Sounds like you're a man who recognizes the value of a good *team*."

Alex paused. "You could say that, sir."

"Just a Navy diver, huh?"

Alex stared at him, eyes hard. "Is there another question you're trying to ask, sir?"

Barnes laughed. "No, I think you answered it. You don't like the limelight much, do you, son?"

Alex continued to look straight at him. "No, sir. I don't."

Barnes held up his hands. "All right, all right. I'll leave you with your thoughts. But those people were lucky you were out there today."

"Thank you, sir."

With that, Barnes was gone, the door softly clicking behind him.

Hope's face came unbidden to his mind. He only wanted to get home and see her, finally free to imagine what it would feel like to hold her in his arms. To stroke a finger over her tattoo—he was fascinated with the idea of touching it.

He thought about what Barnes had said. No one had ever accused Alex of a lack of courage, but he'd been avoiding his pain for too long. He'd tried to come to grips with his past for years now—by himself.

It hadn't worked.

Maybe he needed to be part of a team. Alex smiled at the irony of it, then envisioned a team of two. He checked his watch again and sighed, his body swaying automatically to the motion of the ship with effortless movement that came with long experience.

CHAPTER 32

*H*ope closed her eyes and took a deep, shuddering breath, getting herself back together again. Finally she straightened, facing the ladies room mirror again. "Alex will come back to you. This isn't the end. Believe, Hope. You wanted a sign, didn't you?"

She turned and marched back to the restaurant.

Word had gotten around, and the restaurant was filling with people. The guests who had been out earlier were now back, and all were in attendance, anxiously waiting. Tommy's wife Priscilla and their two children were at a table. They had an eight-year-old girl and a five-year-old boy. Both sat quietly at the table, looking around with wide eyes. Priscilla flipped her long black braids over her shoulder as she placed two plates down in front of the kids.

Daphne and Sue were still in the same chairs, wrecked and not speaking. Everyone looked at Hope expectantly when she entered. She quickly shook her head and reported no news.

At 4 p.m., she once again relieved Patti. Both of them were openly crying now, though Patti was doing a better job of holding it together at the moment than Hope was, or at least pretending to. After Patti left the office, Hope resumed pacing back and

forth, a hand on either cheek as she tried to physically hold
herself together, breathing in gasps.

*Why have I kept away from him? How has this served me? I can't
believe I've been so blind!*

At 4:30, the phone rang. Hope stared at it, her pulse
pounding.

*I can't. I just can't answer this. What if it's bad news? What if they're
all gone?*

She picked up the phone. It was the Coast Guard.

"May I speak to the person in charge please, ma'am?"

"That would be me, Hope Collins. I'm the owner. What is
going on?"

"Ma'am, we picked up the survivors at approximately 4 p.m.
local time. We confirm ten survivors. How does that tally with
your records?"

Hope collapsed into the chair. "We sent ten out this morning.
That means all are accounted for. Thank you." She shook all over.

"You're welcome, ma'am. Our final head count is a group of
eight guest divers, plus one boat captain and one dive leader.
Sounds like your dive leader kept the group together, which definitely helped."

"Are they all safe? Is anyone injured?"

"Negative, ma'am. All have been checked out by medical and
appeared to be healthy—only some sunburns, and they were
pretty thirsty. The vessel is headed your way now. ETA is approximately . . . 7 p.m."

Hope hung up the phone and sat back in her chair, covering
her face with her hands as relief coursed through her and tears
slid down her cheeks. But she still had work to do, so she pulled
herself together. She automatically turned her eyes to Alex's in his
wall picture, and new strength filled her.

She rose, marching out of the office.

Hope ran to the restaurant to give everyone the good news,
taking a big breath before entering. As soon as they saw her,

conversation halted. She was shocked at how full the restaurant was. It seemed every employee of the resort, plus many family members, were there. No one had left. She recognized staff from other nearby resorts as well. Patti stood up as soon as she entered, her face slack with fear.

Hope's face split into an enormous, relieved smile as she knelt in front of Daphne and Sue and grasped a hand. Radiant hope lit up their faces.

"The Coast Guard picked them up. The entire group. Everyone is safe and they're all on their way back here."

Everyone jumped up and cheered at this news. When the cacophony died down somewhat, she said, "They should be here by 7 p.m. They're all on the Coast Guard vessel now." Hope stood straight, filled with light and shining like a searchlight. Patti came up to her and they embraced. Hope stroked her head as she cried.

AFTER HOPE'S ANNOUNCEMENT, the crowd dispersed from the restaurant to regroup, but they were back in force at the end of the pier by 6:30. Hope pulled Patti aside, and they agreed if the reporter called back to give him a full update.

"We've got enough to deal with, though. Hopefully he'll get the info off the scanner," Hope said.

She smiled as Alex's friend Robert approached, a divemaster who filled in for him when needed. "Thanks for coming. Your support means a lot."

He was a local thirtysomething, thin with a shaved head and a killer smile, not that it was in evidence tonight. "Hey, do you have another dive boat lined up?"

Hope gave a shaky laugh. "No. I'll find one tomorrow."

"I might be able to help with that." She turned sharply to him. "The dive community's pretty tight here, you know. A friend called me today. He has a boat that's not bein' used right now. We can drive it up here tomorrow and take your group if you want. We can fill in until Alex and Tommy are ready to get back to work."

Tears sprang to Hope's eyes as she hugged him. "Thank you so much. You don't know how much that means to me. I'm sure Alex and Tommy will appreciate it too."

THE COAST GUARD vessel turned on all its exterior lights as it approached, lighting up the night in a starburst of promise. The assembled crowd grew silent, full of nervous anticipation as it launched the Zodiac. The first load of people came toward the pier, heads on swivels as they surveyed the crowd and tried to find individuals. A tide of murmuring rippled around the crowd as a swell of emotion overcame everyone.

I'm so grateful they're all safe. I care about all these people. It's not only one head I'm looking for.

But where is he?

The first boatload of survivors ascended the ladder as the Zodiac sped back to the main vessel. They weaved through the crowd, stars of the hour. Tear-streaked faces and embraces were all around Hope as she waited. More tears prickled her eyes as Sue and Daphne reunited with their husbands. Happiness filled Hope, as well as pride. She had managed the emergency with tact and a large amount of elbow grease.

When the second boatload departed the ship, she spotted Alex immediately and slumped, eyes brimming and relief over-flowing. She never took her eyes off his head as the boat bobbed and floated over the water, ever closer. It finally pulled alongside the ladder, and she lost sight of him. Hope's heart pounded as guest after guest climbed onto the dock to happy cheering. Her mouth ran dry as she waited. Ben and Mary came aboard and embraced Patti.

Tears sprang from her eyes as Tommy climbed up and fell into

Priscilla's arms. They were both crying openly, as were most others. The two children wrapped their arms around both. Hope watched the reunion with a great swelling of happy emotion and greater anticipation.

Then her gaze drifted to the ladder, tunneling down to a laser beam. Alex climbed onto the deck, the last out of the small boat, looking around him.

Hope breathed in gasps, both hands over her mouth.

Standing tall, he whipped his head left and right, eyes searching. There was a piercing intensity about him she'd never seen before. Finally, he spotted her off to the side.

She ran toward him. They locked eyes.

Ignoring everyone else, Alex marched toward her. As if by instinct, people parted around him. As she flew into his arms, he crushed her to him.

They held each other, neither saying anything, just existing together at last. Hope buried her head in his chest, breathing in the scent and presence of him. Finally appreciating he was *here,* in her arms. Right now. She broke down and sobbed with relief.

He bent down and whispered in her ear, "It's ok. Everyone is fine. You don't need to cry."

"Oh, Alex. Thank God. You're here. You're finally here."

Hope basked in his warm, solid embrace, crying into his chest as he swayed a bit on his feet. Eventually, she opened her eyes. The crowd had thinned a bit. She looked around, making eye contact with Patti. Hope beckoned to her, and she hurried over, starting to cry. Alex unwrapped one arm from Hope and embraced Patti too, whose tears turned to sobs. Seeing Patti made Hope's tears start anew.

"Jeez, a guy could get a swelled head hanging around with you two," Alex said, his voice hoarse and cracking as the three embraced in the warm, tropical night.

CHAPTER 33

*T*he next morning, Hope studied the buffet, taking a to-go container from the stack and filling it with heaping servings of scrambled eggs, hash browns, and bacon, plus six pieces of toast. She added three pats of butter on top.

Hope lit up when she saw the pastry bar. On impulse, she grabbed another container and filled it to the brim with assorted pastries, donuts, and croissants. *There, that should do.* A large black coffee completed the ensemble, and she stacked everything carefully before making her way down the pier. She had a feeling her mission this morning was going to be difficult, and food always helped.

Alex kept strong emotions close, especially anything relating to weakness, unless he deflected them with humor. Last night, when she had finally stood with him, their arms around each other, Hope felt his bone-deep weariness as he swayed on his feet.

As much as she wanted to bask in their reunion—and more— she had bit down on her own emotion and sent him up to his apartment to rest, going back to her own house. As tiring as her day had been, he was far more exhausted.

Hope was sure he hadn't been down for breakfast yet. It was

only 7 a.m. and the area was silent as she padded up the stairs to Alex's apartment. She stuck the coffee in the crook of her elbow and was getting ready to knock when she gazed through the windowpane embedded in the door. Alex stood over a small kitchen table, wearing nothing but boxers.

Hope gasped as she looked more closely.

He faced the door, looking down and standing over a steaming cup of coffee as he leaned on the table with both arms. The muscles of his arms flexed from the strain, each sharply defined with tension. She narrowed her eyes at his white fingers, tented up as if he didn't want to put full weight on his hands.

His face was a vivid portrait of pain and weariness, and he took deep, heaving breaths with his eyes closed.

Oh, Alex.

She quickly stood aside. Alex was a man who allowed no one to see his deepest self. *Especially* what she just saw. She contemplated coming back later or leaving the food on his doorstep. *Oh, stop being such a coward!* Before she could second-guess herself anymore, she knocked on his door.

"Hang on. Give me a minute," came the hoarse reply.

Hope moved back to the window panel, but the room was now empty. Then Alex appeared, dressed in a staff T-shirt and board shorts and walking fully upright, though more slowly than usual. Surprise registered as he recognized her and opened the door, but he quickly covered it, his mask firmly in place.

"I brought you breakfast." She held up the containers and smiled.

"Really? Thanks. I was getting ready to see who was on the dive board for this morning."

"Uh, can I come in? Or do you just want me to hand you this and bolt?"

He laughed and stepped aside. "Please, enter."

Hope swept into the apartment. "Nope, Alex. You're taking today off. Robert came by yesterday and found us an extra boat, complete with a captain, until we can get a new one. I've got it all covered."

She put the containers down on the table, which stood between an open-concept living room and kitchen. The apartment was nearly bare—nothing on the walls and no personal pictures or decor. Only an adjustable weight set in one corner. It was sterile, without life and so different from the Alex she knew. She peeked to the side at his bedroom with a queen-sized bed.

He has lived here for five years?

Alex came over to the table, still standing as he opened the containers. "You joining me? I can't eat all this."

"No. I just thought you might be hungry after yesterday."

His eyes softened. "Thanks, but I'm fine. I don't need today off."

Her heart beat faster in her ears.

Here we go.

Hope started gently. "You went through one hell of an ordeal yesterday. I can hear how hoarse your voice is. You probably talked for hours. You've earned a break—take today off."

"I slept great last night, and I feel pretty recovered." He smiled softly. "I'm fine. You worry too much."

Ok. Gentle didn't work—let's try strength.

Which was just as well. Her anger increased, and she narrowed her eyes at him, her hands clenched. "Don't be a stubborn ass. It won't kill you to rest a little. I've already made arrangements to cover today. It's a done deal—you're off today."

She drew herself up to her full height, which wasn't as intimidating as she wished, considering Alex was more than six inches taller. "Alex, as your employer, I forbid you from working today."

"No. I'm working." Now he wore a satisfied smirk, arms crossed.

"Goddammit, do I have to handcuff you to the bed?"

The smirk turned into a wide grin. "Oh, excellent suggestion!"

This is not the day for that.

She met his eyes, her chest tight now. "You are *not* ok." Hope pressed her lips into a thin line and threw her hands in the air. "Why is that so hard to admit? You *never* take a day off. What is so horrible about relaxing a little? God! I'm not asking you to knit me a scarf, just to stay home. Would you stop being such a . . . a . . . *man*?" It was the worst insult she could come up with on short notice.

He laughed. "What would you suggest, a golden retriever?"

Hope sagged and looked at her hands, gritting her teeth as she tried not to tear up. "Look, I saw you. Just now, before I knocked on your door." She met his eyes as he tensed. "I didn't mean to pry, but you were right there in front of me. I saw your exhaustion." She was shaking. "You looked like you could barely stand up."

The tension in Alex's shoulders eased a bit, and he walked stiffly over, brushing the hair from her brow. "I'm standing just fine now. Ok, I'll admit I'm not twenty-five anymore, but I'm perfectly able to lead two dives. Send Robert home."

It rose like a tsunami inside her, the tears and rage welling and building on the stress of yesterday.

There was no denying it this time.

The pressure and the fury continued building within her. She ground her teeth, and her shoulders started shaking.

Finally, she lost control.

Hope pounded his chest with both fists, screaming, "Damn you! Do you have any idea what I went through yesterday? Do you know how scared I was? For hours, I didn't know if you guys were alive or dead. HOURS, Alex! It was awful. Guess how I spent yesterday afternoon? I had to organize a command center for an emergency, complete with a whole meal for the entire resort on no notice. I had to answer to a goddamn reporter about something I had no information about.

"Oh, and best of all? I had to comfort two wives who were afraid they were widows!" Hope glared at him, eyes blazing. "I sat next to that phone in the office, staring at it. I didn't eat. I didn't drink. Why? Because I knew none of you could either. I paced back and forth in that damn room for HOURS!"

The anger fled, and the tears built again. She stared at the floor, chest heaving.

No! No tears, dammit.

Hope took a deep breath to gather herself, then looked back up at him and continued in a much softer voice, anguished. "I didn't know if *you* were alive or dead. Do you have any idea how that felt? I stared at that goddamn phone, willing it to ring, yet terrified it would."

She deflated, mirroring his position on the table with her hands resting on it.

Hope said in a soft, exhausted voice, "Please, just do this for me. Take one day and rest. That's all I ask. I *need to know* you're ok."

Tears slid down her cheeks—she couldn't control them.

Alex had stood silent throughout her rage, eyes wide and shattered. Now he jolted, hurrying over to Hope and wrapping her in his arms. At his touch, she lost control all over again, averted grief this time instead of anger. She clutched him to her, sobbing out her fear and misery. He held back tightly, stroking her head as he slowly shifted from foot to foot, almost slow dancing.

Her throat was sore with the force of it as she completely let go, holding back as tightly as he held her.

Eventually, her sobs slowly lessened, turning to occasional hiccups. She finally quieted, and Alex took her arms and pressed her back so they could see eye to eye. "I'm so sorry. I shouldn't have been teasing you. I never thought about what you might be going through." His voice cracked. "I never in a million years meant to hurt you. Never."

Hope sniffed and pressed against him again. "This is the third time I've cried my eyes out in your arms, you know. You'd probably never believe this, but I've made it a life goal never to let a man see me cry." She laughed weakly. "I guess I have changed."

His face was pressed tightly against her head. "The last thing I want is to see you cry. I'm so sorry." He took a deep breath. "God, I'm an asshole."

She had to laugh at that, still pressed against him. "Maybe we both are. God knows I've jumped down your throat over pretty stupid stuff. I feel like you see me at my worst. Things haven't exactly been tranquil since I arrived." She was able to smile now, feeling better having gotten it all out and at home in his arms. "I'm surprised you haven't run screaming from here and found somewhere else to work."

Alex pulled back and wiped the tears off her cheeks, smiling at her. "Eh, it's not so bad. I've been through rougher things. Not many, but a few have been worse."

"You jerk. I'm thinking about heading to the humane society tomorrow to look at golden retrievers." She hugged him, feeling a brief pressure on the top of her head. *Did he just kiss my head?*

His chest expanded as he sighed. "Ok, I'll stay home today, but only because *you* asked. Besides, I've got some scuba equipment I can work on instead."

Her anger flared again. Hope pulled away from him and jabbed her finger into his chest. "Oh, no you don't. Rest, I said. I mean it, Alex. Don't you mess with me."

He held up his hands, smiling now. "Ok, Boss Lady. I'm a man who knows how to follow a direct order."

She sniffed again. "I need to blow my nose. Where's some tissue?"

He shrugged. "I don't have any, but there are paper towels there in the kitchen."

"Paper towels, great." She walked toward the kitchen, shooting him a dirty look.

"Hey, I'm not a tissue kind of guy."

She ripped off a sheet and blew into it. Reading him correctly, she opened the cabinet under the sink to throw it in the trash and washed her hands. "That's better. I'm glad it's settled."

Hope took another deep breath and pointed at him. "Now, sit down, shut up, and eat your breakfast."

She widened her eyes as Alex came to attention, saluted her crisply, and replied, "Yes, ma'am."

Well, he's done that a time or two.

Then he moved to the table, sitting down and inspecting his food.

"I'll come and check on you later." Smiling, she ran a hand across his shoulder as she walked toward the door.

"Hey, Hope?"

She turned with a raised eyebrow.

"If I change my mind and call you, will you come back with the handcuffs?"

"Oh, behave." She laughed as she went out the door.

Hope's smile faded as she descended the stairs to see four of the divers from Alex's group yesterday standing under the palapa, looking lost. "Good morning, guys. How are you feeling today?"

Ben turned to her, his bald head red and sunburnt. "We were hoping to find Alex."

She relaxed. "He's taking today off. If you want to dive, we have arrangements all made and a new boat will leave at 9 a.m. as usual but with a different divemaster."

Mary laughed. "I'm not sure I ever want to dive again without Alex."

I know the feeling.

"We didn't get a chance to thank him yesterday," Ben said. "After we got picked up by the Coast Guard, we never really saw him again. And things were so crazy here on the dock when we got back, we didn't see him then either."

"He might have needed some time to decompress a little." Hope paused. "I don't know what you guys went through out there, but I know Alex pretty well. And I doubt he just laid on his back staring at the sun all day. I'm sure he'll be around sometime soon, and you'll be able to talk with him." She regarded the group. "Are you guys doing all right?"

"We're still trying to process it, I think," Mary said. "It was such an unbelievable experience. Every diver's worst nightmare. You're right about Alex, though. When we first surfaced, he was terrifying. He was very blunt about our situation and that we had to listen to everything he said. I started crying. I don't think any of us understood how much trouble we were in—only Alex."

She shifted from one leg to the other. "But after he had our full attention, he got us to start talking about ourselves. I know it was to distract us and keep us calm, but it worked. He even started cracking bad jokes."

She paused, staring at the ocean. "I'd never want to repeat that experience, but I knew we were going to be ok. I don't know what I'm trying to say, just that I felt safe the whole time."

Hope smiled. "Actually, that sounds just like Alex."

CHAPTER 34

*L*ater that afternoon, Hope walked up to the pool bar, tired but satisfied. She'd changed into her favorite sundress and strappy sandals, wanting to enjoy herself after a very long day. "Clark, can I get a bucket of beers?"

"Comin' right up."

He had a calendar near his blender with a weekly countdown on it. "This competition means a lot to you, doesn't it?"

"Oh yes. If you're gonna do something, do it right." Clark reached down and produced a galvanized steel bucket. "This job has been really good for me. A few years ago, I fell in with a bad crowd. Broke into some cars and got caught. Aunt Patti got me the position here and vouched for my good behavior, and they dropped the charges. I don't want to let her down." He put six Leatherbacks in the bucket, filling it to the brim with ice. "Thank you for your support, too. Steve never seemed to get behind me, so I appreciate your encouragement."

Hope squeezed his arm. "Clark, if anyone can win this competition, you can. Whatever you need, consider it done."

"You want to try my latest inspiration? I'm still workin' on it, so not sure it's quite there yet."

"Bring it on."

Clark busied himself mixing her cocktail as she looked around. Guests relaxed in the pool and on the beach, everyone happy. It was as if yesterday had never happened. Clark set the glass next to her, and she lifted it to her lips absentmindedly, continuing to check people's moods.

Hope took a big drink and nearly gagged, the mixture of sourness and bitterness overwhelming.

"Well? What do you think? I'm thinkin' it needs somethin'." Clark watched her with anticipation.

"Keep working, Clark. You'll get there," she wheezed as she stood and picked up the bucket. "I think you're right. It still needs a little something." She waited until she was out of sight before hacking.

The sky broadcast streaks of pink and lavender as she knocked on Alex's door. As Hope looked through the window in his front door, he rose from his couch and walked stiffly toward the door, slightly favoring his right leg. Alex brightened when he noticed it was her, making her stomach flutter.

"Room service." Hope held up the bucket with a smile, determined to make up for the morning.

"Oh, you are exactly what the doctor ordered. Let's go out on the deck."

They sat at his table outside. Alex used the bottle opener on the bucket to open two beers, which they clinked together.

"So, how are you feeling now?"

"Better than this morning." He held a hand up. "And I've been a good boy and watched baseball on TV today. What have you been up to?"

Hope took a big drink, then sighed and closed her eyes. "Damage control. Everyone in the group is doing fine, and they're all worshipping you, by the way. There was a small article in the paper about it, but it was pretty sparse. I was afraid the reporter was going to make some big exposé out of it, but he wrote a good, factual article."

She waved her hand. "Back to the guests. I'm giving all eight of them full refunds for their stay and a fifty-percent credit for their next booking. I talked to them today." She turned to him. "You managed that whole ordeal like a real pro. Sounds like you scared the hell out of them to start, then pulled them together to get through it. I really owe you. Thank you."

"They did great out there." Alex smiled slightly, gazing at the ocean with a faraway look before turning to her. "I'm really sorry this happened."

Hope's mouth dropped open. "What are you apologizing for? If you hadn't been there, I don't even want to think about what might have happened. Yet again, Alex saves the day. The last thing you need to do is apologize."

He shifted in his chair, grimacing. "It comes with the territory. I did what I had to."

"Oh, what happened was just an average day at the office, huh?"

He brushed a hand over his chin, scraping the stubble. "No, I have to admit that was a first."

"What happened to the boat, Alex?"

"I don't know. We've had some issues, but nothing major. The bilge pump, maybe? I was leading the dive and got a bad feeling and brought the group back. Hope, I watched that boat sink right in front of my eyes."

"I'm so glad no one was injured. That could have been such a disaster." Alex rested his hands on the table, and looking down, she grew concerned. Grasping his hand, she turned it palm up, inspecting it. There were red marks and flaps of exposed skin that looked surgically cut. "You hurt your hands. I didn't even know."

"It's nothing. They got soft being in the water, and I got a couple of cuts."

She shook her head. "Your average days could stand to be a little less exciting, you know."

He laughed softly, and she let go of his hand. Then, like the day before, she remembered the feel of it on her cheek and the look in his eyes as they nearly kissed.

Hope leaned forward in the chair, her heart speeding up as she spoke softly. "And what about my accident? Was that just an average day too?"

"Oh no. That was different. And don't ever do it again."

"Don't worry, that didn't make my shortlist of experiences to repeat." She tilted her head. "I wasn't sure it even affected you. You seemed so calm the whole time."

Alex leaned forward and laughed. "Oh my God! I was anything but calm. You scared me half to death."

"I think you should consider a new career. You've got a serious poker face." She felt so different from the last time she was here —happy, calm, and at home with him.

His eyes were warm. "I like my current career just fine. It's gotten a whole lot more interesting in the past few months."

Hope thought of several responses to that, but didn't feel like pointing out that a lot of those experiences had been negative.

If he's not going to dwell on it, why should I?

Instead, she let her smile fall into a contented sigh. "It hasn't been boring."

Hope got up to stand at the railing. The sky radiated shades of red and orange. She inhaled the salty air, listening to the sounds of the water lapping against the wooden pilings below. Because the apartment was elevated and out over the water, it commanded a full view available nowhere else in the resort. The flat light made the surface of the ocean appear like shimmering mercury, more like liquid metal than water.

"Oh, Alex. This is beautiful." Hope took it in, holding the rail with both hands, the wood warm under her hands.

He replied, "Yes, it is."

Then his chair scraped the deck as he rose to stand behind her. Hope was warm, relaxed, and so grateful for his presence. She leaned back against him, just enjoying his comforting solidness as he rested his hands on her shoulders. His thumb stroked her tattoo as they stood together, neither speaking as they watched the vivid colors above.

Eventually Hope closed her eyes, enjoying the moment and for once not thinking about anything else. Alex's chest rose as he inhaled deeply. A wind gust from the side had lifted her hair off her neck and she tilted her head sideways, relishing the air blowing across her skin and cooling it. The breeze was sensuous, like an invisible caress, and she parted her lips slightly.

Then the cool air above her skin became warm.

Hope's eyes flew open as Alex's mouth hovered just above her shoulder, his soft exhalation warming her skin. She froze, hardly daring to breathe but eager for whatever might happen.

With one hand, he pulled her hair away from the nape of her neck as he lifted the strap of her sundress aside with the other and kissed the skin revealed. She closed her eyes again with a shaky inhale.

Alex continued, slowly tracing his way along the top of her shoulder, kissing to the margin of her neck, then up the side of it. She trembled, waves rising from head to feet and back up again.

He hadn't shaved that morning, and the roughness of his chin contrasted with his soft mouth. Hope tilted her head further sideways to give him better access, heart racing now and breath deepening. He continued up to her ear, opening his mouth and flicking his tongue before biting the lobe gently as she moaned.

She quickly turned around and found his lips as their arms went around each other. His mouth was warm and soft, the pressure light. They melted together like they'd done this a thousand times. Opening slightly, he ran his tongue over her teeth. He tasted of the beer they had been drinking. She was sure she did, too.

Hope responded with her tongue, and it was as if this were some unacknowledged signal between them. He cupped the back of her head and pulled her toward him, groaning as she gasped against his mouth.

This was no gentle kiss now.

They crushed their mouths together, frantic for each other. His stubble scraped against her skin, and she pressed even harder against his mouth, their teeth clashing. At last, Hope lifted his shirt and rubbed her hands up the hard muscles of his back and across those incredible shoulders. He responded with a sharp inhale. Their tongues entwined further. She pressed her body against the front of him, feeling how aroused he was. Alex pushed his hips back against her, strong enough to move her backward as he stepped forward.

Then his breath exploded in a strangled moan as he nearly collapsed onto the rail, grabbing it with both hands to keep from falling.

"Alex!"

"Oh God. I didn't expect that. I'm so sorry. It's a pulled muscle in my hip," he said between deep breaths. Leaning over, his eyes were closed and his knuckles were white on the rail.

That's a pulled muscle?

"What can I do to help?"

Alex shook his head, but after several more breaths, he straightened and faced her. "I'll be fine. I'm just a forty-year-old man who feels a whole lot older today."

He brushed his lips against hers and placed his fingers under her chin to keep her head tilted up. With his other index finger, Alex traced a line from the hollow of her neck down the valley of her breasts, making her breath catch again. "You have no idea how much I want you right now." He leaned his forehead against hers. "But I'd do a really awful job of it. And I told you before—you deserve better."

As he put his arms around her, Hope rested her head against his chest. "What's wrong? What aren't you telling me?"

Alex stroked her back, whispering, "Shhhh. Everything's going to be fine. You don't need to worry about me."

I wish I could believe you, you stubborn man. But I can't exactly get mad at you for holding something back, can I?

He accepted her help by putting his right arm over her shoulders. That alone told her how much pain he was in. They made their way back into the apartment and toward his bedroom. They hobbled to his bed, and he worked his way onto it, finally lying on his back with an arm over his eyes, breathing heavily with beads of sweat peppering his forehead.

"You sure know how to show a girl a good time."

Alex smiled but didn't remove the arm from his eyes. "I'm really sorry. I didn't mean for that—" he indicated the deck, "to happen. Well, not today anyway."

He removed his arm to look at her. "It was your hair that did me in, you know. You were so beautiful against the sunset like that. I had to get up and touch you. And I was doing fine with only that until that gust of wind blew your hair and showed the skin on your neck."

He shook his head. "I've been thinking about this for a long time now, and this is *not* how I thought it would go."

She gave him a crooked grin. "Why do we always seem to be apologizing to each other?"

Alex tucked a lock of hair behind her ear. "If I've seen you at your worst, today has definitely turned the tables."

"Anything I can get you?"

"I'd like an entire night with you, with no sleep whatsoever. But I'd settle for another kiss."

Hope obliged, tenderly this time, then rose. "If you need anything at all, you call me." She smiled. "I can be here in seconds, Mr. Monroe."

He reached out and pulled her down to him. Hope wanted

much more but knew the moment had passed. When the kiss ended, he said, "You can have me on my back anytime, Ms. Collins. But next time, I'll do my best to get you on yours."

"I can't wait."

IT WAS dark when Hope approached the stairs leading to her back porch. As she climbed, her heart almost jumped out of her chest at the sound of scraping on the porch, which revealed itself to be Cruz standing at the other end with his tail wagging.

"Were you protecting me, Cruz? You look happy to see me." As she reached midway across the porch, he backed up, looking one last time at her before descending the steps on that side and disappearing.

Hope undressed and climbed into bed. Picking up a book, she read for a few minutes before her text tone sounded—it was from Alex. She rushed to pick up the phone, concerned there was something wrong.

The text was only four words: Sleep tight, Boss Lady.

Smiling, she texted back, You too.

CHAPTER 35

The wooden boards were still wet under Alex's bare feet as he stood on the pier. A passing summer storm had drenched the resort an hour ago, but the sky was now blue with no hint of nature's ferocity. "Ok, Patti. Where do you want me to stand?"

"There, near the edge of the pier, so I have the ocean as a backdrop."

He glanced over at the dive shop, which reminded him of the awkward conversation he'd had with the remaining six divers in his group. They'd finally cornered him yesterday, right before leaving for the airport. They tried to give him an outrageous tip, and Alex practically tripped as he backed out of the dive shop to escape. Eventually, he talked them into giving it all to the rest of the staff. He understood they had needed some closure on the whole episode, but he only wanted to put it behind him.

Alex still wasn't a hundred percent but was fully capable of leading dives again. News of the boat sinking and subsequent rescue had flown around the local dive community, and his friend Robert had really come through, filling in for several days.

In the end, Hope managed to talk him into taking three more

days off. He still wasn't completely sure how she'd done it. Mostly, he would have agreed to anything she asked simply to avoid a repeat of the other morning when she'd broken down screaming and crying at him. He flushed, still not believing how badly he'd misjudged that situation. Alex had so much fun teasing and flirting with her when she was flustered and had thought it was more of that—how wrong he'd been.

As for what had come later that evening, a flush of another kind rose as he smiled to himself. Reaching the edge of the pier, he turned around. "Is this good?"

Patti held up her phone. "Yes! That's the smile I want. You must be thinking nice thoughts."

He laughed at that, and Patti took the picture.

"Excellent." She pointed to him. "That wasn't so bad, was it? Let's go back to the lobby right now and I'll print the picture. I need you to help me hang them. I'm not tall enough."

As they walked toward the lobby, Alex took a deep breath, remembering how it had felt to hold Hope in his arms at last. Like she belonged there. They had hardly seen each other in the past few days as he healed, and she worked frantically to manage all the fires caused by the boat sinking. Just a few stolen kisses and one spectacular but interrupted make-out session in the gear room that only made him want more. He lifted the corner of his mouth.

I'm a forty-year-old man making out in a darkened room.

But he was more reassured that she wasn't going to run off on him again.

His smile fell as he thought about the consequences of the boat disaster. The event could have ruined the resort and everything Hope had accomplished, but the divers in his fated group had been content upon leaving, even Turtle Guy and Teresa. Ben and Mary were planning a return in December. But a new boat was priority one.

As Patti printed his picture, he inspected the staff photos

lined up on the counter, all new in their just-purchased black frames. He was the last one. She was right—he'd been avoiding it. Patti placed the picture in the empty frame and held it up for his inspection, triumphant.

Alex winced. "I look like a grinning idiot."

"You just stop it. You look very happy. It's a wonderful picture."

He returned to the photos, stopping when he got to Hope's. Patti must have taken it in front of the lobby with the flame trees as a backdrop. Hope's hair and face were lit by the sun, and she smiled at the camera, looking radiant. His breath caught as he stared at her mouth, remembering the feel of it. The taste of it.

Worst timing ever . . .

"Ok. So how do you want to arrange these?" He could see the big blank space on the wall but wasn't about to suggest to her how to hang the pictures.

Patti went down the line and picked up Hope's picture. He grabbed the hammer and nails, and they walked over to the wall. "Let's start there," she said, pointing up. "Hope belongs on top."

Alex couldn't help the broad grin that spread across his face as he took the photo from her.

Of course, Patti noticed and slapped his arm. "You bad man," she said, but she was laughing too. "She is a beautiful woman, isn't she?"

"You're fishing, Patti. Besides, I'd never kiss and tell." He caressed the picture after he was done. In the next row down, he hung the pictures of Patti, himself, Tommy, and Gerold.

Hope's raised voice came from the office. "I know we sent that police report. You must have received it by now. This delay is not acceptable. We need the insurance payout as soon as possible to buy the new boat. You need to do better than this."

Alex and Patti turned to each other with wide eyes. Hope had spent the past few days battling with the insurance company. The bureaucracy on St. Croix was notoriously slow, but he had faith in her. It might take a few months, but she'd prevail. He figured she'd finance a new boat until the insurance company finally paid out.

Alex had been busy looking for a replacement boat, only today locating one in St. Thomas. He'd move heaven and hell to make sure they got another boat, and he was worried about the effect of all of it on Hope. She'd been working nonstop.

"I understand that," Hope said. "Look, it's not my fault if you can't organize any of your crap."

Alex grinned.

"Fine. I'll fax over another copy of the police report, and I'm going to call you every five minutes until you tell me you received it. What's the number? I'll send it *again* in a few minutes. You can expect my call shortly after." The phone slammed down, and he shared another look of mock alarm with Patti.

"Alex!" Hope bellowed. "Are you still out there?"

He turned to Patti with his best expression of horror. "Save me, Patti. I'm scared to go in there."

She tried not to laugh. "You better hurry. She'll only get angrier if you make her wait."

"I'm coming." He crossed to the office and immediately recognized Hope's exhaustion.

"Did you send that police report to the insurance company?" Hope was pressing the palms of both hands against her eyelids.

"Yes. I faxed it twice, yesterday and again this morning."

She lowered her hands and paced. "I knew it. Damn bureaucrats. They wouldn't proceed on the case until the police report declared it an accident. And now that we've sent it, they're stonewalling again. Thanks. I'll find it and send it again."

"Hey, you doing ok?"

"Yes, this is just incredibly frustrating."

Alex peeked out the doorway to make sure no one was looking, then gave her a brief but very thorough kiss. She softened against him. "I've got a lead on a dive boat. Come see me after you're done." He drew his finger down the bridge of her nose and returned to Patti. They were hanging the next row with the kitchen and bar staff when Hope got on the phone again.

"Look, I have the confirmation in my hand that says you received it. It has to be sitting right there on your fax machine. Would you please go check?" There was a pause. "What do you mean, you don't have any more time available to talk to me? Listen, we have sent you that police report a minimum of three times. This is ridiculous. Maybe I need to escalat—no, don't you dare hang up—"

Silence.

Then, "Oh, you *bastard*!"

There was a rustle, and Hope stormed out of her office, throwing her purse over one shoulder.

"I'm going to Christiansted. And I'm not coming back until I have our money."

Alex turned to Patti. "I'm glad I'm not that guy."

AFTER HANGING THE PICTURES, Alex walked down the beach toward the pier. The loaner boat was moored at the end. It was small but reliable, ideal for using until they found their own. Tommy stood in the stern, hosing down the deck. Alex hadn't talked to him since the rescue.

Tommy was facing away as Alex stepped on board, but turned as the boat shifted in weight. "Hey, man. Good to see you out and about."

"Feels good to be out of that damn apartment. I was afraid Hope might kill me if I tried to break out of jail, though."

"You'd probably deserve it." Tommy laughed before growing serious. "You doin' ok? Your hands all right?"

"They're fine. I had a pulled muscle in my hip. That's what laid me up the last couple days, but I'm good to go now. I'll be back to work tomorrow morning."

Thank God it was only a pulled muscle after all.

"Good to hear. Hasn't been the same without you."

Alex sat on the side bench. "Tommy, what do you think happened out there?"

"I haven't thought about anythin' else. I guess we were wrong about that drydock. She'd had that slow leak for a while now, then Jason ran over a damn reef when he was fillin' in for me last week. And, of course, the bilge pump failed again." Tommy sat opposite him.

"That damn bilge pump." Alex shook his head. "I was there with Jason—it's not like he ran us aground. A wave just tossed us against the reef."

"The best I can figure, that bump might have knocked the driveshaft seal loose and she started takin' on water. And without a workin' bilge pump . . ."

"Yeah, that makes sense. This is my fault. I should have told Hope we needed to dry-dock the boat, regardless of the cost. I just didn't want to floor her with how much it would be. She's been watching the bottom line pretty carefully." Alex ran a hand over his face. "Too late now."

Tommy laughed, and Alex looked up, startled. "Stop bein' such a prick."

"Great, you too? Turtle Guy wasn't enough?"

That made Tommy laugh harder. "Yeah, I was startin' to wonder if I was gonna have to pull you off that guy." Then he became serious. "That's not what I'm talkin' about, though. Man, why are you always so hard on yourself? This was an accident. The boat hit some coral, loosening the seal, which failed on our trip to the dive site, and when the damn bilge pump broke again, she sank. That's how it usually happens—a bunch of little things happen at once and cause a big thing."

Tommy met Alex's eyes. "Out there, you told me not to blame myself. Now I'm tellin' you the same thing, man."

CHAPTER 36

*H*ope trudged with exhausted steps, in need of a drink.
Upon her return that evening, she grabbed a bottle
of white wine from the restaurant refrigerator along with a glass
and made her way down the pier, inspecting the newly installed
swing. Wood framed to match the palapa around it, its four-foot
waterproof vinyl cushion enticed. She sat down on it, enjoying the
back-and-forth motion as she poured a glass.

Hope had experienced a moment of guilt walking by Alex's
apartment without alerting him. He wanted to talk to her about a
new dive boat, but she couldn't face it tonight. Not after her
battle. The past few days had been beyond exhausting, and she
was running on fumes. Her eyes grew heavy with the gentle movement of the swing.

"Hope, what are you doing?"

Yelping, she dropped the bottle on the wooden deck and
nearly broke her glass before whirling around. Alex stood there,
brows lowered.

"Don't you ever make any noise?"

He sat next to her. "I was about to text you, then I noticed you out here. I've been worried about you since you stormed out of the lobby earlier. Why are you sitting out here alone?"

She poured a generous amount of wine into the glass and handed it to him. "Here. I've only got one glass. You take it—I can just drink straight from the bottle."

"I take it things didn't go well at the insurance company?"

Hope gave a low growl. "The agent was a malignant little troll with a very high opinion of himself." She put the bottle down. "I set the police report in front of him, sat down, and told him I wasn't moving until he approved my claim. He told me this was *highly irregular*, and he couldn't possibly do anything for me today. So I smiled sweetly at him and told him he better get comfortable because I wasn't leaving without my money. That was . . . about 1 p.m., I think." She laughed. "By 4:30, he was visibly sweating."

"You sat in his office for over three hours?"

"You're not the only one who can be stubborn, Mr. Monroe. I asked if he preferred pizza or pasta for dinner, and he finally caved. He had the claim approved by five and said the payment would hit our bank account in five to ten business days."

She rubbed her eyes with both hands. "He emphasized that he was doing it as a one-time courtesy, and I should be very grateful. So I said, 'Well, hopefully you're enough of a gentleman to give me the couch to sleep on because I'm not leaving until that payment posts.'"

Hope laughed and looked at Alex's astonished face. "Oh, he was so mad! I think he was desperate to get rid of me at that point. So he got started processing the wire transfer, and I came around his desk to watch him do it. I didn't trust him an inch, little bastard."

Alex's laughter had been building during the last of her story.

"What?"

"Nothing—go on."

"In the end, I got it done. He said since it was finalized before 6 p.m. the payment should post sometime tonight, so I left. He probably locked the door after me." She wrapped an arm around the frame of the swing. "I drove home like a maniac and refreshed my bank balance for the next two hours. The payment posted about eight, and we now have $100,000 to buy the new boat."

Hope picked up the bottle again and held it up to him as a toast before taking a big swig. Setting the bottle back on the ground, she continued to lean forward, rubbing her face with both hands. "I cannot believe how tired I feel right now. I could go to sleep just like this."

"That looks really uncomfortable. Come here." Alex gathered her up and shifted her sideways so her legs were across his lap, and he cradled her upper body in his arms.

"I felt like I slayed a dragon an hour ago. What happened?"

"The adrenaline wore off. Now you've got the hangover."

"I'm not a big fan." She yawned.

"No, it's not much fun."

"I imagine you know all about adrenaline hangovers."

"Huh? What do you mean?"

"The rescue. Your adrenaline had to be pumping pretty good that day."

He had tensed but relaxed again at her explanation. Then he laughed. "I can't believe you got all that done in one day." Hope melted against him as he continued stroking her hair. "Why are you down here by yourself? Why didn't you come get me?"

"Look at me! I can hardly stay awake. Would you want to hang out with me right now?" She frowned. "Oh wait, you are. Alex, this isn't a very good decision on your part."

"I never said I was smart." He kissed her and leaned her head against his shoulder.

Hope snuggled into him, her eyelids feeling like they weighed a thousand pounds.

~

Sunlight streamed into the room when she awoke. Hope darted her gaze around the room, not recognizing her surroundings. Finally, everything snapped into focus.

I'm in Alex's bed!

She yanked the sheet up and looked down—she was fully clothed. Next to her, the other side of the bed was still made. She had a vague memory of Alex helping her stumble up the stairs last night.

Hope flipped the covers back and stood, feeling remarkably refreshed. Opening the door, she looked across the room at the couch, a rumpled blanket at one end. At the other end of the apartment, Alex stood at the patio door with a coffee cup at his mouth.

As if he sensed her, he turned and brightened upon seeing her. He set his cup down on the counter before rushing to the coffeepot, where a second mug was already waiting. He poured and brought the cup to her. "I don't have any cream. Is black ok?"

"It's perfect. Thank you."

"How are you feeling?"

She swallowed her coffee and smiled. "Wonderful, actually. I don't really remember coming up here last night. I've never had wine affect me like that before."

"It wasn't the wine. You've been running yourself ragged the last few days, and it caught up with you." Alex checked the clock on the wall. "I need to get to work. Why don't you join me on the morning trip? I'm splitting the groups with Robert, so I can add another tank no problem."

She thought about it a moment and said, "You're on. I think that's exactly what I need."

He closed the distance between them, cupping her face in his hands. His kiss sent waves of desire through her. "Don't be late, Boss Lady."

∿

HOPE WAS the last to board the boat, dressed in a staff shirt and a long swim skirt. Just looking at the boat made her heart pound. Robert had informed her the owner needed it back soon, which made purchasing a new one an immediate priority, and she still hadn't talked to Alex about it.

Both morning dives were relaxing and fun. Hope was fully confident again and recovered from her near-drowning. Alex paid extra attention to her with errant touches and looks, though he hardly let on it was on purpose.

After returning to the boat from the second dive, she shook her head, smiling as Alex climbed back on board, looking more like a Christmas tree than a dive guide with his BCD decorated with a magnetic slate, various pointers, lights, compass, reels, SMB, and other strange things she couldn't guess the purpose of. *Is that a magnifying glass?* He sat, sliding the tank into its holder in one practiced motion in his usual spot closest to the stern.

Hope pulled her wetsuit off, wrapping herself in a towel and wrestling her unruly hair into a staff baseball hat. Tommy began the trip back home as Alex removed the regulators from the tanks.

Wanting to stay out of his way, Hope made her way to the stern platform, standing near the ladder to warm up in the sun. The boat left a large white wake behind it, creating a serpentine as Tommy turned the wheel periodically.

Eventually, Alex appeared at her side. He wore his staff T-shirt and had his hands clasped behind his back, both of them facing the wake. He bent closer and whispered in her ear, "Do you have any idea how sexy you are right now?"

She laughed, then replied in a low voice, "You're blind. I'm wearing a towel and my hair is so awful I have to wear a baseball hat."

He turned to her, hands still clasped, and even though they were both wearing sunglasses, she could feel the intensity of his gaze.

"I think you look amazing in that hat." He leaned closer and said, "And that towel gives a man all kinds of ideas."

"Oh? What kind of ideas?"

He smiled wider, and a tremor ran through her body as she locked her gaze on his mouth. "Maybe I'll have to show you sometime." Turning back to the group, he said in a much louder voice, "Ok folks! We're almost back. Time to gather up your stuff." He brushed her hand as he left, walking back up to stand with Tommy.

Attempting to cool off after the conversation, Hope returned to the bow and redressed. Alex had been talking on his cell phone. Now he turned to her, eyes wide with excitement. "Hey, you want to have lunch? I've got some news on that boat I was telling you about."

~

Alex was at her corner table when she arrived at the restaurant, and she sat across from him.

"I think this boat is a great opportunity, Hope."

"It sounds exciting. Tell me about it."

He opened his phone and showed her several photos. "It's a forty-six-foot Newton, outfitted for diving—used but in great shape. My friend knows the owner and vouched for him." Alex's excitement was palpable. "This boat is a lot bigger, and I think we need that. We're getting more guests, and we could use the extra room since we might need to split into two groups permanently."

"If you say it's what we need, that's good enough for me. How much is it?"

He leveled his gaze at her. "Well, that's the thing. It's $150,000. It's been maintained regularly, and it doesn't have many hours on it at all. Believe it or not, it's a great buy."

Hope slumped, exhaling heavily. "Ouch."

They dug into their sandwiches, giving Hope time to think it over. "I can come up with the extra money, but that leaves me pretty thin. I never thought the day would come that I'd be thinking about buying a six-figure dive boat." She paused, then came to a decision. "Nothing ventured, nothing gained, right? Let's do it. Is it here in St. Croix?"

Alex shook his head. "It's in St. Thomas. I can fly over in the morning and drive it back. I'd probably be back here by early afternoon."

"You? Not Tommy?"

"No, I want him here with the dive group." Alex's face broke into a broad smile. "Besides, I hardly ever get a chance to drive. This'll be a blast."

"Ok, let's move on this. We don't have long before Robert's friend needs the boat back. If you give me the man's number, I'll call and get things rolling."

SEVERAL HOURS LATER, the boat was hers. The owner, a local with the wonderful name Baxter McBride, had texted her a multitude of photos and several videos. They filled out the bill of sale via fax, and she had him fax her a copy of the title to make sure he actually owned it. She wired the money to his account and told him she expected to take possession in the next day or two.

Hope met Alex on the beach, informing him she now owned the new boat.

He grinned at her. "You do know how to get things done. Let me call Robert and see if he's free. If he can take the morning dive, I'll go to St. Thomas tomorrow."

"Nope. *We'll* go to St. Thomas."

"Are you sure? St. Thomas is over forty miles from here. We need to come back through an open water channel." Alex paused, watching her. "It could get rough, Hope. It won't be like the boat trips we've had around here."

She shrugged. "I'm not afraid of a few waves. Besides, I

checked the forecast, and it's supposed to be beautiful tomorrow. If I'm spending this much money on a new boat, I'm making damn sure I'm there to take possession. Text me when you get the details worked out."

She turned and looked back at him, eyebrows raised. "Besides, somebody has to keep you in line."

CHAPTER 37

*T*he morning dawned clear and perfectly tropical as Hope and Alex arrived at the St. Croix airport at 6:30. Hope was full of excitement for their day of adventure. Alex had driven them in his old Land Cruiser with plans to pick it up later that day. At the check-in counter, he insisted on buying both their tickets.

"You've already outspent me on this trip by six figures—this is the least I can do."

As they passed through security, Alex asked for a manual security check.

"Why'd you do that?"

He turned, eyes wide with horror. "Have you ever seen the images those things produce? You can see everything. I have to preserve my modesty, you know."

"Hey, I went through it. What about my modesty?"

A slow smile crept across his face. "Oh, that is a completely different situation."

They made their way to the gate and sat down to wait.

When it was time to board, Hope groaned. The plane was

tiny, with only eight seats, one on each side of the aisle. "I hate these things. You feel every little bump."

"What were you expecting? A 747 for a twenty-minute flight?" Alex laughed. "I've flown in them lots of times. You'll be fine." He put his arm around her as they walked across the tarmac, Hope trying to ignore the ball of anxiety in her gut.

A few minutes later, she was tightly buckled into her seat, maintaining a death grip on the armrests. She darted a glance across the aisle at Alex, who was sprawled out with one leg in the aisle, leafing through the in-flight magazine and completely unconcerned. She mock glared at him and without looking, his face broke into a smile.

"I knew you could see me over there."

He put the magazine down. "You want to sit in my lap? We can ask if they'll allow it. Might get lucky."

"You're impossible." But now she was smiling a little.

The front door shut, and the plane taxied out, speeding bumpily down the runway until it became airborne. They were about twenty feet off the ground when they hit the first jolt of turbulence. Hope increased her death grip and looked over at Alex. He was fast asleep, with his head leaning against the window.

Twenty endless, turbulent minutes later, they touched down with a hard thump on St. Thomas and she breathed an enormous sigh of relief.

Alex finally woke up and stretched, turning to Hope. "We there already?"

She glared as he grinned at her.

Thank God we're taking the boat back.

~

THEIR TAXI WOUND around the narrow two-lane road and up and down steep hills until they arrived at a restaurant named Rock

City Grill. Alex opened the front door and ushered Hope through. It was only 8 a.m. and the place was deserted.

"At least the door was unlocked," Hope said before calling out, "Hello?"

A pair of swinging doors to their right opened and a man with shining dark skin approached and boomed, "Well, good mornin'!" He looked to be in his late fifties with salt-and-pepper hair.

"Mr. McBride?" Hope asked. At his nod, she introduced herself and Alex.

"Call me Baxter!" He beckoned to them as he walked toward the rear of the restaurant. "Come on—she's in the canal out back. You're gonna love her!"

The group made their way through the dark restaurant and emerged into the bright sunlight. After the cave-like interior, Hope dug her sunglasses out of her bag to ease the strain on her eyes. The dive boat was tied up in front of them, alongside a brick-paved walkway lining a canal that ran behind the building.

The boat was blinding white in the sun, sleek with a half-covered main deck and a large open fiberglass area on the bow, perfect for sunbathing. From the main deck, a ladder extended to a small second-story elevated wheelhouse. Baxter and Alex continued onboard so he could show off the boat's features while Hope made her way down the walkway to the stern. Alex deposited a large backpack he'd been carrying under the covered canopy and climbed the ladder to stand with Baxter behind the steering column on the elevated bridge.

Hope inspected the stern to read the name. "*Surface Interval*, huh?"

Baxter beamed down at her. "Great name for a dive boat, yes?"

Hope boarded the boat and climbed the ladder to the elevated wheelhouse, inspecting the gauges in the wood-grain console while the two men discussed aspects of the throttle system. They returned to the main deck and inspected the engine. The boat was spotless, and all the surfaces were in good condition. She was very pleased with it and could tell Alex was impressed.

"I think I've got everything I need to know. It's in great shape. You ready to head out, Hope?"

"Yes, let's go." She bounced up and down on the balls of her feet.

Baxter stood up. "No, wait! I have somethin' for you both. Wait right here." He disappeared into the restaurant, only to return a few minutes later with a large picnic basket in one hand and a bottle of champagne in the other with a Styrofoam cooler tucked under that arm. "My wife insisted on sendin' you off in style! Have a nice picnic lunch on the way, compliments of the McBrides."

Hope was touched at his thoughtfulness and thanked him for the bounty.

"I know a small islet where we can stop and have lunch," Alex said to her. "It's about forty-five minutes from the resort and south of the main channel. I'd like to get across the channel as soon as possible, though. The seas will be lower in the morning."

Hope turned back to Baxter. "Could I use your restroom? I'd like to change before we leave."

"Of course! Follow me."

Alex grabbed a pair of board shorts out of his backpack and followed them back into the restaurant.

LOCKING THE BATHROOM DOOR, Hope changed into her bikini, smiling at herself in the mirror. While waiting for her flight to St. Croix at O'Hare airport in March, she'd entered a swimwear shop and purchased a black string bikini and matching fishnet cover-up. At the time, she'd been self-conscious and embarrassed just buying it but determined to make a new start.

Now she inspected her reflection, proud of her transformation, both inner and outer.

She stood tall and straight, wearing the bikini with confidence. It showed every curve of her toned body and full breasts. She'd never worn the bikini but had decided to pack it today, realizing its time had come. Still, the fishnet cover-up was pushing it a bit far, so she brought out the spare she'd carried, black with a gold crescent moon and stars printed on the front. She slipped back into her flip-flops and left the restaurant.

As she climbed aboard, Alex was already behind the wheel in the elevated bridge. The roomy lower deck had a large covered forward section for divers to get out of the weather if needed. Plastic tank holders were installed in the open-air section toward the stern, in front of the dive platform with its twin ladders.

Hope climbed to the wheelhouse and stood next to Alex. "I just renewed your Coast Guard captain's license, Mr. Monroe, so I know I'm in excellent hands today."

"Pretty sure I can get us back without getting lost. Not one-hundred percent, but pretty sure."

"Well, we can always call the Coast Guard if we need to."

Alex flinched, then laughed. "Absolutely not. Once in a life-time was plenty for me." He drew her in for a quick kiss. Hope's heart sped up. She flashed back to that evening on his deck, the feel of his back muscles under her hands and the taste of his mouth. She took a deep breath and sat on the padded bench next to him.

Baxter threw the lines into the boat, and Alex started the engine, working them sideways away from the dock. He glanced at Hope before turning to the front again. "It'll take us about an hour to get out of the lee of St. Thomas, so the first hour should be pretty nice. Then we hit the open channel. The islet I mentioned isn't too far away after we cross the channel, and the resort is forty-five minutes from there. All told, I'd guess we'll be back early afternoon—one or two o'clock."

Hope spied the large fiberglass area at the bow beneath where they presently stood. It looked very inviting. "You mind if I get some sun on that deck?"

"Not at all. Improves the view substantially."

She descended the ladder. After applying sunscreen, she reached for her towel and made her way out to the sundeck. The morning sun was soft and warm, and white puffy clouds danced across the sky. Hope waved to Alex, then spread out her towel and sat down on it with her arms hugging her knees.

They had left the canal behind and were in the open ocean now. The blue water was nearly flat, and Alex throttled up to full speed. She breathed in the fresh, salty air, smiling at the freedom of it. Hope removed her cover-up and lay down on her back, escaping the wind. Wearing sunglasses, she could watch Alex without fear of being caught looking. He wore a baseball hat turned around backward and sunglasses. His shirt was off, and he stood in an easy, relaxed posture.

He was also staring right at her.

With a contented smile, Hope lifted her arms above her head, stretching her legs out. Closing her eyes, she drifted off to the gentle motion of the boat.

Hope awoke to the sudden decrease in volume as Alex throttled down and put the boat in neutral. "What's wrong? Why are we stopping?"

"Nothing's wrong. But you should probably get off the bow. We're about to head into the channel, and if you stay up there, you're gonna get soaked."

"Really? Ok." She looked around as she put her cover-up back on, noting the whitecaps further out. Hope made her way to the half-covered main deck where Alex was securing items.

They climbed the ladder to the bridge. There was a long, padded bench seat behind the wheel and console. Hope sat down as Alex pushed the throttle forward, and they were underway once again.

Five minutes later, she experienced the first big dip as they hit a trough. He throttled down as they rose over the next wave, then up again on the far side to the new trough. Their speed was much slower than before. Hope opened her eyes wide as a wave crashed over the bow, completely covering where she had sunbathed minutes before.

They continued like this until a big wave sent them airborne, only to slam down into the trough. Hope bounced up from the bench with a loud "Oof!" as Alex whooped and laughed out loud. His excitement was infectious, and she laughed too.

She was thoroughly enjoying herself, but after thirty more minutes, her butt was getting sore from all the bumps. Hope turned to Alex, who was still grinning like a lunatic. "Are you sure this is safe? It's rough out here."

"No, this isn't rough. This is great!" He looked at her and became more serious. "It's ok, Hope—we're fine. This is calmer than I expected."

"Wow. Ok."

"I did warn you, you know."

"Yes. Yes, you did. At least I'm not getting seasick." They continued for another hour. After the euphoria wore off, Alex got more serious, piloting the boat with skill.

Over two hours after they had entered the channel, the waves were decreasing, and land was ahead. "Is that St. Croix?"

"Yep. I'm guessing we've got another thirty minutes or so until we get to the islet."

Once he closed in on the north shore of St. Croix, Alex turned the boat west and eventually left the large island behind. The ocean steadily became calmer, and he was able to increase speed. After another twenty minutes, Alex throttled back somewhat as he skirted a small land mass and turned the boat south.

"We're here," he said with a smile.

CHAPTER 38

*T*he tiny island was a glorified sand bar with shrubs and stunted trees dotting the interior. It formed a horseshoe shape with the open ends pointing south and creating a protected bay, complete with a sparkling white sand beach. Hope brightened. "Wow, I didn't think much of it when we first got here, but this part is really pretty. It's super small, though."

"That's why it's called an islet, Hope, not an island."

"Very funny."

Alex slowed further, watching the depth gauge closely. "Ok, this is good." He pushed a button, and the anchor clanged as it was freed. "We're on bare sand here, so it's safe to drop anchor. We can't get any closer without risking grounding her."

He turned to her with a broad smile, both arms held out from his sides. "Welcome to Horseshoe Key! You up for a swim to shore and then lunch?"

"Sure. Wait—how are we going to get the picnic stuff to shore?"

He opened his backpack. "This is a dry bag. We'll put all the picnic supplies in here along with anything else you don't want to get wet."

Hope peeked inside. "You brought a first aid kit? Really?"

"I'm a good Boy Scout. It's easy to fall and crash into something when the boat's in rough water. Much better to have the kit and not need it than the reverse." Alex stacked the food on top of a blanket, adding the chilled champagne and two plastic glasses. He grinned. "The guy thought of everything."

Hope reapplied her sunscreen, collecting her towel and placing it in the dry bag before removing her cover-up and adding that too. Alex shrugged into the backpack, and they set off, swimming at an easy pace.

The sandy beach rose at an angle from the water before flattening out. Alex chose a spot framed by some shady trees, then kneeled and opened the bag. He removed the blanket and spread it out, handing Hope her towel. She dried off and thought about replacing her cover-up, but the sun on her shoulders felt so good she decided to go without.

Alex spread out the food. There were two lavish turkey sandwiches, a salad, rolls, fresh fruit, and the champagne. Alex popped the cork on the bottle after Hope firmly declined opening it, handing her a full glass. "Here's to new beginnings."

"I will certainly drink to that."

They clinked their glasses together and drank, eyes locked on each other.

Forty-five minutes later, it looked like they'd hardly made a dent in the food. Alex became pensive at times, but then he would make a quip, making her think she was imagining things. Alex poured the rest of the champagne into their glasses as Hope refused his proffered mango. "I can't eat any more."

After returning the food to Alex's backpack, they lay on the blanket, watching the ocean as they finished the champagne. Hope couldn't help anticipating where things might go next, smiling as a current ran through her body.

"Are the waves getting bigger?" Hope asked.

"A bit, I think. They usually do in the afternoons."

"I'm going to hit the water. I feel sticky and want to rinse off."

With his eyes closed, Alex replied, "You shouldn't swim so soon after eating. Your stomach will cramp, and you'll drown."

Hope threw back her head and laughed. "Well, I'm sure you can prevent that. I know from personal experience your rescue skills are first rate." She stood.

Alex rose too. "Ok, but you saw what happened when you ignored my first warning about the rough crossing. Who knows what might happen now?"

"I'll risk it," she said, walking into the warm water as sand stirred up around her feet. "How did you know about this place, anyway?"

"It's a great dive site. See that arm of the horseshoe?" He pointed to the west. "You can see the reef there. It slopes down to a hundred feet. We don't come here often because of how long the trip is, but maybe with the bigger boat we can start doing longer three-tank dive trips."

A wave washed over Hope's head. She wiped her face after surfacing again. "That's a good idea. We can start all sorts of stuff now. The bookings are really picking up, and more guests mean more money to do things."

Alex swam to her as another wave washed over them. He shook the water droplets off his head. "You're doing a great job with the resort. It's like a new place."

"Thank you." She smiled at him, her stomach a constant flutter now.

Oh, those eyes!

"It hasn't been easy, but I think things are turning around now," Hope said as another wave broke over her head. "Let's go back to the beach. I'm getting pummeled out here."

They turned and headed back to shore, getting tossed around. Hope stood when the water was at waist level, and a large wave toppled her over.

Then Alex's arms were around her, spinning her toward him as she fell against his chest. "Whoa, there. Take it easy." He helped her to her feet, still holding her against his body.

He smiled at her. "Don't worry, I won't let you fall." The smile fell away as they held each other's gaze. "Unless you want to fall . . ."

Heart pounding now, Hope became very aware of their bodies touching and their arms around each other, his skin warm under her fingers. Those blue eyes drew her in, and the moment froze.

Slowly, Alex lowered his mouth until his lips brushed against hers, barely touching. Hope reached up a hand and pressed the back of his head toward her as she opened her mouth and brushed her tongue lightly across his lower lip.

The effect on Alex was electric. He groaned and crushed her to him. Hope kissed him back, her hands firm across his back, feeling the hard muscle underneath his skin.

He loosened his hold, lips still firm against her. One hand ran down her spine, while the other reached around to cup her breast, gooseflesh rising on her skin in their wake. The warm water swirled around her, competing with his touch. As his hand reached under her swim top, Hope inhaled sharply then pushed against him, feeling the rigidness between them.

Alex pulled away, water beading on his face as he grasped her face in both hands. "I really need to hear you say you want this."

She whispered in his ear, "I'm done running away. I want you so much."

He grabbed a handful of her wet hair, pulling her mouth back to his.

Another big wave picked them up and set them back down, unbalancing them both. Alex broke the contact and turned around. He led her back to the beach, drawing her down onto the blanket with him.

As he removed her bikini top, she couldn't distinguish the sound of the ocean over the blood rushing in her head. His mouth tasted of champagne and salt—she couldn't get enough of him.

After brushing her lips one more time, he continued down her neck then lower, his mouth circling her breasts until she moaned.

Alex lifted up on one elbow. "God, you are so beautiful."

Hope didn't trust herself to respond to that, so she pulled him down to kiss him again, running her hands across his chest and pausing to enjoy the contrast of soft skin with firm muscle underneath. Finally, she traced her fingers lower and squeezed softly. His breath caught at that, and she smiled against his lips.

He broke off their kiss and sat up, pulling off her bikini bottoms. He shrugged out of his trunks and lay down again, the full length of their naked bodies touching as she pulled his mouth back to hers, immersed in the feel of it all as he slid his hand over her hip.

Then he stopped.

"Oh, *hell!* We're on a deserted island here. Hope, I don't have any protection . . . what are we——"

She placed a finger against his lips and smiled. "Shhhh, it's ok. I've got an IUD. I'm safe, Alex."

He relaxed and leaned his forehead against hers. "Me too." He laughed quietly. "I haven't done this in a really long time."

Alex closed his eyes and kissed her before she could respond. He moved his hand over her hip, finally stopping between her legs. Hope heaved a breath, giving herself over to the sensations, her pulse pounding in her ears as his touch sent jagged sparks through her.

Kissing him deeply, she drew her nails down his chest. Hope slowed her hand as it continued down and across his abdomen, softly now, the muscles underneath rippled at her touch. Moving on, she slowly caressed down his side, tracing a light touch against his hot skin.

Then she encountered a massive ridge of scar tissue that completely covered his right hip. Shocked, Hope paused, and Alex tensed all over.

Her heart raced at the sheer violence of the wound.

That is a topic for another time.

Quickly continuing, she lifted her hand to stroke down his thigh, then up the front of his leg, feather-light until she took him in her hand. He moaned softly against her mouth and pressed his hips forward.

A flood of emotion built within her, understanding at last what this meant to him. His wound was only exposed when he was naked, figuratively and literally. What Hope just discovered on his right hip was the key to this man.

But she had more enjoyable things to concentrate on now.

Alex rolled over onto his back, taking her with him as their mouths remained locked together. She ran her hand down his chest and hip once again, the mass of scar tissue not surprising her this time and letting *him* know it didn't bother her. Feeling the soft breeze cooling the hot skin on the back of her body, Hope moved her hips from side to side, grinding against him.

He rumbled deep in his chest and rolled them back over. They were both breathing hard now, sharing the same air between them as their mouths devoured each other.

"Alex, I want you. Now," she breathed into his ear.

He moved on top of her, and she inhaled deeply as he entered her, every nerve calling out. His eyes were full and brilliant, and he looked at her as if she were the only thing in his world.

They maintained eye contact as they began moving together, first very slowly, and then faster. Alex grasped both her arms and lifted them above her head as their fingers intertwined. She was immobilized by his body. Lost in his eyes, full of desire and trust, she was safe with him.

Alex gasped, closing his eyes and burying his face in her neck as their movement increased. "Oh God, Hope."

Everywhere their bodies touched became slick with sweat. Glancing at the blue sky, Hope tightened her grip on his hands, breathing ever faster as the sensations within her built, wave after wave, as she closed her eyes and locked her mouth onto his shoulder. Alex gripped her hands tighter in return, crying out with her.

HOPE STRETCHED ON THE BLANKET, the breeze cooling the sweat on her body as a bead ran down her side. Alex languidly kissed her, then rolled onto his back, pulling her with him so she lay alongside, her head nestled on his chest. Feeling the comforting beating of his heart beneath her ear, Hope slowly stroked his chest, enjoying the feel of it beneath her fingers.

Continuing downward, she softly caressed his side, slowing the pace when she reached his area of scar tissue. She lightly drew her hand down the massive wound, closing her eyes as she silently asked the question.

His heart raced next to her ear.

After hesitating, Alex began in a flat, emotionless voice. His entire body was coiled tension, contrasting his soft, clipped words. "It was an IED. In Syria. We ran right into an ambush. Sixteen of us went out that night. Eight were killed in action, four badly injured, and four made it back ok. I was airlifted to Germany after they stabilized me somewhat. The doctors told me later I coded twice on the way. They rebuilt my hip there. It's pretty much a mass of metal. After a few months of that, I came back stateside and did my rehab at Walter Reed in Bethesda."

He took a deep breath. "But it was the end of my Navy career. That was when I became a full-time dive instructor and moved here five years ago."

Hope was dizzy and short of breath, stunned at his revelation. Under her ear, Alex's heart beat even faster than before. His chest moved with each deep, rapid inhalation.

A tear slipped from her eye and ran down his chest as his entire body became even more rigid.

"Don't feel sorry for me, Hope. I don't need your pity." He spat the words out like brittle ice chips.

She raised on her elbow, meeting his eyes. "I don't pity you, Alex. I've seen who you are. I *know* who you are. But that doesn't mean I can't cry at a sad story. It only means I wish I'd met you sooner. That I could have been there to help you."

Eyes glittering with unshed tears, he pulled her back down tightly to his chest. "You're helping me now, baby. More than you'll ever know."

CHAPTER 39

*a*lex pulled Hope tight against him, entwining his legs further with hers. His heartbeat gradually receded to its normal, steady rhythm as he relaxed. A lightness spread through his chest. It had definitely been worth the wait.

He'd done it—finally told what happened—and the world hadn't ended.

Quite the opposite.

Hope didn't show any signs of running away. He smirked at the sky. *We're on a tiny island. Where's she going to run?*

He'd tried to think of a way to bring up his wound while they were eating, but couldn't do it, deciding instead to let things play out. He doubted they were done with the conversation, anyway. That was a huge surprise he'd dropped on her. And he had his own reckoning to begin.

She brought his hand up to her mouth and kissed it. "Why? Why have you kept this so deeply hidden?"

He sighed as his mind clouded once more. "I had to. It was the only way I could deal with it. Eight of my best friends died. Horribly. Throwing myself into work kept me from thinking too much. And the last thing I want is anyone feeling sorry for me.

The only time I felt alive was in the water." Alex tipped her face toward his. "Until you came into my life."

Hope reached up, kissing him deeply, then brushed her lips over his closed eyelids, and the dam he'd built began to crumble at last. She lifted onto her elbow, tracing a finger down his chest and abdomen as her gaze sharpened. Her eyes examined the scars scattered across his lower abdomen, her face showing only tender concern.

Then she found the other one.

She traced her finger across the three-inch angry gash near his groin, nearly hidden in the thatch of hair.

Alex exhaled, his eyes closed. "That's the one that almost killed me. The hip was bad, but only needed a series of operations to rebuild. Shrapnel hit me there and severed some blood vessels. I didn't ask the details, didn't want to know."

"No, I don't blame you." She traced back up his body and cupped his cheek. "I'm so glad you're here. There's nowhere else I'd rather be right now." She smiled, a gleam in her eye now. "And I'm pretty happy that wound wasn't a couple more inches to the left."

A faint smile crossed his face. "Yeah, one doc liked to joke how I came pretty close to singing in the Vienna Boys' Choir. Though I wasn't very grateful at the time."

Hope shook her head. "I was an empty shell when I got here. I left nothing behind in Chicago, and I really needed a new start." She paused. "I haven't had the best experiences with men, and I tried to resist you from the start. But when the boat sank, and I thought I might have lost you, all I could think about was how stupid I'd been."

"Then I acted like a complete idiot after I got back. I still can't believe I made you cry like that. I'm so sorry."

She smiled. "You're starting to make up for it now."

"I'm sure going to try." Relief rolled over him like a warm blanket. Alex rolled her over and kissed her deeply.

The relief was quickly replaced by something much more urgent as the heat between them grew again.

AFTER THEY HAD FINISHED the second time, Alex turned them onto their sides, fitting himself tightly behind her. Hope could feel every inch of where their skin touched. He used one hand to slowly stroke the side of her breast. Over time, it became slower and slower until it stopped altogether mid-stroke and his breathing deepened and steadied.

Hope inhaled a shaky breath, coming to terms with the feelings inside her. Alex had just shared the innermost facet of himself with her, the part of him kept deeply hidden and protected. Her breath was building, emotion surging as she thought about what he had been through. Then she tamped down on the emotion hard.

Stop it. He made it clear he doesn't want your tears.

"Everything ok? I can hear you thinking from back here." He snuggled closer to her and cupped his hand around her breast.

"Yes, everything's fine." Hope placed her hand over his, and within seconds his breathing deepened again. She now knew this man better than anyone else did, and he trusted her completely. Still, she thought he hadn't shared everything yet.

He's not the only one, is he?

The thought brought disquiet with it and she took a deep breath, pushing it from her mind. What she'd experienced on this beach with Alex had been different, very different. Hope was falling more deeply for him than any man since—she stopped the thought in its tracks.

That's the last thing you should be thinking about right now.

But the seed had been planted.

Would she only get hurt again? Hope cleared her mind and relaxed. Listening to Alex's deep, regular breathing and the steady sound of the ocean waves lapping on the beach, her eyelids grew heavy.

SOMETIME LATER, she awoke. The sun was well past its zenith, hot and merciless now. Hope was uncomfortably warm but still reluctant to move. Her mind was fully present and fully conscious of the man with her. She didn't want their escape to end, but she was feeling decidedly hot and sticky now. Alex was close behind and had moved her hair aside so he could rest with his lips against the back of her neck.

Hope stretched, and Alex pulled her tighter against him and nuzzled her neck. The sun continued to beat down. Sighing, she said, "Alex, we should probably get back to the boat soon."

"Yeah, I know." He made no effort to move.

"I'm afraid I might be getting sunburned. We've been here a long time. I put sunscreen on before we, uh, before, um . . ." Feeling his lips widen into a smile, she dug her elbow into his side. "You enjoy seeing me uncomfortable, don't you?"

Alex rolled her over onto her back, serious. "I never want to see you uncomfortable." His face widened into a grin. "But I love seeing you flustered." He kissed her and jumped up, right leg strong and steady. "Let's go back to the boat."

Hope folded the blanket while he gathered their swimsuits. She handed it to him as he finished putting their clothes in the dry bag.

"Wait," she said as he zipped the bag shut. "I need my swimsuit, you know."

"No, you don't. I said we were going back to the boat. I didn't say we were done yet." Alex pulled her to him, and his kiss seared through her. "Every boat needs to be christened, you know."

∼

As they swam toward the boat, Hope luxuriated in the warm water, sensuous against her bare skin as it washed her clean. As they approached, Alex pulled himself up onto the stern platform. Hope followed, her arms flexing, and the appreciation in his eyes was evident.

It was also evident he wasn't finished with her yet.

He went over to the dry bag, then returned with her towel and wrapped it around her naked body. He whispered in her ear, "I get to wrap it around you this time. I've already told you what this towel does to me, and now I've finally got you alone without the swimsuit underneath."

"Hmmm, I don't think you actually said what it does to you."

He laughed softly. "I said I was going to show you."

After drying her midsection, Alex drew the towel down each arm, his lips never leaving hers, eyes closed. Hope reached up to hold on to the metal grab bar bolted to the ceiling of the canopy as he lowered to his knees, the waves crashing on the outer edge of the islet as she inhaled the salty air.

Running the towel down each leg to dry her, he planted a series of kisses across her lower stomach, slowly moving from one side to the other, the breeze cooling her wet skin as his tongue moved on.

Hope was on fire now, embers radiating throughout her body.

Alex stood back up and nuzzled her ear. "I noticed, you know."

"What?"

"The second time, on the beach. I got more out of it than you did. I intend to make up for that now."

"Alex, it's ok. I got every bit as much—"

He silenced her with a finger to her lips. "Hush."

Alex lifted her against his stomach, and she wrapped her legs around his waist. He carried her underneath the canopy and lay her on her back on the side bench, climbing on top of her. He spent a long time with her breasts, investigating thoroughly.

Eyes closed, Hope reached above her head and grabbed both sides of the bench she lay on as he continued to move downward. She was making soft moaning sounds, but she didn't care.

After that, she lost all conscious thought.

When she came back to herself, she was breathing in shuddering gasps. Alex climbed back up toward her head, wiping the back of his hand across his mouth. He crushed his mouth to hers as he entered her powerfully. Hope arched her back, feeling the bolt of sensation as both her arms clenched his back.

There was no tenderness this time.

They crashed together again and again. Her climax built once more—this time Alex was right there with her. Biting down hard on his shoulder, she gripped his back as both of them gasped.

He collapsed on top of her as she wrapped one arm around his waist, holding him close to her while she stroked his hair. The sun descended toward the horizon as she pulled him to her as tightly as possible.

What happens now?

~

THE MOUNTAINS OF ST. Croix looked like brilliant emeralds in the late afternoon sun. Hope stood next to Alex as he drove the boat, cradled against his chest as he held her close with one arm.

She turned to the west with a jolt of alarm. The sun was near to setting.

"Alex, how close are we to home?"

He inspected the shore. "Less than ten minutes. We're almost there."

She glanced again at the sun. "Wait, what time is it? I put my watch away when we got on the boat in St. Thomas."

"Yeah, so did I, and I silenced my phone. We're pretty late." Alex picked up his phone. "It's almost six. And I've got three missed calls from Patti, and several texts."

"Didn't you say we'd be back by early afternoon? Oh, I think we're in big trouble." She started laughing.

He pulled her close for a kiss, his chest rumbling. "I think we got a little distracted. And I did warn you that swimming after lunch might be dangerous."

"You did. Well, I can't go back to the resort like this. Can you stop for a minute? I'm going to hop off the back and wash up a little." Alex throttled down and put the boat in neutral. Hope removed her clothing, not wanting to get her swimsuit wet again now that it was nearly dry. "What about you?"

"Oh, definitely."

Hope lowered herself into the water and resurfaced to find Alex right in front of her, drawing her into a tight embrace. She laughed and pushed him back. "Oh, no you don't. We're officially back on the clock now."

"Hard-ass."

Smiling, she got dressed. Alex climbed aboard completely naked, and Hope sharpened her gaze at the straight lines of multiple surgical scars running down his right hip. He used his hands to push the water off his body, then changed back into his board shorts.

Hope couldn't resist looking at him—he was a beautifully built man, and she loved watching the muscles move under his skin.

She widened her eyes, putting a hand to her mouth.

"What?"

"Oh no." She laughed. "You have to get your shirt on before we get home! You've got bite marks on both shoulders."

He pressed a hand against his skin, inspecting the damage. "Well done. I'll wear them as a badge of honor."

"Oh, shut up and put your shirt back on."

He did, but his smile faded. "I better call Patti. I've already put her through a lot—the boat sinking wasn't that long ago."

Hope nodded, encircling his waist. "I know. I feel bad too."

She ran a finger down the center of his chest. "Having regrets already?"

Alex pulled her to him, kissing her deeply. "Not a chance." Then he pulled away with a sigh. "I'll try to keep this short. Wish me luck."

He climbed up the ladder to call Patti. "We're fine, Patti. It's ok. I'm sorry—we didn't mean to worry you. We were out of cell range." There was a pause. "Less than ten minutes out now." He winced and held the phone out from his ear. "Calm down. We had rougher water than I was expecting, and I wanted to show Hope some things on St. Croix she hadn't seen before."

He said this last part to Hope with a broad grin as she rolled her eyes.

"I lost track of time a little. Look, Patti, the water is rough out here—I need to concentrate. We'll be there in a few minutes. Bye." He hung up. "Well, that was fun."

Hope glanced at the flat, calm water and pressed against his chest. "Seems like Golden Boy is in trouble. Though I noticed you took the blame instead of sharing it with me. Very gallant of you."

"No sense in both of us being in the doghouse."

Half Moon Bay appeared, and Alex angled the boat in, becoming pensive. He throttled down and cupped her face in his hands, his eyes full of emotion. "Thank you. This has . . ." He flushed. "Well, it's been one of the best days of my life. I've felt alive today in ways I haven't for a very long time. It's hard for me to . . . open up about my injury. Being with you helped. I've spent years now just trying to bury it."

"Oh, Alex. Thank you for trusting me." His eye contact was too much for her, and she wrapped her arms around him. "Today was . . . I don't even know how to describe what I'm feeling. I don't want it to end."

"Me either. But Patti's probably got binoculars trained on us right now—I think it's time to face the music."

That brought more uneasiness. She hated feeling insecure but couldn't help it now, afraid this would all come crashing down. He turned back toward the console, and she pulled him toward her again.

"Stay with me tonight," Hope said into his chest. "I need you with me."

"Nothing would make me happier." Alex tilted her face up to his, a corner of his mouth lifting. "But realize, Ms. Collins, this might be another dangerous situation you're getting yourself into."

"Promise?"

"I told you. I keep my promises."

CHAPTER 40

The palapa at the end of the pier came into view. Hope was surprised to see a crowd milling around. Patti and Clark stood there, and a pang of guilt rolled through her. This big step wasn't only about her or Alex. The whole resort was excited about the new boat.

Alex was soon in his element, inviting everyone aboard so he could show it off. Even Patti seemed to be more impressed than angry, which Hope counted as a major win.

Alex was talking with a female guest who also owned a commercial dive boat. It sounded like they were comparing notes. Two more guests came on board, and Hope moved back to give them room, feeling uncomfortable at the crush of people around her as her earlier disquiet returned. Alex had a crowd clustered around him. After her day of intimacy alone with him, the crowd of people seemed loud and abrasive.

A knot of anxiety built, churning in her abdomen.

The man next to her was gesticulating wildly, and she moved back further to keep from being hit by a flailing arm. Besides, no one wanted to talk to her—they only had eyes for Alex. She turned to see him and the woman leaning over the side bench to look at something. They straightened up as she said something, and both started laughing. She touched his arm, and the knot in Hope's gut turned into a stabbing pain.

Stop it, for God's sake! Think about what you shared with him today. He's just being friendly with her.

But the familiar sensations started to creep back in, the ones she'd fought so hard to overcome—the dread, the insecurity, the fear. *This is* your *boat—you have every right to be here!*

But the old voices were back in force now.

No, you don't know anything about this. Why are you even here? You don't belong.

Clutching her cover-up tighter, Hope kept moving back to avoid the crush and soon found herself next to the dock. It was a simple matter to hop off the boat onto the wooden planking, where she stood trying to regain her confidence. She looked at Alex, surrounded by people, laughing and relaxed as he demonstrated every feature of the boat.

You really think he's still interested in you? He already got what he wanted.

She clenched her fists, reminding herself of his assurance that he'd come up to the house. *You thought he'd actually keep his word?*

With a deep sigh, Hope turned and walked up the pier.

She made a determined effort to silence her inner demons by being productive. Hope stopped at the kitchen, picking up two sandwiches, some chips, and a prepared salad for dinner.

It didn't last.

She walked down the beach to her house, feet leaden now. Shoving the food in the refrigerator, she slammed the door and whirled around, leaning her arms against the island counter as acid burned a hole in her stomach as she fought back tears.

"He said he would come. Give him time."

She hated how shaky her voice was.

Hope turned around and took a large glass out of the cabinet, filling it with tap water. She drank it in one shot, then went out on the porch and stood at the wooden railing, gazing at the pier and feeling empty inside. She could imagine Alex enjoying himself as the women gave him appraising glances. Hope banged her hand into the railing so she could feel the pain.

With a frustrated groan, she went back inside, aimlessly straightening her living room. Trying to fill the time, she cleaned the kitchen counters next. She looked at the wall clock. It had been well over an hour.

They probably invited him to have a beer at the bar. You're the last thing he's thinking about. Hope shut her eyes, then she raked both hands through her hair, only to get them caught in the thick, tangled strands.

That's what I need!

She spun around and marched toward her bedroom, entering the bathroom and turning on the shower. Undressing, she inspected herself in the mirror. She looked the same, but now everything was different.

Or was it?

Hope stood under the showerhead, hands leaning against the wall on either side of the handle as she let the hot water wash over her, her fingers white against the wall from the pressure she was exerting.

You know he's going to break your heart. You never should have let him in this deeply. He's not coming.

She tried to force the thoughts out and concentrated on calming herself. Eventually, she stood straight and wrapped her arms around herself, still fighting back tears as the steaming water poured over her head. Eyes closed, her fingers parted her hair, trying to separate it into more manageable sections before shampooing.

Then a second pair of hands were in her hair, stroking it and gently squeezing the water out. He slid his arms around her waist and pulled her back to him as she choked back a sob, relief washing over her.

"Where did you go?" Alex murmured in her ear. "I didn't think they'd ever let me out of there. Then I looked around for you, but you were gone."

"I . . . I didn't feel like I belonged," Hope nearly whispered. "There were too many people, and I wanted to be alone with you." And quietest of all, "I didn't think you'd come to me."

"Hope, nothing could keep me away from you, not after today." Alex turned her around, looking at her sharply. "And you always belong with me."

Tilting her face up, he brushed his lips against hers tenderly, as if she were a porcelain doll that might shatter any moment. "Are you ok?"

"Will you wash my hair?"

"Of course." He poured the shampoo into his hand and rubbed it into a frothy halo around her head. Then he walked her back under the stream of water to gently rinse it off, enfolding her in his arms after.

After enjoying his closeness for a few moments, she said, "Now the conditioner."

"Um, is it like the shampoo? Rub it in and rise?"

Hope laughed softly, relaxing now. "Yes."

He was smiling too. "My hair's pretty short, you know. I don't use the stuff." Alex rubbed it in, gently massaging it into her scalp while she closed her eyes and leaned into it. He brushed her lips with his, moving her once again back to the stream of water, where he ran his fingers through her hair over and over, his forehead against hers.

She was still full of emotion, but the tears threatening now were ones of relief and hope.

After he finished rinsing, she washed his hair, and they stood there, silent, holding each other under the hot, steamy water as Hope relaxed into him.

She pressed her mouth to his ear and whispered, "Thank you for keeping your word."

Alex clasped her face with both hands. "Hope, that is one thing you never have to worry about."

He enveloped her in his arms once again, his chin resting on top of her head. "Someone hurt you, didn't he?"

"Yes."

"I'm so sorry."

Hope closed her eyes, her arms tight around his waist as she ran her hands softly up and down his back while they rocked back and forth. She tilted her head back and pressed him down to her lips, at last feeling warm and secure—where she belonged.

HOPE EXITED first and was setting the table with food when Alex appeared. "It looks nice in here—a lot different from before. You've made it your own."

"You've been here before?"

"I had dinner with Steve and Susan a few times. I like it a lot more now."

"It took me a few trips to town," Hope said and pointed to the living room wall and two large stretched canvases of abstract seascapes. "I bought those two watercolors from a street vendor in Frederiksted."

"I think I know the guy you're talking about. I've always liked his work too." Alex poured two glasses of wine and made a toast. "Another toast to new beginnings?"

After touching his glass, Hope swirled the red liquid, the corner of her mouth twitching. "The first time I noticed you drink wine was at Sara's going-away dinner. I had you pegged as a beer guy."

"I like wine. But it's a lot more enjoyable when you have someone to share it with, so I don't really drink it." He paused for a moment. "I can tell you and Sara are very close."

"Yeah, we are. She's the one person in my life I know I can always trust. We learned to depend on each other early on."

"Sounds like there's a story there."

Hope nodded. "Not that unusual, unfortunately. Our father deserted us when I was twelve and Sara was eight. Our mother was a wreck, so I grew up fast. The truth is, we were much better off without him. He was hardly ever there. And when he was, he was . . . scary." She shook her head. "Mom never saw it that way, though. She was always waiting for him to come back. He never did."

Alex took her hand. "I'm sorry. That sounds rough."

"We all have our crosses to bear, don't we?" She gave him a small smile. "And both Sara and I turned out fine, so I count it as a victory."

He squeezed her hand, lifting it to his mouth. "Sara isn't the only one you can depend on, you know."

"I know." She looked down as tears rose in her eyes again. They paused to finish the meal, Alex seeming to understand she needed some time.

"So, has your hip been all right since that night on your deck? It wasn't that long ago."

He glanced at her, then dropped his eyes again. "Yes, it's doing much better now. I was afraid I'd torn something in there again, but the next morning it felt better than I was expecting. Which is good, because I wasn't looking forward to another surgery."

"How many surgeries did you have?"

"Six total, over a year's time. That's why I swim so much. The doctors said it was the best exercise to keep my hip stretched out and strong."

Hope reached out to squeeze his hand before pouring the rest of the bottle and standing up. "Let's go sit on the porch. It's a lovely evening."

She opened the slider and stepped out, hearing a soft whine as she caught movement near the stairs. "Hi there, Cruz."

When Alex appeared behind her, the dog started barking. "Oh, hush. Alex is a good one." She turned to Alex, smiling. "I think he's mad there's some competition now." Cruz barked one final time and scurried down the steps into the nearby jungle.

"I didn't know you had a dog."

"Well, I don't, exactly. He started coming around soon after I moved in. I think he's a stray—he's very skittish. He's slowly warming up to me, though he still won't let me touch him."

Alex wrapped his arms around her shoulders, murmuring in her ear, "I have the advantage then. I'll let you touch me, you know."

They settled on the couch, Hope's head in the hollow of his shoulder and his arm draped around her. A nearby jasmine was in bloom, the warm floral fragrance bathing her in its scent, and there was a nearly full moon on display. Both complemented her now-euphoric mood. "I'll try to be a little more awake than the last time we snuggled up under the moon. Oh, that insurance guy! How long were we down on the pier before you finally gave up on me waking?"

"It was about 1 a.m., I think."

"What? That's hours later than I thought—I'm sorry. Alex, you should have woken me up."

He smiled, brushing a lock of hair behind her ear. "I was sitting there on a beautiful night with you wrapped up in my arms and sound asleep against my chest. I could have stayed like that all night. The only reason I got up was because I was afraid you'd get stiff and sore after so long in that position. I was in heaven." He kissed her forehead.

"Oh," she whispered. "Let's go inside. This time you don't have to sleep on the couch."

CHAPTER 41

*C*onsciousness returned to Hope in layers the next morning. First, a general awareness of contentment and warmth. A dove outside cooed gently, and a wonderfully sore Hope stretched, snuggling deeper into the covers. She hadn't thought anything could top their idyll on Horseshoe Key, but they'd surpassed it last night.

Several times.

Her mind flashed to her conversation with Sara on the Frederiksted pier and she broke into a wide, satisfied smile. If what they had experienced wasn't an A, she couldn't imagine what was.

Reaching out one hand across the bed, she was met with only cold air. Hope spun around. The other side of the bed was empty, the covers thrown back. *He left already?* She relaxed—Alex wasn't going anywhere.

Just then, the delicious scent of freshly brewed coffee drifted to her, and she smiled, inhaling the scent.

"Oh good, you're awake." Alex walked into the bedroom, dressed only in shorts and carrying a cup of coffee. "I found creamer in your fridge, so I assume you're a coffee with cream kind of girl, but I don't know about the sugar. I need to know how you like your coffee, baby."

She sat up, feeling like her smile might break her face.

Oh, stop acting like a teenager.

"No sugar, just cream." She took the mug and drank. "It's exactly how I like it. "Thank you."

Alex sat on the bed, and his kiss brought back delicious reminders of the previous night. "You getting up? I need to get the new boat ready for today's trip."

She put the mug on her nightstand, checking the clock and snuggling back down into her pillow. "No, I've still got some time before I need to be up. Besides, I'm not sure I can walk just yet."

Alex rewarded her with a wide smile. And was that a gleam of pride in his eyes? Oh yes, definitely. "Careful now. There's more where that came from."

~

HOPE WENT to the lobby office and tried to work, though her thoughts kept returning to the whirlwind of the day before. To a man she'd done her best to scare off. Alex refused to be scared. Instead, he'd shared his own deepest trauma with her, asking her to help.

A flush of guilt came over her. She needed to share the rest of her story. Tonight. And she thought Alex hadn't told his fully either.

They were both people who didn't like to talk about their pasts, but it was time for that to end—completely.

THERE WAS a full dive schedule that day, including an afternoon trip. She'd popped down to the boat prior to the afternoon departure, inviting Alex to dinner afterward. A warmth spread through her at his delighted acceptance.

They shared a long dinner full of the expectant glances of a newly formed couple. When given the choice of chicken or steak, Alex hadn't hesitated at choosing steak, and she got a small thrill at learning something new about him.

After leaving the restaurant, they walked hand in hand along the beach toward her house, a luminous moon shining down on them.

Hope glanced at Alex before diving into the deep end.

"I want you to know how much yesterday meant to me, and last night too. But Alex, I still have some questions about you."

He squeezed her hand, defensiveness nowhere to be seen. "Ask away. I need to start dealing with this. It isn't easy, but I'll do my best."

"You told me you were a diver in the Navy. I thought at first you went around picking up anchors or something. Yet you were wounded while in Syria—that doesn't sound terribly diving-related to me. Since you told me, I've been trying to figure why a diver would even be in Syria."

She stopped and turned to him. "Alex, who *are* you?"

He drew her into his embrace and kissed the top of her head. "A man who loves you very much."

She glanced up at him with a small smile, a warm flush rising at hearing those words. "I love you too. Now stop evading the question."

He steered them down the beach, walking slowly. "I don't mean to. I'm sorry—you get so used to not talking about stuff that it's hard to bring it up."

She fought to keep her face still at that.

You're the last one to be throwing stones here, Hope.

Alex paused, his brow furrowed. "I believe there are things worth fighting for, and dying for if necessary. I *was* a Navy diver, Hope—it's just not all I did. I was part of Navy SEAL Teams for over fifteen years. We were hunting an ISIS cell in Syria when we were ambushed. That's when I got wounded."

"Oh. You were a Navy SEAL?"

He nodded.

"That makes a lot more sense than looking for anchors."

He laughed, but it didn't reach his eyes. "Actually, you'd be surprised how often people lose things that would be very bad if they fell into the wrong hands. I did a fair amount of finding lost items."

That gave her an icy feeling in her stomach. Then she stopped. "Why didn't you tell me yesterday when you told me about your wound?"

His face clouded with pain. "I should have. I'm sorry. Telling you about my wound . . . was hard. Really hard."

He ran his hand over his face, rubbing fiercely and meeting her eyes. "I'm really proud of being a SEAL. What I did out there was important, and I was damn good at it. Then, in one night, everything was gone."

She squeezed his hand but let him continue uninterrupted.

Alex heaved a sigh. "When you tell people you're a SEAL, they tend to ask a lot of questions. If you tell them you were one for fifteen years, they wonder why you stopped. Until I met you, I just couldn't go there.

"When we were on that beach yesterday, I didn't want it to be about my past—I wanted it to be about who I am *now*. Talking about that day is still really hard." He stared at her, his eyes naked and wounded. "But I'm trying, ok?"

"I know you are. And I love you for it." She brushed his lips with hers. "Are you not supposed to talk about what you did? Is it classified?"

"Some of it is, but being a SEAL? No, it's fine." He paused again before looking at her. "You know that saying about fight club?"

She smiled. "The first rule of fight club is don't talk about fight club."

"Yeah. It's more like that." Shrugging, he continued, "I've been calling myself a Navy diver since I made SEAL Teams at age nineteen. You get used to it after a while."

Hope sighed. "Now I'm really going to have to give you a raise."

He laughed and pulled her close, lowering his mouth to hers. Hope ran her hands through his short hair, kissing him back hard. Eventually, she pulled back and looked into his vivid eyes.

Alex stared intently at her, then raised a brow. Without his saying a word, Hope understood he was asking if she had anything to tell him. She turned around in his arms, leaning back against him.

It's time. How much more could he possibly do to prove he's different?

~

"I'm the last person to get upset about you withholding something," Hope said. "That's something I know a little about too. And I understand how hard it is to talk about. But we're starting something new, and it's time to get everything out in the open."

She paused, a knot growing in her stomach. "I know what's it's like to have your life turned upside down. It happened to me. Twice. Last night I told you about the first time. That was my first lesson about men—they leave."

He wrapped his arms above her chest, holding her closer as he squeezed her shoulders. "I'm not going anywhere."

"I know."

Hope trembled and took a deep breath, leaning further back and drawing strength from Alex. "I told you some of what my life was like when my dad left. I took odd jobs to make money and worked throughout high school. My mother was terrible at holding down a job.

"I graduated and went off to college—my grades were good enough to get a scholarship." She paused. "And for the first time, I could do what I wanted, make decisions for myself. I was still working and sending money home to Sara, of course. But I was practically drunk on the freedom of it all."

She took another shaky breath, then said the words she'd never told another man. "And that was when I met Caleb. I'd dated some boys in high school. Nice boys. But I was a grown woman now and fully capable of making good decisions." She barked bitter laughter at that. "Caleb was everything the nice boys weren't—older, mysterious, handsome, intense. I fell wildly in love with him."

Alex pressed his cheek to her head.

"It started with him being angry and possessive. Then, when he started saying things to me that were . . . terrible, I got very good at making excuses for him. Next . . . he hit me, but I reassured myself that he was always sorry." She laughed, no humor in it whatsoever. "I was so naïve. Within three months, he had me completely dominated."

Alex's chest moved behind her as his breath caught. "It's still incredible to me all these years later. How he managed to manipulate me into thinking *I* was the one with something wrong."

She spoke barely above a whisper. "That I deserved to be treated like that."

Pausing, she took a deep, shaky breath. "And then I ended up in the emergency room . . . broken."

Alex's arm spasmed around her.

Hope's voice strengthened, and she stood tall. "And that's when the excuses stopped. The police came to take my statement and pushed hard for me to press charges against Caleb. So I did. And I testified against him. He was convicted and sent to prison. And I've never heard from him since."

Her upper body moved back and forth with the force of Alex's breathing. But he didn't interrupt.

"Now, of course I was smart enough to realize that not all men were like Caleb. But I made it a top priority only to get involved with men I could walk away from. That was lesson number two—

never feel so deeply you can't walk away. I refused to let myself fall hard, thinking that kept me safe." She shook her head. "It only made me numb and dead inside. But that's how I've operated for years now."

Alex still gripped her shoulder, and a fine tremor ran along his arm.

"Until I met you." She placed her hand over his and took a heaving, deep breath. "I can't walk away from you, Alex."

His breath exploded out behind her. "Oh my God, Hope." He inhaled deeply, nearly a sob. "If you need me to promise you, I will."

She turned around, pressing the side of her head against his chest. His heart hammered under her ear, and his entire body trembled.

Oh Alex, you couldn't be more different.

She stared into his eyes, putting every ounce of intent possible into her words. "Sometimes I think I don't know anything about life. But the one thing I do know, beyond any doubt, is that you would *never* hurt me like that. You don't need to promise me anything."

She smiled. "Well, I wouldn't mind if you promised to love me. That wouldn't be too bad."

He met her gaze, his face grave as he cupped her face. "I love you more than you will ever know." Then his expression softened. "And hopefully you know by now how I feel about promises."

She smiled. "I do."

Hope turned back around, his arms still encircling her as she gazed out at the moonlit ocean. "That first time on the beach. You covered me with your body and held my arms over my head, our hands locked together. That should have sent me into a tailspin of panic. But it never even crossed my mind. I only felt enveloped and protected. I felt *safe* with you. I always have—since we first met. And yesterday I was completely free, and that awful numbness was gone."

She snorted softly. "Then it all came crashing down on me last night. That's why I was such a mess. I've worked so hard to start over here, to finally put it behind me. But I guess the old demons had to have one final shot. And then you came to me. You'll never understand what that meant.

"This whole experience has taught me that there are risks in life worth taking. The rewards can be so incredible, and I've learned there are people who will always be there for you. I feel alive again." She brought his hand up and kissed it. "Telling you I love you seems so inadequate to describe what you've brought to my life, but it's the best I can do."

Alex kissed the top of her head and held her a little tighter. "It's no more than what you've brought to my life. I know something about being numb and dead inside. When that bomb went off, I lost my whole identity, my purpose. I was so lost when I came here. Little by little, I've clawed my way back—well, somewhat."

He paused, resting his cheek against her head. "But when you arrived here, I realized there might be more to life than just existing. You showed me something worth caring about. I *matter* again because of you. You helped me get that back. I need to start coming to terms with Syria, and I've learned I can't do it alone. I need you. I love you." He kissed her temple. "I've been finding hope without even looking for it."

Hope smiled and leaned back against his chest. "We've got each other and this incredible place. There's nothing else we need. I can't wait to see what tomorrow brings."

An errant breeze brushed against her face. She closed her eyes, breathing in the fresh, bracing scent of the ocean as the palm trees sighed around them. Alex had moved the strap of her shirt aside and begun kissing along the length of her tattoo, moving from chrysalis to butterfly. Hope opened her eyes and smiled.

"I got that tattoo shortly after Caleb was convicted. It represented my life as a work in progress—what the end goal was. I knew I was a very long way from the butterfly. But over time, I was no longer in the chrysalis either. I've existed for *years* somewhere along that black line."

She turned around once again and looked into those crystal blue eyes, a smile forming. "But Alex, I'm finally flying now."

～

Hope and Alex's Story Continues in
Defending Hope

Keep reading for an excerpt

AUTHOR'S NOTE

Thank you for reading *Finding Hope*! This has been a real labor of love for me, and I hope you enjoyed getting to know Hope and Alex as much as I did. I first got the idea to write a novel during The Covid Summer. 2020, that is. My hours were drastically cut at my day job as a pharmacist, and I needed something else to be productive with.

So I set out to write a scuba diving romance novel. I've been diving since 1998 and have read many books involving diving. One of my biggest frustrations has been all the details of diving that authors get wrong. And I'm not talking about knowing the maximum operational depth of thirty-two percent enriched air. I'm talking about things like "Brawny McBiceps shrugged into his diving vest and took a big pull from his oxygen tank."

Yech. So much wrong with that sentence. And don't get me started on goggles and flippers.

I set out to make the diving accurate. Now, I must admit to an advantage here—I'm married to a scuba instructor. He vetted all the scuba passages (skimming the love scenes!) and served as my technical advisor. I assure you any errors in the diving scenes are mine, not his.

Also, if you were wondering how realistic it was to have someone win a dive resort in a raffle, I can assure you this very thing happened in 2016 in Micronesia. The description I used for the sinking of *Deep Diver* was taken from a real-life incident that occurred in Mexico, though the circumstances were different. Alas, there is no Half Moon Bay or its namesake resort on St. Croix. Frederiksted and Christiansted are real towns, however I took some poetic license with their details.

If you want to keep up to date on their adventures, be sure to sign up for my newsletter. As a special thank you, I have an exclusive Half Moon Bay novella available just for my newsletter subscribers. It's completely free! You can sign up for my newsletter at

www.erinbrockus.com

And if I could make a request, if you enjoyed *Finding Hope*, would you leave a review at Amazon or your favorite platform? Reader reviews are the lifeblood of independent authors and ensure I'm able to keep writing more books. Even a line or two helps tremendously.

Thank you, and keep your head in the clouds and your feet in the sand!

By the way, the MOD for thirty-two percent Nitrox is one hundred eleven feet (at an oxygen partial pressure of 1.4). Just in case you were wondering.

Erin Brockus
June, 2021

DEFENDING HOPE EXCERPT

*A*ugust . . .

HOPE COLLINS SAT in her home office, staring out the window with a dreamy smile. Her email tone sounded, snapping her attention back to the matter at hand. All morning she had been trying to keep her mind on business.

And failing.

Her computer screen displayed the website for Half Moon Bay Resort in St. Croix. Hope had owned the resort for five months, though it could have been a lifetime ago that she'd lived in Chicago. As she tried to prepare for a staff meeting that afternoon, Hope's mind was repeatedly diverted by thoughts of a certain dive guide who worked at the resort.

Of course, dive guide didn't exactly describe Alex Monroe, any more than what a person saw of an iceberg described its entirety. In addition to leading dives, Alex was the dive operations manager of the resort. And as Hope had discovered recently, he used to be a Navy SEAL before being terribly injured in an ambush that had ended his career.

And there was one other position he'd recently added to his resume. Hope closed her eyes and took a deep breath as the dreamy smile returned. But instead of inhaling Alex's intoxicating scent, her nose wrinkled at the stuffy scent of her home office.

Frowning, she rose, crossing over to the window and opening it to admit the fragrant tropical breeze. It was time for the meeting, so she left the house through the back sliding glass door, pulling her shoulder-length chestnut hair into a ponytail as she walked up the beach. The resort was located on the western edge of the island, making for stunning sunsets but sultry afternoons.

As she passed four guest bungalows, she waved at a couple relaxing on their porch, enjoying their afternoon with a beer. Soon, Hope approached the heart of the resort, a restaurant and a brick patio next to an infinity pool on her right, and on her left, a long wooden pier with a complex of rooms halfway down and a thatch palapa at the end. The resort boat, *Surface Interval*, was tied at the end, ready for the next day's dive trip.

As Hope climbed the stairs onto the pier, she checked to make sure her white tank top and skinny capris were in order, then wrinkled her brow. *Should I have changed into a staff shirt?* Since she'd been working from home, she hadn't worried about her appearance. With a shrug, she continued. *Too late now—and it's not like anyone at the meeting cares.*

Thunder rumbled over the mountains to the east, and a threatening roil of clouds crowned the jagged peaks. But the last thing Hope wanted to be reminded of were storms. The resort had recently weathered a major one when their boat sank. She'd recently bought the replacement, the boat tied at the end of the pier.

As Hope strode toward the dive classroom, the boards under her sandals were still wet from the afternoon rain, and the air smelled delicious, a mixture of fresh rain and damp wood. She'd called an informal meeting amongst herself, Alex, her star chef Gerold, and Patti, the general manager of the resort.

The dive classroom was the best place to hold it, being private and blessedly air-conditioned. The room was a simple affair, a wooden box twenty feet square with three rectangular tables lined up behind one another. Two long whiteboards hung side by side in the front, and a tall bookcase stood in one corner.

She was the last to arrive. Patti sat at the back table, her blue staff shirt hugging her ample frame. Alex and Gerold bantered back and forth at the middle one. Gerold still wore his white chef's coat, his dark skin a pleasing contrast.

Hope sat on the table facing them before placing her feet on the seat of the chair in front of her. Slapping her thighs lightly, she said, "Thanks for coming."

Alex smiled widely and winked one vivid blue eye at her. As usual, she feasted on him with her own eyes. His short, sandy hair was still damp from a recent shower—he lived in an apartment above their current location. His good looks and warm smile never failed to get a reaction from her. Hope pulled herself back together. She had unconsciously mirrored the position Alex had taken when teaching her scuba class. "How does it feel to be on that side of the classroom, Alex?"

Gerold and Patti both grinned as he leaned back in his chair, saying, "Well, I seem to have gotten used to taking orders from you, so I guess we're just taking things to the next level."

Hope didn't miss the gleam in his eye, but ignored it. "I wanted to give you all an update on some plans I have for the resort and get your input. One of the major projects I wanted to tackle this summer was a total revamp of our website and creating a cohesive brand for the resort. But that's going to cost some serious money, and with the new boat, I've had to modify my plans a bit."

Alex's teasing smile disappeared. The previous resort owner, Steve Jackson, hadn't wanted to spend the money necessary to complete extensive repairs to their venerable boat, so Alex and the boat's captain Tommy had nursed it along with the plan of dry-docking it in the fall for an extensive overhaul. Unfortunately, a series of minor issues had snowballed into the boat sinking disaster. They had lucked into an even better replacement boat, but Alex blamed himself for the accident.

She continued, leaning forward. "The one part of the project I am definitely going ahead with is adding an online booking portal to the website, and I'm increasing our advertising budget with the PR company.

"I've looked at a lot of other resorts' websites, and I plan to offer *only* four-day and seven-day packages on the portal. One package of accommodations plus meals, and another with that plus a two-tank dive trip each morning. We'll still have our Miami travel agency for phone bookings, of course, but guests would have to call to book anything but the four or seven-day packages.

"Most people prefer to book online since they hate calling. And if their only choices are four days or seven, hopefully they'll pick seven and we'll get more revenue. What do you guys think?"

"A lot of dive resorts run on a standard seven-day schedule, usually Saturday to Saturday," Alex said. "We're small enough that I don't think we need to mandate a specific day of the week, but it's a great idea. It will give the divers a better chance to know us, and for us to know them."

Hope nodded. "The main reason I wanted to bring this up is because I think it will make us busier, and we're going to need to hire more staff. Patti already has a new housekeeper working, but Gerold, we need to get you a sous chef. Somebody who can fill in when you're off. I'll admit I had fantasies about applying for the job, but I don't think that would work well for either of us." She laughed.

"I told you, there's always a job for you in my kitchen."

Hope enjoyed helping when Gerold was shorthanded, but she

was no substitute for a real sous chef. "You can definitely do better than me."

Hope's attention drifted to Alex, whose gaze was locked on her chest as he eyed it intensely. She ignored it as she directed her next statement at him. "You've been able to get fill-in divemasters when you've needed them, but I'm wondering if we need to put Robert on the payroll permanently."

He widened his eyes, snapping out of his trance. *What has gotten into him?* "I don't think so. When he's not available, I can use his friend April. But the day may come."

Hope nodded, glad he was paying attention again.

Patti cleared her throat. "While we're together, I wanted to make sure Charles is workin' out. I've had no issues with him, but I hired him mostly because his father was desperate for him to get a decent job and start on a new path. And his dad has always been my favorite cousin." Patti was a St. Croix native with an extensive local family.

Alex's and Gerold's faces went blank. "He seems fine to me," Gerold said.

Alex nodded, shrugging. "We work in different parts of the resort. I've hardly had any interaction with him. He's a big guy—he should get a job as a bouncer."

Hope held her tongue regarding their new landscaper. Patti had told her Charles had completed several stints in jail. It was mostly for petty crimes, but he made Hope uneasy. He was a hulking man, though that was advantageous for a landscaper.

But working here had done wonders for Clark, their bartender. After a minor scrape with the law, Clark was now a model citizen, so Hope wanted to give Charles a chance. Patti would never hire him if she thought he was dangerous.

"Good," Patti said. "I told him he's on a tight leash, so hope-fully this will be the change he needs."

Hope turned to Alex and Gerold again. "I'd like to start a regular schedule of days off for you guys. Patti and I already have something worked out to get her two days off each week, but both of you work way too hard." They opened their mouths to speak, but Hope held up a hand. "We'll have to wait until we have extra staff in place, but I'm serious. I want each of you to work toward at least one regular day off each week, ok?" Gerold nodded, and Alex stared at her levelly.

Oh, you stubborn man.

Patti spoke up. "What about you, Hope?"

"What do you mean?"

"When was the last day you took completely off?"

Hope thought for a moment. "The day we got the new boat." She slid her gaze to Alex, who slowly winked, again devouring her with his eyes. That had been a big day for them. The memory brought a pleasant jolt through Hope's body. She and Alex had spent an incredible day on deserted Horseshoe Key.

A day that had also brought revelations.

The same ambush that had nearly killed Alex also proved fatal to eight members of his platoon, which he'd revealed when they'd first made love. His wound covered his right hip and there was no hiding it. For years, he'd been so traumatized by the experience that he'd buried it deep and refused to discuss personal matters, let alone get involved in an intimate relationship.

Alex was a complicated man—charming and affable, unless matters turned to subjects he was uncomfortable with. Then he shut down.

"That was weeks ago, child." Patti glared at the back of Alex's head. "You have to start takin' better care of yourself. Let me know what I can do to help. *Someone* needs to look out for you."

Alex pressed his lips together and gave an exasperated grunt. He was turning around when Hope intervened. "Patti! I'm ok. It's fine. Answering guest surveys from my laptop while sitting on the porch is hardly working, and I've had plenty of days like that. Besides, this meeting isn't about me."

She and Alex hadn't been open about their new relationship,

but they hadn't hidden it either, so it was no surprise the staff had figured it out.

"How can you say that?" Alex asked. "We wouldn't be sitting here if it weren't for you. Patti's right—if we're taking a day off, you are too. Though I'd like to see her try to get you to do something you don't want to."

"Ok, fine. I surrender. Happy now?"

Alex gave her a private smile. "Yes, very happy."

Chapter 2

AFTER THE MEETING, Hope ambled to the end of the pier, finding it deserted and enjoying the cool shade under the palapa while she peeked over the edge. Colorful fish darted below. She was leaning forward and examining a bright blue fish when someone clasped her hips, steadying her.

She yelped.

"Careful. Don't want to fall in the drink."

After her heart started beating again, Hope turned around to face Alex, who was dressed in his work uniform of a staff T-shirt and board shorts. Instead of reprimanding him for sneaking up on her, she stood on her tiptoes and kissed him. "I think the meeting went well. Patti and Gerold are on board, and I'm excited about longer bookings."

Alex returned his lips to hers, speaking against her mouth. "I don't care."

Hope pulled away. "What?"

"You show up to a staff meeting looking like that, and you think I can pay attention?"

She looked down and lowered a corner of her mouth. "I'm wearing a tank top and capris."

"Believe me, I know." He cracked a small smile and brushed

her hair away from her forehead. "That outfit brings back a memory for me. You've affected me since you first arrived on St. Croix, Ms. Collins. I've been attracted to you since the second time I saw you. Though I fought like hell against it."

"Really? That long ago? Wait—why the second time?"

Alex's smile widened. "The first time, I wasn't sure I liked you. You were distant when we met on the dock, but then I learned why. Steve sure didn't do you any favors. But the second time—that was a different story. It was early evening, and I was sitting on my deck when you walked below me and stood right here. You wore tight jeans and a white tank top." He ran his gaze down her body, then back up. "God, you were gorgeous and ready to take on the world. I'll never forget it."

She was all warm and fuzzy inside. "I don't remember that at all. What did we say to each other?"

"Nothing. You didn't even see me. I was pretty stunned at my reaction. I wanted to keep the moment to myself and not let reality screw it up."

"Probably just as well. You weren't the only one fighting your feelings." She squeezed his waist. "I think the reality we have now is pretty good, don't you?"

"Oh, yes."

Hope smirked. "I hate to burst your bubble, but I bought these capris in Frederiksted. There's no way this was what I wore that night." Located a few miles south of the resort, it was one of the two major towns on the island.

"It's close enough. The whole package blew me away. It does even more now."

Hope's eyes were riveted to his as her heart pounded with his admission. "I love you."

"I love you too." He brushed her lips with a feather-light kiss. "But I have to finish up. Later?"

"You'd better believe it."

After finishing work in the lobby that afternoon, Hope shut down the front-desk computer. She panned her gaze around the room, making sure all was in order. The lobby was a single-story cottage-style building, and she left the ceiling fans spinning to cool the room in her absence. Feet sinking into the sand, she nodded at a guest powering through a beach run as she walked home. After he passed, a small frown crossed her face. She'd been a steady runner while living in Chicago. *Maybe it's time to take it up again.*

Hope's text tone went off the minute she walked into the house. The open-concept living area contained a kitchen near the front and a great room facing the ocean, with the kitchen island between. Sitting at the kitchen table, she smiled at the sender's name—her sister, Hurricane Sara.

∾

Order *Defending Hope* today!

ALSO BY ERIN BROCKUS

Jamaican Escape: A Short Story

Tropical Chance: A Half Moon Bay Novella

Half Moon Bay Series:

Finding Hope: Half Moon Bay Book 1

Defending Hope: Half Moon Bay Book 2 (Fall 2021)

ABOUT THE AUTHOR

Erin Brockus writes contemporary stories set in exotic, tropical locales. She features mature, realistic characters, romance, and adventure, with a focus on the ocean--especially scuba diving.

Erin was born in 1969 in Washington state. A great love of creative writing as a child got pushed aside by the expectations of Real Life and she went to college to become a pharmacist.

After practicing pharmacy for over 25 years, it was time for a change. So she reduced her hours as a practicing pharmacist to devote more time to writing.

She was introduced to scuba diving in 1998 by her husband. They have since traveled worldwide enjoying scuba diving, and the exotic locales they visited formed the ideas for her characters and stories. Erin has even been known to don a drysuit and explore the cold, murky waters of the Pacific Northwest. She is also an avid runner and cyclist.

Erin lives with her husband (a scuba instructor) in eastern Washington state. Finding Hope is her debut novel.

Made in the USA
Middletown, DE
21 September 2021

48730059R00182